Diana K. P

The Finest Little Village

Diana K. Perkins

The Necessary Parts

Copyright © 2024 by Diana K. Perkins
1st Edition
ISBN 978-1-7327983-5-9

Disclaimer: This is a work of fiction. Any resemblance to actual lives or persons is purely accidental and should not be taken as fact. To bring realism to the novel's setting in Windham Center and surrounding areas, some of the historic characters, buildings, businesses, churches and roads referred to are or were actual structures or institutions.

This book is number eight in the Shetucket River Milltown Series. It is set in 12 point Times New Roman with chapter heads in 24 point Blackadder ITC and cellphone texts in 11 point Arial Narrow bold.

Cover: "Bird's Eye View" Painting by Annie Wandell

Produced by   Shetucket Hollow Press
1 Shetucket Drive, Windham, CT 06280
Author's website:
http://www.dianakperkins.com

Acknowledgements

I want to thank my readers:
Michelle Giffin, Barbara Morton, and Susan Shand, whose thoughtful feedback made this a much better story.

A special thank you goes out to Attorney Barbara McGrath and to Probate Judge the Honorable John McGrath, who helped greatly in sharing their knowledge about the probate system and filing wills. Any errors regarding wills and the probate system are entirely mine.

A heartfelt thank you to Windham artist Annie Wandell, who does beautiful scenes of our village and wooden replicas of our village houses, and who gave me permission to use her Windham Center village painting "Bird's Eye View" on the cover.

A special thank you to Suzanne Blancaflor and Barbara (Boo) Morton, who had no idea their home would be one of the primary settings for the heroine Frances's adventures.

I also want to sincerely thank my faithful editor, Blanche Boucher, who generously allowed me to use several of her haiku in this story. She always finds those (really, hordes of) nasty little grammatical errors that plague me and improves my work; she has my enduring gratitude. You can be sure that any grammatical, punctuation or spelling errors are due to my post edit fussing.

- Diana K. Perkins

The Finest Little Village -

Dedicated to

Gwen Bruno

whose tireless effort,
along with the board and
volunteers from
Windham Preservation Inc.,
to restore this historic gem,
the Windham Inn
in Windham Center,
is heroic.
We hope you succeed.
Thank you.

Inn Layout

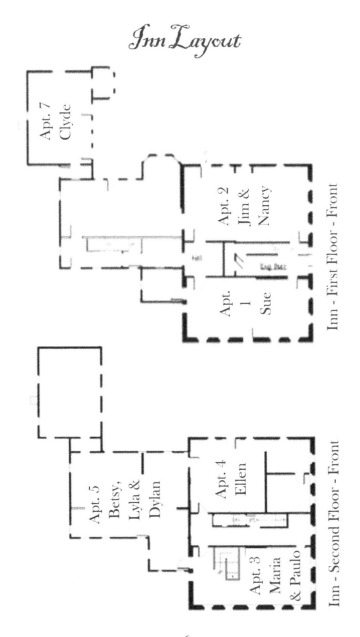

Apt. 7
Clyde

Apt. 2
Jim &
Nancy

Apt.
1
Sue

Inn - First Floor - Front

Apt. 5
Betsy,
Lyla &
Dylan

Apt. 4
Ellen

Apt. 3
Maria
& Paulo

Inn - Second Floor - Front

The Village of Windham Center

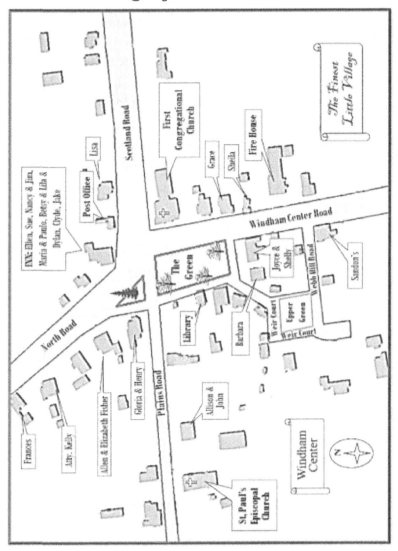

A copy of this map is available on line at:
https://dianakperkins.com/home-2/books/the-finest-little-village/

Author's Note

This mystery set in the village of Windham Center, Connecticut, is fictional, as are the characters, but of course writers often draw from real life to create their characters. The relationship between Haggarty and Frances is highly unlikely. Most codes of conduct would not allow state detectives to collaborate with a civilian, even a retired state detective, in such a manner. But it was fun to imagine.

As reflected in the book I am something of a foodie, so at the end I've included recipes for many of the dishes described.

Much of this story takes place at the Windham Inn, a historic building which is not, as in the story, currently in use. It has been condemned, but with the efforts of a number of dedicated people it will be saved and hopefully returned to its once vibrant use as apartments and perhaps a small café. The major group working on the Inn's preservation is the nonprofit Windham Preservation Inc.; you can follow their efforts and events online at https://windhampreservationinc.org/. Some of the proceeds from the sale of this novel will go to support this effort. For more information about this beautiful historic village please visit the Windham Inn, where informational maps of the village town center and homes mentioned in this novel are available on the front door or contact WPI (above) to have one mailed to you.

Diana K. Perkins - Author's Note

The village of Windham Center has some of the most talented artists and craftsmen in Eastern Connecticut (and perhaps the whole Northeast), along with an impossible array of professionals and scholars. Many of us wonder about this vortex of artists, craftsmen and musicians, and what draws so many into our rich and dynamic fold. Our village also hosts many of the events in the novel. Soup night is a real thing here, and Jazz in the Garden is a yearly fundraiser for our little library.

In my opinion to live in this little village is a gift and a privilege. It is not only the quintessential New England town center, with lovely old homesteads surrounding a historic green, but the villagers themselves are kind and generous and during this time (the decades from 2000 to 2020's) it housed the finest group of citizens one could ever ask for.

Hats off to this Finest Little Village.

The Finest Little Village -

Chapter 1 – The Fall

If I were to choose the person in our village who would be the least likely to be murdered, it would be Ellen. If you think that's a strange way to think about someone, I must say it's all the more strange because she was the first to be murdered, at least the first I remember. There had been one a few years ago, not in our town, Windham Center, but an adjoining town, South Windham, where a dear elderly library volunteer was murdered for her fortune, which all went to the nonprofits in the end.

But Ellen?

I could believe it because I saw it–well, sort of saw it. I was taking my usual morning walk to the post office, next door to the old inn where Ellen lived in one of seven rental units. I was passing the inn when Sue slammed open the front door and screamed, "Help! Help!" When I turned toward her she yelled, "Thank goodness you're here, Frances! Something's happened to Ellen!" I ran as quickly as my old bones could carry me, stumbled over the curbing, recovered and dashed inside the open door.

The hall light at the bottom of the stairs threw an oddly warm comforting glow on the scene in front of me, also illuminated by the open door behind us.

Ellen was at the bottom of the stairs, in a crumpled heap that looked a lot like a pile of laundry except mixed in with the clothing were limbs all akimbo, not at all assembled in the way God intended.

"What should we do?" Sue's voice coming from behind me was alarmed.

"Start by calling 911," I said in an also alarmed but annoyed tone. I mean, wouldn't that be the most obvious thing to do? Sue, flustered, replied, "Of course, of course."

She rushed through her still-open apartment door and I heard her pick up the receiver of her remote phone and drop it, then stutter into it.

As she was on the phone describing what had happened, I had a few moments to take in the scene. To me it was pretty clear that Ellen was in serious trouble and I didn't want to disturb anything, but I did reach down to her arm, which poked out at an alarming angle, to look for a pulse in her still-warm wrist. I found a very faint one. I did nothing further because my sixth sense and training as a detective always had me on the alert–even the most mundane-looking of accidents could be caused by something other than what seemed obvious.

Sue's call got almost immediate results; I heard the alarm at the firehouse go off. The firehouse was only a stone's throw away from us and the cars of volunteer firefighters and EMTs were already whizzing by the inn to get to the firehouse emergency vehicles. In less than three minutes after Sue's call the ambulance was rushing down the street toward us. Sue stood in the inn's front door, watching me as I took out my cellphone and photographed the scene and the body from several different angles up the stairs from where I assumed she'd fallen. A small puddle of blood was collecting by her head, which was toward the door, her face and neck twisted away from Sue's apartment on my left. The ambulance alarm stopped. Sue watched me take several photos in the seconds it took for the paramedic to come through the door.

"Is she alive?"

"Just barely."

"You don't think this was an accident, do you?" Sue asked me as the emergency response team came in and I stepped carefully around Ellen to where Sue was standing.

"I don't know."

We watched as the paramedic did just what I had done, feel for a pulse, first at her wrist and then at the side of her neck. He gently turned her over, trying not to cause any more damage to the obviously broken body with its limbs dangling loosely in odd positions. Sue gasped and retreated into her apartment. The mobile gurney clanged as the other emergency worker pulled it noisily from the back of the ambulance parked in the post office lot.

Ellen was wearing a long, medium-weight mauve wool coat, a cream jersey top, grey cuffed wool trousers and loafers. One of the loafers was still on the stairs, halfway up. The coat was wrapped around her oddly, like cellophane wrap in some spots but hanging loose in others. The bulkiness of the coat hid the frailty of her body. You could tell this was a person who might once have lived a high life and was accustomed to finer clothing.

"Do you know her?" I nodded. "Good. Could you help me fill in some details on the paperwork?" I nodded again and replied. "My name is Frances O'Connor. I live around the corner," and tipped my head in that direction.

"I retired from detective work over a decade ago. I can help you with what you need." He looked relieved.

"I'm Medic Roland Smithe. I live on Plains Road. I'd shake your hand, but…" He lifted a rubber-gloved hand and did an air shake at me. I smiled.

Roland and the other emergency worker tried to straighten Ellen out enough to get her onto the gurney beside her. As they gently lifted her onto it she exhaled a puff of air and her arm dropped limply off. They belted her on and the EMT put over her face an oxygen mask connected to the small tank next to her on the gurney.

"This looks like an accident, don't you think?" Roland sought confirmation.

"It certainly does, but…. I got some photos if you think you'll need them." As I spoke I heard another siren screaming from South Windham. A state police cruiser sped up, lights flashing, and parked next to the ambulance. Out stepped a tall, trim trooper putting on his grey Stetson. He walked up briskly, surveying the scene.

The training of the state police is thorough. They are taught to observe and remember and document all they see at a crime scene: weather, vehicles, bystanders, anyone leaving the scene. Trained to maintain the safety of bystanders and first responders, scanning the area for anything hazardous, be it chemical, electrical, animal or weapons, and neutralize anything dangerous. They arrange for medical assistance. They secure the scene, ensuring that no one contaminates the area, keeping bystanders at bay. Once done, they interview bystanders and anyone obviously related to the possible case.

Chapter 2 – The Find

The trooper walked up to Roland and spoke to him in a low voice. Roland, busy securing the gurney inside the ambulance, replied, pointing toward Sue and me in the doorway watching Ellen being readied for the ride. The trooper walked over to us, nodding a quiet greeting.

"Hello. I'm Sargent Haggarty. Are you the ones who called in the 911?" We both nodded. "Do you have time to talk to me?" We nodded again. More sirens, one from the ambulance with flashing lights now headed down North Road toward Willimantic, one from a second state police cruiser pulling in beside Officer Haggarty's cruiser. A young, bright-looking female trooper emerged and approached, scanning the areas Haggarty had, taking it all in.

"Officer Kimball, could you please secure the scene while I interview these ladies?" The trooper nodded, went to her cruiser and pulled out a small suitcase.

"You live here?" He addressed Sue. "Is there a back door that we could use so we don't disturb the area?" Sue nodded and led the way around to the left to the second entrance. As we went into her kitchen she looked pale and was shaking. "Why don't you sit down and have a glass of water," Officer Haggarty suggested gently. "I'll be back in a moment." He left.

Sue fidgeted with the electric kettle. "Can I get you a cup of tea or coffee?"

"Yeah. Are you okay?"

"I can't believe this happened! I just can't believe it!"

"Maybe a shot of brandy would be better than coffee. Have any? I can run over to my place and grab a bottle…"

"Oh, yeah, I think I have some right here." As Sue rummaged through a cupboard, clanking bottles. She stood up and fussed around the counter collecting cups, saucers, sugar bowl, spoons, and an old tin that had Tetley printed on it in fancy script.

"Did you say tea or coffee?"

"Brandy."

"Oh, yes, what am I thinking? You did say that…." From the bottle she poured about two fingers into a small water glass. "Sorry, I don't have any brandy. Will sherry do?" Not waiting for my reply, she poured a second glass and held it out to me, her hand shaking.

"Why don't you sit down? You've had quite a shock."

She nodded and sat at the table, where I joined her and took a sip. Haggarty knocked on the door. He had a clipboard in one hand and a camera in the other.

"Come on in, Officer." I motioned him toward the empty chair. From the radio attached to his shoulder came static and a garbled voice saying something like "10-37 Route 6." He ignored it, laid the clipboard on the table and sat down.

"Hello. I'm Sargent Finn Haggarty." Addressing himself to Sue he leaned across the table, one hand open to her, the other pointing toward the name tag on his jacket.

Sue shook his hand. "I need to get some information from you. Do you have time to help me fill out this report?" We both nodded. He glanced at his watch and wrote down the date and time. "Could you give me your name and the address here?" He wrote as Sue answered in a soft voice. He turned to me. "What is your name?"

"Frances O'Connor. I live just a few houses from here, twenty-three North Road. I used to be a state detective." He gave me an appraising look and smiled.

"And what is the name and address of the woman who… fell?" Finn was being diplomatic. The radio hissed.

Sue replied, "Ellen. Ellen Richardson. She lives upstairs in apartment four. I'm in apartment one, across the hall is apartment two, above me is apartment three and Ellen lives in apartment four, above apartment two, top of the stairs and to the right." I watched Finn write down the apartment number and not lose patience with Sue's more than adequate details. "Her apartment is a little quieter than mine, me being on the corner and all. The big trucks and motorcycles make a lot of noise. The apartments in the ell are much quieter." Finn nodded.

"So, tell me what you remember. What happened?" Sue looked out at the hall and frowned.

"It's cold. Can I close that door?" Without waiting for an answer she went to the door, leaned out, probably to see the other officer draping crime scene tape, closed the door and came back to the table. Her eyes were watery. "I don't know what happened." She took a sip of the sherry. "Can I get you something to drink? Tea, coffee?" She made a squeaky chuckle. "Sherry?" Finn shook his head.

"No, thank you. You were saying?" Finn's pen was poised above the form on the clipboard.

"I don't know what happened. One minute I was making myself an English muffin, the next minute I heard a racket from the hall, a loud noise like something falling down the stairs and maybe a scream or shout; I'm not sure. I ran to the door and she was right there at the bottom of the stairs. The front door was slightly open. For a few seconds I couldn't even figure out what I was seeing and I just stood there, trying to wrap my mind around it. Suddenly I realized it was Ellen because I recognized her coat. She loved that coat. I pushed the door open, saw Frances walking by and called out to her. She came and told me to call 911. That's it. That's the whole story."

"Thank you, Ms. Gallen." Finn, still writing, was professional and patient. "Ms. O'Connor, what did you see?"

"When I came in I saw Ellen like Sue said. I checked her pulse and found a weak one. We didn't touch anything else. I took some photos. I can email them to you." He nodded.

"What do you think, Ms. O'Connor? Do you think there is anything suspicious here?"

"Well, from a casual viewpoint I would say it was accidental.   I'd be interested though in knowing any autopsy results and if you do a tox screen…" I was hoping professional courtesy would allow him to share any findings with me.

"Thanks. Let me see what I can do." He smiled. "Is there anything else you can remember? Anything at all?" Sue shook her head. "Well, if you think of anything please give me a call." He handed each of us his business card. "An investigator will probably drop by later today or tomorrow. Don't be surprised, and please don't use the front door until after the investigator gives you the okay. I'll check with the other apartments here and ask them to avoid the front stairs and door for a while. They all have rear entrances, right?" We nodded. "Do you know who her attorney is or have any information on next of kin? That would be very helpful."

Sue responded, "Her attorney is Kelly. He lives up the street. She lives alone, but she does have a cat, Harold. I can take care of him."

"That's not a problem?"

"No. Several of us have each other's keys, just in case we need to get in for some reason."

"Okay. Does your key open all her doors?"

"I think so. Can I go up with you to get the cat?"

"Let me help." I looked at him hopefully. He nodded. "Okay, but please don't touch anything."

Sue rifled through a kitchen drawer and produced a fuzzy fob attached to a key. Haggarty led the way up the side fire escape stairs to Ellen's side door. It was slightly ajar. "Does Ellen usually leave this open?"

"Not usually, but sometimes on hot summer days..." Which it was not; this was December.

Finn put on white booties and rubber gloves and stepped cautiously into Ellen's living room, motioning for us to stay back, but I poked my head in. It was spotless.

"Okay, don't touch anything. Wait here. I'll look for the cat." Just then Harold, a big black and white tom, came around the corner and stopped dead, looking nervously at the strangers.

"Here kitty, kitty." Despite Officer Haggarty's sweet voice, Harold arched his back.

"Let me try. He knows me." Sue coaxed, "Here, Harold, come here. I have a treat for you." Harold, having none of it, spun around and dashed behind the couch. "Damn you, Harold," Sue muttered under her breath. "Now what?" She looked at Finn.

"Listen, I'll let you in here but you can't do anything other than get the cat, okay?" While he was speaking he handed us booties from his pocket. We put them on and followed him into the living room. "Wait for me." I watched as he ducked into the kitchen and paused at the table, where Ellen's purse lay open. Gently lifting the flap he peered in and pulled out her wallet, which he carefully opened to reveal her license. He photographed it with his cellphone, flipped to a credit card and photographed that and several more cards, then opened the cash pocket and took another shot. As Sue watched him I looked around the kitchen. I noticed a calendar attached to the refrigerator and leaned toward it but couldn't make out what was printed on today's date. Finn moved on and we followed.

"Here, Harold," Sue pleaded and made kissing sounds. "Come here, sweetie." We saw him peer from the shadows behind the couch. I went around the other side as Sue went toward him. I clapped and he bolted into Sue's arms. At first it seemed like he would fight her, but she turned away from us and crooned to him and he surprised us by starting to purr. "I think his litterbox is in the bathroom." Sue pointed toward it and Finn went that way. I followed.

"I'll get it." I looked at Finn to see if that was okay. He nodded. I cautiously walked into the bathroom and picked up the pan and box of litter. I looked around. Nothing. Nothing out of place; neat as a pin. As I went back out through the kitchen I took a moment to check the calendar on the old green refrigerator and read the note on today's date.

"Gerry, don't forget. "

Chapter 3 – Harold

Sue and I went back down the fire escape to her side door. Sue put Harold down, took a bowl from the draining rack and an open can from the refrigerator, scraped some morsels into the bowl and put it on the floor. "Just a little leftover tuna." Harold made for the living room. I sat at the kitchen table, sipping sherry and waiting for Finn to join us, while Sue set up Harold's litter in her bathroom.

We waited.

Sue looked into the hallway and probably saw the small puddle of blood and crime scene tape. She jerked her head back in and shuddered.

"Come on over here and have a little more sherry." I poured some into her glass. "Why don't you sit down with me?" She looked agitated as she told me, "I checked her plants. They were damp, just right, blooming. I think we should get them. If we leave them they will die." She sipped the sherry. "What about the Morrises? They don't know. When they come home and see crime-scene tape across their front door they'll freak out. I mean, wouldn't you? Wouldn't you freak out if there was crime scene tape across your front door?" She took another sip.

When we stepped out into the hall Sue stopped at the small puddle of blood and couldn't bring herself to climb the stairs. "This is just horrible. When can we clean this up?" She stood there while I took another photo.

"This is creepy. Who usually cleans up these kinds of things?"

"I think it's mostly relatives, although I've heard there are companies that specialize in cleaning up crime scenes." She looked at me strangely.

"What do you think? Was she going out? Maybe to the post office or to Barbara's? She had her coat on and wasn't carrying her purse and didn't lock her fire escape door, so she must have been going somewhere close by, don't you think?"

"That makes sense."

Sue called Harold, who came out from the living room, wound his way around the corner and rubbed against the door jamb, tail up, in no way nervous.

"Yoo-hoo! Anybody home?" It was Barabara from across the green. She'd come to Sue's side door.

"Yes, just a second; we can't let Harold out." Sue tried to stop Harold from escaping as she let Barbara in.

"Oh, hi Frances. I didn't know you were here."

"Come on in, Barbara. Sit down and have a glass of sherry." I knew she too would need one.

"Someone said the ambulance was here this morning and there's crime scene tape outside. What's going on?"

News travels like wildfire in this little village. I was surprised there weren't a half dozen people here by now but I knew there would be soon, especially with the tape around the front, which certainly would draw some attention.

Even the usually loud traffic didn't speed by but slowed down and crept past. Rubberneckers, I thought.

"Sit down, Barb. We've had a tragedy." There was no other way to explain it. We were a diverse but engaged community and something like this struck us all. Barbara looked fearful.

"What happened?" Her eyes darted back and forth between us. "It's Ellen, isn't it?" She looked at Harold, who was investigating the bottom of the kitchen cabinets.

"Yes, she fell down the stairs." Sue paused, looking at me. "They took her off to the hospital. She didn't look good."

Barbara gasped. "You're kidding! What happened?" She took the water glass of sherry I pushed toward her as we began to explain the last hour's happenings.

Trooper Haggarty knocked at the side door and let himself in. We were all sitting around Sue's kitchen table.

"Don't get up." He put his hand out to motion us down. "I just got some bad news." We looked at him and knew what it was. "Ellen has passed away." Sue gave a low gasp. "I'm very sorry."

"Thank you, officer." I stood up and shook his hand again. "We'll be close if you need anything else."

Chapter 4 – Barbara

Of course, when a small, tight-knit village experiences a tragedy, all the villagers come together. It was no different here. We were the definition of a true village community, something I think is unusual in this day and age when everyone is online on their computers, tablets or iPhones, so you would imagine we'd be completely isolated. But not here. We would come together for the smallest event–a promotion, a retirement, a birthday; all those and more were causes for celebration. Before I moved here I hadn't experienced true commitment to a community, and now I didn't think I could live without it. Where some might have found it intrusive, most of us were happy to join in. There were outliers, but they were in the minority.

So when this happened we all came together, in the beginning at Sue's, who was the focus because she'd seen it and lived close. But gradually we visited with each other in little groups and discussed it. We all had questions, not about what happened but more about Ellen and her life– what did we really know?

I knew they needed to process it, to bring their comforting casseroles and soups somewhere, but Ellen lived alone, without husband or kids. She'd divorced decades ago and the kids went with him, living with his second wife somewhere by the shore. She had only Harold, some houseplants, the people living at the inn and of course others in the village. They were her people. So the casseroles and soups came to Sue's house and mine and to little nightly gatherings at homes throughout the village, two or three families or just a plus one. I tried to attend everything. I was curious about this woman who, although an important part of the community, was still so mysterious to me.

Barbara, Ellen's dear friend, lived diagonally across the green. They had lunch together frequently, sometimes going out, other times in each other's home. I, like the others, lived within a stone's throw of the green, the town center that so many of the old seventeenth and eighteenth-century houses faced, cheek by jowl, so much closer to each other than most homes could ever be built today. On the green sat a tiny library, which had started out in 1832 as a bank. When the bank moved to Willimantic the building lay vacant until the Windham Free Library took it over in 1896, and now it housed among its treasures a carving of Bacchus riding a keg done by British Revolutionary War prisoners. Other buildings in the village included the post office, the inn now converted to apartments, and several old churches. When Windham Center had been the county seat and the courthouse located there, it had been bustling with several taverns and inns and lawyers' homes and offices. When the county seat was moved to Brooklyn and the pace of manufacturing grew wildly in Willimantic, growth in Windham Center slowed, then reversed until it became what some might call the sleepy little town it is today, with beautiful homes and historic buildings.

I was one of those fortunate enough or silly enough to buy one of these homes. Fortunate enough because the village is lovely, silly enough because these old homes needed quite a lot of love, work and cash. Nevertheless I was happy to be included in our little community.

I invited Barbara to my house for wine and cheese. Among the many subjects we touched on, naturally Ellen was at the top.

"I was going to visit her that day, you know, Tuesday. We had planned a couple of days earlier to get together but she called at the last minute and told me she had to cancel. Well of course I had to say okay, but you know, I'd already made the brioche, and that's best served warm with lots of butter, so I was a little miffed. I feel bad about that now. How did I know what was going on with her? How did I know what would happen?"

I nodded and poured a little more wine into Barbara's glass, cut a few more slices of summer sausage and cheese, rattled some fresh crackers out of their box onto the board and freshened up what I hoped was an inviting though modest charcuterie.

"Don't feel bad. Regrets are worthless. She knew you cared. Otherwise why would she have invited you over that day?"

"Yeah, you're right." Barbara took a sip of wine, sandwiched pieces of sausage and cheese onto the rice cracker and crunched into them. "I guess it's just that it's not the first time she'd left me in the lurch. Remember those playhouse tickets I gave to Cheryl and her husband? They were supposed to be for Ellen and me, and at the last minute I had to find someone to take them." She sipped again and raised her voice a little. "They were good ones too, close to the stage, and I paid a pretty penny for them." She sighed deeply. "I don't know… it all makes me very sad. I really wanted to resolve that, feeling sort of like second fiddle. I never forgot that and I wanted to talk to her about it and get past it, put it away, and then…"

I nodded. "So did she ever explain why she couldn't go with you?" Another sip of wine for me.

"No, that's just it. It was sort of a mystery. She would allude to something important but wouldn't tell me what. I was one of her best friends, at least that's what she always said, so why didn't she tell me what was going on? I just don't get it." The conversation circled around the regret drain. It seems that so often when we've experienced transgressions by others or ourselves, it's the regrets that hang us up. If we're normal God-fearing people with a fair amount of guilt, we have a need to resolve them, put them behind us before we can move on. Otherwise we never heal, never forget, but just stay vulnerable to the next time a small comment opens up the wound again, our sensibilities always hovering just above it. I felt bad for Barbara; I really did. I knew what she was experiencing and hoped at some point she could let it go.

Just then the doorbell rang and Sue's head appeared.

"Hey, mind if I pop in for a few minutes?"

Chapter 5 – Sue

Sue, like so many of us, felt comfortable inviting herself in. She pulled up a chair and sat down, and I set her up with a plate, glass and napkin.

"Sure, we're just shooting the breeze. How are you doing?"

She smiled. "I'm okay. You know how it is. Harold has settled in, eating the houseplants and spilling litter around the bathroom." I poured wine for Sue.

"Barbara, how's your knitting coming? Almost ready with your Christmas wares? How are the sales at the shop? Things moving much?" Barbara was a very talented knitter. Using the finer wool available mostly from local farms, she'd developed a small following of people who loved the fisherman's knit styles and boiled wool mittens, hats and warm scarves she made. I watched her pick up a cracker and slice a piece of cheese with her gnarled fingers, thick with arthritis. I imagined the long winter evenings when those fingers were kept busy with lanolin-coated yarn that probably helped keep them supple.

"Oh, not bad. I sold two sweaters, got orders for two more, and got rid of at least six pairs of mittens and matching hats, so I feel like it's going well this season." I smiled at her. I too had a pair of her mittens, which seemed indestructible and warm even when soaking wet. She got a pretty penny for them, but they were worth every cent. She ran her fingers through her beautiful head of curly grey hair "But my husband seems to spend most of my profits on his damned guns. I don't know what possesses him. He just loves to collect these old things and get together with his buddies down at the Rod and Gun Club and shoot into a sandpit. How can that be fun?" She punctuated that by popping into her mouth a thick slice of sausage on a cracker, crunching and talking with her mouth full. "Really, what fun can that be?" She realized she'd blown out a couple cracker crumbs and then covered her mouth with the napkin and laughed to herself, blowing out a couple more. "I guess I'm just an animal. That must be my appeal to him." We all laughed at that.

"Sue, what are you up to? Any new woodcuts?" Sue was a woodcut artist–well, really she linocut block prints. She had been a historian and worked in the museum, but after she lost her husband she downsized into the apartment at the inn and became part of our community. She'd always been artistic, and when she took a course in cutting linoleum blocks for prints she found a niche that fit her perfectly. She could work at her kitchen table with a set of special carving knives and some block, a brayer and a paper press, turning out beautiful cards. Many were rustic linocuts of our village that she was able to sell for enough to keep her in what she called pin money, but I had a hunch it helped her a fair amount and gave her the artistic outlet so many of us needed. I loved that despite appearing somewhat scatterbrained, she was able to tackle some of the more complex issues of the conservation commission board she served on, offering a strong down-to-earth point of view. She had to be almost seventy but she kept her shoulder-length hair in a pageboy, dyed to a vivid auburn that might have been close to her original color, although now her white roots were showing.

"Well, Harold has become one of my favorite subjects now. I just designed one of him with a limp mouse in his maw. I know it sounds gruesome, but it's actually quite cute and I think it will be a great addition. I've done a couple more sketches of him, one curled up on an afghan in the sun. I'm sure this new Harold series will be a hit." She looked pleased. We nodded our agreement. "I don't know if Harold misses her. He seems pretty content just sitting in the window watching the world go by – unless it's a loud truck using its Jake Brakes. Then he retreats to his bed." She took another bite of cracker layered with herbed cream cheese. "I think it was a bit quieter in Ellen's apartment."

I was glad that so far we'd not fixated on Ellen, but I knew that would happen sooner or later. I'd heard back from Finn Haggarty and I really didn't want to talk to them about it.

"Anything else happening at the shop?" Of course the holiday season was the busiest time of year for this little shop in Willimantic that featured wonderful art and hand-crafted items. It was sad that so many talented artists and crafts people didn't have a busier downtown to sell their wares. Our struggling little downtown had seen better days, but it was gradually coming back and hopefully would be bustling once again. Willimantic, like so many other nineteenth-century mill towns, suffered when electricity allowed manufacturing to relocate from the dams and rivers that were once their source of energy.

Most manufacturing then went south and eventually left the country altogether. We did have a fine little college in town and a really good selection of eateries, so empty store fronts were gradually filling up.

"It's picking up." Both spoke and smiled at once.

Sue added, "We're featuring a special artist each day, posting online and giving out little treats like cookies and Hosmer's sparkling water." Sometimes the co-op will take things and also the museum. You never know where the best sales will be. Don't you find that, Barb?" Barb nodded and gracefully picked up an almond-stuffed olive with a toothpick.

Sue continued. "I know we have busy schedules, but wouldn't it be fun to have a game night? I'm thinking of having something like that. You know, wine, cheese, anything others want to bring. We could play cards or board games, and the boys could watch football or whatever sports they want if they aren't interested in playing. What do you think? Maybe after the holidays, not monthly like so many things, just once, or maybe twice a year. I almost go stir-crazy during the winter and just don't get out enough." Barb took a sip of wine and she and I nodded in agreement.

"When's the carol sing and tree lighting? Isn't that coming up?" We looked to Sue.

"I'm not sure. Next Saturday? I know they were just here with the fire truck and tall ladder fussing with the lights, so it must be soon."

Chapter 6 - Investigators

I was actually a little surprised that Finn got back to me. It turned out that the tox test returned some odd findings and Ellen's body had signs of a struggle. When the coroner had a look he found some strange marks and sent bloodwork out for testing. Finn said he'd like to visit with me and talk more about it. I imagined he was worried that he'd removed the body from a possible crime scene and there might be repercussions. It had been only a day and an investigative team would be coming out shortly to go through her apartment. He asked me to email him the photos, which I did, and he also asked me not to discuss this with anyone, not even Sue. I knew from my working life that the more people who know details the greater chance there is of too many details getting out and possibly fouling up an investigation, and not only that but details get changed and pretty soon people no longer remember the facts as they had shared them originally. An investigation can become mud in no time, and if there are guilty parties paying attention–and they are always paying attention— they could learn valuable details and understand what might have been found. Really, perpetrators were often paying so much attention that detectives might share false information in an attempt to snag them or lead them to think they knew less than they actually did. It was a cat and mouse game.

So I felt it important to steer most of the conversation away from Ellen. Yet I was still very curious about the woman. What was she like? Did she have relatives other than the estranged husband and kids?

Sue had told Finn and me that Ellen's lawyer was Attorney Kelly, who lived in town, next to me on North Road. I'd contacted him that evening. Knowing she didn't have any next of kin living with her, I assumed he or the coroner would file her will with probate and would want to know what had happened. He seemed appreciative and said he'd contact the coroner to get her death certificate and start the filing process.

Finn Haggarty texted me to expect an investigator to visit later in the day and I told Sue to give me a call when he came.

Sure enough, early in the afternoon she phoned to say Investigator Carlos Lopez had arrived with Investigator Kimball, who'd been there the previous day. I told her I'd be right over and threw on my warmest parka just in case I was stuck outside for very long; I'd found I didn't tolerate the cold as well as I once did, even with the extra pounds of insulation I'd put on.

Their van was parked out front, backed up to the inn as the ambulance had been. The rear doors were wide open and they were both busy with several aluminum suitcases that lay with contents in view: swabs, numbered tent signs, cameras, spray bottles, flashlights, notebooks, collection bags and bottles with numbered labels–all manner of equipment to support their investigation.

Sue waited at her window and opened her side door when I arrived.

"They already came in and introduced themselves. You remember Inspector Kimball from yesterday?" I nodded. "And the other one is Inspector Lopez." From her front window we watched their progress. Soon they approached the front door, wearing white Tyvek suits, berets, booties, and rubber gloves. A few people had parked at the post office and now stood in the driveway, looking on and talking together. We heard the inn's front door open. Sue looked out from her door to the hall.

"Hello, Ms. Gallen. It's okay if you look, but please don't come into the hall. We'll tell you when we're done."

"Okay. We'll stay right here."

Inspector Kimball had a camera with a bright light and snapped photos as she entered the hall. She put down little plastic tent cards with numbers on them and took photos. Next to the small puddle of dried blood she put an L scale with inches and centimeters marked on it. Each time she took a photo she wrote notes about it in a notebook, then advanced the film; investigators do not use digital photos because they are too easily manipulated with photo editing software and AI. After she'd taken several photos in the hall and on the stairs, Investigator Lopez came in and sprayed the whole area, then turned on the flashlight. "Ladies, if your lights shine into the hallway it will be hard for us to get good photos. We need darkness." Sue turned off her living-room light and he switched the hall lights off and shone his flashlight on the stairs, from the bottom to the top. It was a UV flashlight and the luminal he'd sprayed made any blood glow bright blue. We noticed more smudges and splatters partway up the stairs. Kimball started photographing. We closed the door and went back to the kitchen.

"I wonder when they'll let us use the front door."

"I don't think it will be too much longer, maybe today or tomorrow." Sue had picked up the local paper and spread it on the table. Ellen's death had not made the front page but was on page 3.

> **Elderly Woman Rushed to Hospital**
> Ellen Wolfe Richardson, of Windham Center, retired Professor of English Literature at UConn, passed away yesterday after she apparently fell down her stairs. State Police are investigating this as suspicious. More details to come as information is uncovered.

Harold slid sleekly around the corner from the bedroom, rubbing against Sue's leg, and aimed for his food bowl. The activity on the stairs did not seem to affect his appetite.

"I wonder if they will help us get those plants from Ellen's apartment." Sue went to the door, cracked it open and peeked out. I heard Inspector Lopez say, "We're almost done here, Ms. Gallen. Once we've finished you can use your front door. We've got a few more questions so we'll stop by in a little while."

Chapter 7 – The Questions

"They're doing something with the handle on the front door, maybe taking fingerprints. We can use it pretty soon." Sue tuned her small flat-screen television to the local news. The weather forecast predicted snow. "Gee, we haven't gotten any snow this year yet. It would be nice to have it before Christmas, just for the beauty of it. But I'm grateful I don't have to shovel – just clean off my car. We have someone to plow out the parking and shovel the front walk." We watched news highlights until a knock at the door startled us both. It was Lopez, holding a clipboard and no longer wearing the white suit and booties.

"Hello, Ms. Gallen." He held out his hand to shake. "Can I come in?" Sue led us all to the kitchen table. "I have a few questions. Do you have a couple of minutes?" Sue nodded and introduced me.

"This is Frances O'Connor. She lives nearby, and she was here yesterday when it happened." He leaned across to shake my hand too.

"Hello, Ms. O'Connor. Inspector Lopez. You must be the retired detective." He smiled and I returned his smile and nodded. "So what do you think, Ms. O'Connor?"

"I don't know, but it looks like an accident."

"Yes, it does look that way. Did either of you go up the front stairs to her apartment?" We both shook our heads. "Well, her door was open and so was the fire escape door, and when you found her the front door was ajar too. Is that correct?" Susan nodded

"Yes, the front door was slightly open, but I didn't go up the front stairs and went up the fire escape only with Officer Haggarty, not before, and yes, that door was open too."

"Don't you think it's odd that in December, when it's quite cold, all Ellen's doors were open?"

We looked at him, then at each other. Sue said, "Yes, it is odd, I mean, we do have the heat jacked up kind of high, but still, not so much that anyone would want all their doors open." He looked at each of us and waited uncomfortably for Sue or me to say something else. That's an investigative tool: ask a question, get an answer and wait, wait for more, wait until the person being questioned feels uncomfortable, feels the need to say more, and maybe says something they hadn't intended to say, maybe changing their story after they realize they'd slipped up.

"Did you hear anything yesterday morning other than her falling down the stairs?" He watched Sue as she leaned back and looked at the ceiling.

"Not really. I mean, you know, I think I heard someone go up and down the stairs. Nothing unusual; people go up and down the stairs all the time. The three apartments above use those stairs."

"So you heard someone go up and down the stairs. Please try to remember. This is important."

"I guess so. I don't know. I didn't really pay that much attention."

"Have you seen or talked to Ms. Richardson lately?"

"I saw her a couple of days ago, when she asked me if I could pick up some kibble for Harold when I went shopping. I did and dropped it off upstairs and she paid me for it. I didn't see anything odd, although she did seem stressed or something, a bit more short than usual. She could be kind of crotchety–we all knew that–but she had a heart of gold underneath it all. She'd do anything for you. God, I'll miss her." Lopez watched her. "That's the thing–she would tell you what she thought in no uncertain terms. She wasn't one to smile and sweet-talk to your face and then talk about you behind your back. If she had something to say, she'd say it."

"Do you think that made enemies?" Lopez jotted down a note.

"Well, I don't know. You either liked her or you didn't. I think if she offended you, you likely deserved it, and then you might just avoid her. Why? Do you think someone tried to hurt her? Did someone do this to her?" Sue looked intensely at him.

Chapter 8 – Don't Forget The Plants

"We think she may have died under suspicious circumstances. That's why we're here, so if you noticed anything, anything at all, it could be important."

"She was alive when they took her out, wasn't she, Fran? You saw her. She was still alive, right?"

"Yes, but barely," I confirmed.

"Ms. Gallen, she died on the way to the hospital. They've taken her body to the UConn Health Center in Farmington, where the medical examiners and death investigators do their work. They've taken blood and tissue samples from her brain, kidneys, liver, eyes and other organs which might hold clues, but the results are not back yet. They're checking for evidence of trauma, contusions, abrasions and bruising that might have occurred prior to the fall and they will try to determine if any bones broken were not consistent with her fall." He paused.

"That's crazy. Who would want to kill her? That's just insane. She's just a fussy old lady. No one would kill her. I mean…" Sue's glance went from him to me, then back to him.

"Here is my card, Ms. Gallen. Please call if you think of anything else." He handed both of us cards and stood up.

"Wait. Can we get the plants that are in her apartment? They'll die if we don't get them."

He smiled. "Sure, let me go up and get them." Lopez left and a few minutes later several potted plants were on Sue's kitchen table. "You can use the front door now. We're taking down the tape. I think we've gotten everything we need. Remember to call if you think of anything." He left, and we watched him and Inspector Kimball pack up the van and drive away. The crime scene tape was gone. The only telltale sign of the event was the puddle of dried blood and smudges on the bottom of the stairs.

"Do you think they found anything suspicious?" The obvious might not have been obvious to Sue.

"I don't know. I guess we'll just have to wait and find out." I inspected one of the violets. "Can I keep this one? I think I gave it to her, and she took good care of it. It will be a nice memory of her."

"Yeah, sure. I think I can keep the rest of these alive and hope that Harold doesn't eat them." Harold had jumped up onto the kitchen table where the plants were and was inspecting them. When he started to nibble one Sue grabbed the squirt gun she used to show Harold his boundaries, and with a little squirt Harold hopped onto the floor and licked his coat where it was wet, looking regally insulted.

"Shouldn't we clean up the blood? I mean it's not only unpleasant, it seems disrespectful to Ellen, just leaving her blood there like no one cares, people just stepping over it." I nodded. She went to a cabinet and pulled out Windex, paper towels and rags. In the hall she sprayed the dried puddle and watched as it slowly reconstituted and became a somewhat brighter red again. She wiped it with paper towels and sprayed it again to liquefy the next layer of not quite dissolved blood. Gradually she got it all and put the paper towels into a paper bag. "I'm going to incinerate these, sort of like a cremation. Just a small measure of respect for this old friend." Her lips were pressed thin as she tried not to cry.

Chapter 9 – The Village

Soup night was coming up the next Sunday and I hoped if I moved around enough into the little clusters of conversations I would catch some interesting tidbits about Ellen. I was becoming obsessed with her. Superficially she seemed well-liked; although straightforward she was thoughtful, polite, generous, and often kind. Who would want to murder her (at least I assumed it was murder)? Who could possibly want to do it? Barbara was one of her good friends, but she had several others and I needed to spend some time with all of them. What was a retired detective's hobby but rooting out all the information and facts that our little village had to offer? Of course I had other things to keep me busy; an older home always had things to be fixed and gardens to be kept and a lawn to be mowed. I was constantly making small adjustments to hinges that came loose or locks that needed greasing, or contacting this contractor or that plumber or another electrician. I was pretty handy and grateful I could manage most of the smaller and carpentry-related fixes, but the plumbing and more complex electrical were beyond me, and I was getting on. This aging stuff was difficult; I'd had no idea how difficult it would be. When I looked in the mirror now I saw almost someone I didn't know. White hair, thinning but still long and pulled up into a sloppy bun, wispy dangling pieces haloing my head; eyes not as clear and needing cheaters just to read the paper; skin getting papery and weird spidery lines on my cheeks and neck where an occasional odd hair stood out long and stiff like an errant weed. What the heck had happened to me? I was one of the healthiest and strongest people I knew and now I was starting to bend over and lean forward and wanted to sit more than stand. It was hard to adjust to this aging stuff, and I couldn't decide whether it would be best to "fight against the dying of the light" or "age gracefully," neither of which I was ready for. I tried to keep busy and that wasn't hard in this little village. Something was always going on: dinners, gatherings, trips to a show or just shopping together. It would be harder to have free time than to be busy, and I understood why some of the villagers chose to be more reclusive or at least not as involved as many of us were.

Soup night consisted of visiting the home of a participant who volunteered to cook two soups, one vegetarian and one with meat or seafood. People would come with their own bowls, napkins and spoons that they would bring home unwashed. They were also expected to bring a bottle and something extra, a sweet or savory dish. The hosts supposedly did not have to clean up but they usually did. Guests of course didn't always bring something; if they were too busy to cook they came empty-handed. There were no hard and fast rules so occasionally I'd just bring cheese and crackers or nothing, but mostly we all brought something and spent the evening eating and visiting and gossiping. It was loose and always pleasant.

The people in this village were diverse but almost all were kind and engaged and engaging. Those who perhaps had fewer social skills were encouraged and those with more were encouraging. There was always a level of conversation that made for a warm, pleasant hum, like a beehive without stings. It was very rare for anyone to be unpleasant, and any interpersonal issues were either smoothed over or taken "off-line" to be handled at another time. There were cliques. Some of the cliques had to do with interests, say sports. Some were crazy for football, or gardening, or cooking, sewing, art, music, carpentry, or fix-it. Some might have been defined by assumed social status. There was a clique of gay people and one of live-theatre enthusiasts; people moved smoothly from one clique to another. The one topic we often avoided was politics; since views diverged, we tried to keep that at a minimum to ensure smooth and unflustered evenings. Such a wide range of interests and careers left no lack of topics to chat about on soup night, but I knew this night would have one topic that rose above the rest, and I would be there, moving from group to group, talking, nibbling, listening.

I made some of my favorite cookies and found a bottle from the case I had bought. I myself didn't drink alcohol, but I didn't mind if others did and didn't want to cheap out on bringing something nice, so once or twice a year I'd pick up a case of wine along with some favorite non-alcoholic drinks for myself.

Soup night tonight was at the Sandons home, the old Webb house near the green, one of the village's most historical homes. It was said that from its elevated porch Lafayette had addressed his troops.

I was ready.

Chapter 10 – Soup Night

The mood was festive since it was near Christmas. Everyone seemed relaxed though perhaps slightly keyed up, like children on Christmas Eve. Bowls of soup, salads and casseroles were downed with gusto, and chatter and laughter filled the air as the wine flowed. I filled my bowl and moved from group to group. The whole event was fluid as villagers glided smoothly from one group to the next, from one topic to the next, sometimes engaging in long, serious discussions, other times just stopping for a fleeting moment to see if the subject matter interested them and moving on if not. Someone might show the latest cellphone photo of a grandchild or new puppy or discuss the town budget or the theme of next year's fundraiser for their favorite nonprofit, or any manner of topic. Friends might meet again after a month or so, or after returning from a long summer at the beach. My ears were attuned as if any and all talk interested to me, and mostly it did, but when Ellen's name came up my radar pulled me to that conversation. Soon a number of people were talking about her, so many that I couldn't take it all in and got frustrated trying.

Barbara, who knew her so well, lamented her loss and spoke eloquently of her kindness and generous nature. Lisa agreed and added to Barbara's comments. Allison moved closer and said she'd never felt so comfortable talking with anyone as she did with Ellen, who never criticized her when she brought up her troubles; she shot a glance at someone but I couldn't make out who. Then Sue spoke and everyone quieted.

"I found her that morning. It was weird. I'd heard a loud noise in the hall and when I looked out, the front door was a little open and I was going to close it and investigate the noise, and there she was...." Sue started to choke up and Barbara put an arm around her shoulder.

"That must have been shocking." Allison filled the awkward pause.

"It was. Frances was there. I called 911 and they came and took her away, and later the investigators came." Sue recovered and everyone listened, several of them looking at me near the doorway. She described the detectives and the luminol sprayed on the stairs and walls and how the blood spots glowed when you couldn't even see a trace with your bare eyes, and how they finally removed the crime scene tape on Ellen's door when they left.

I watched everyone's reaction. They were glued to Sue's words, occasionally looking over to me when she gestured my way as she spoke. People from the other rooms stood as close to the doorway as they could. No one moved around; everyone listened to Sue. Shelly, who stood next to me, leaned close and spoke low, just loud enough for me to hear.

"I didn't know her very well. She always seemed like a cold fish to me, kind of snooty." I turned to her and she raised her eyebrows.

"Well, I know I shouldn't speak ill of the dead, but don't you think she was a snob?" I kept gazing at her with what I hoped was no trace of understanding on my face. "I mean, she never was rude to me; she just wasn't friendly. Almost everyone is warm and welcoming here–well, almost everyone." She gave me a sideways glance, I chuckled, and the tension was broken.

I said, "It was probably a holdover from being an English Lit professor; she had a doctorate. You know, she probably used her attitude to intimidate students, keep them in line." At my words Shelly raised her eyebrows again, pursed her lips and uttered a drawn out melodic "Ohhh. I guess."

Several people asked Sue questions and I strained to hear. Then Tom turned to me and smiled.

"So, what do you think, Frances? You're an old detective. You must have some thoughts on this." I liked Tom. We'd been friends for years and even though he had a husband, we felt like soulmates and could, especially when we were alone, be frank with each other. I leaned into him, quietly signaling that it was for his ears only.

"I want to see how people are reacting, so we'll talk later, okay?" He nodded and gave me a knowing look.

I saw a few people turn away and head toward the dessert table, either having had enough or going to discuss it further. I edged my way out to follow them as Sue continued talking.

I browsed the desserts: lemon bars, chocolate chip cookies, Barb's refrigerator cookies, an ornate tray of Italian cookies probably from Motta's Bakery, walnut spice meringues, a nice spice cake with walnuts sprinkled on top of the icing. Others were browsing too, sampling what appealed to them.

"These walnut spice meringues are deceptively delicious." Two women had moved beside me and tasted one. They were newcomers who had bought a home on Mullen Hill and I didn't know them very well. "I don't remember your names. I'm Frances. I live on the other side of the green a few houses down on North Street." I held out my hand.

"Shirley, and this is my wife Freda. Nice to meet you."

"So I guess you didn't know Ellen at all."

"No, but we heard someone talking about her. Sad, isn't it?" We all nodded. "Wow, these meringues are great!"

"You heard Sue talking about Ellen?"

"Yes, but someone else was saying that she was quite a B I T C H." Shirley spelled it out and chuckled nervously. I wanted to know who the someone was.

"Really? I'd always heard she was well-liked. I guess you just never know, do you?" We were near the doorway where Sue and the others were gathered, and people were moving into the dessert room. With a knowing look Shirley, gently elbowed me and tipped her head toward someone who'd just come in. It was Lisa, one of Ellen's friends. I walked over to her.

"Try the meringues; they are delish." I smiled. "Hey, are you busy on Tuesday? Want to have lunch? I'm making quiche…"

"Love to. What time?"

Chapter 11 – Lisa

Lisa lived on Scotland Road just up from the post office. She and her husband had been there for several years, raising their children and sending them off to college, and now had a few grand babies.

I'd made a broccoli mushroom quiche, one of my specialties. Lisa chatted about her husband, who always seemed busy now that he was involved in town politics, and of course about her children, their careers, and her grandchildren. I listened patiently, knowing I would have to wade through her personal business before I could get her to talk about Ellen. Finally, after working our way through a couple slices of the quiche and a cup of coffee with a few of the meringues I'd held back from soup night, I felt I could approach the topic I was most interested in.

"Sad about Ellen, isn't it?" Lisa eyed me, trying to decide if this was what the whole lunch invitation was about. I shook my head. "I mean around Christmas time. Who wants to have a death in the village? It seems to taint everything, doesn't it?" I made an effort to sound sincere to this suspicious woman.

"Yeah, you're right, it does seem to hang a cloud over us. At least no close relatives need to be under that cloud, or at least I don't think there's anyone other than her ex-husband and children who probably hardly knew her, and I doubt that he cares. She never sees them, hasn't seen them in years." She took another cookie and sipped her coffee.

"Did you know her very well?" I knew that she knew her fairly well and hoped to get her to talk a little.

"We were pretty good friends, but you know, she could be fickle. Sometimes she just didn't want to talk to or be around anyone, and she made that very clear."

"Really? What do you think that was about?" I was genuinely curious.

"I. Don't. Know." She spoke the words separately, pausing a second between each one. "I think she was writing, you know, either a diary or journal, but I'm not sure of that either. She could be rather mysterious. I know she read quite a lot and was always at the library taking out the latest bestsellers, but also some classics, biographies, and all manner of periodicals. She was voracious." Lisa was not only Ellen's friend but was also on the board of the library, so she paid attention to what was being taken out to ensure they had a steady stream of whatever people wanted to read. "She didn't even have a television. You know it seems everyone has a gigantic flat screen these days, but not Ellen. If she wanted to watch something she'd use her iPad; she had a big one. Once in a while she'd come to our house to watch something. She loved historical drama and some of those seem to come across better on a big screen." I let her go on, hoping she'd say something I could put together to make sense of this. "You don't think this was an accident, do you?" Lisa was suspicious and direct. She sat erect and held her head as though she were a model and body-conscious; obviously she was once a beautiful woman. With a practiced motion she brushed her too-long bangs out of her eyes.

"No. The police think it may not have been an accident and they are starting an investigation. They may even come by and want to talk to you."

"But I don't know anything." Her shoulders and hands went up.

"I'm sure you know that I was a detective." She nodded. "Well, as a detective I can tell you that any tiny bit of information, put together with whatever else they might have, can sometimes be just that tiny thing that finishes off the puzzle, that connects it all together to make sense." She nodded. "I know it seems intrusive, and unnecessary, but what if there is a murderer on the loose? What if there is someone preying on elderly women…? That's not out of the question. We just don't know what happened, and if a person caused it, wouldn't you feel better knowing who, and why? Could it be someone from earlier in her life? Was it plotted out? Was it spontaneous? Could it be someone from the village? There are so many questions and I personally want answers."

"I understand." She nodded, yet her voice still had a tone, maybe resentful.

"Did she go out with many others from town?"

"Well, she would go out with Barbara and me, and Allison. Sometimes all four of us would go together, sometimes to Willibrew, sometimes to the Harp, once in a while to Stone Row but that was when we wanted to splurge."

"So she really didn't have too many friends?"

"Um, once she was out there, people would recognize her and say hello, mostly former students, or she'd introduce us to faculty she'd worked with if they came over to chat. But she didn't seek them out; they'd come to her. I think she was quite popular when she was teaching. Even after she retired–what, maybe fifteen years ago–people still remembered her and she remembered them. She had a remarkable memory for people and names. I'm so bad at names. Anyway, a few of the ladies in town would go down to the senior center to play mahjong or do tai chi, but they could never persuade her to go. You know sometimes there are some fun things going on down there, but she wouldn't go."

"I see. So, you've never seen anyone angry with her or say really mean things about her, or threaten her?"

"No. Not really. I know she wasn't the kindest person. I mean she was blunt, and at times said what she thought even if it wasn't what people wanted to hear, but really, no one else would tell people the truth. You know how you might tell someone their slip is showing, or they have a crumb on their face, or something like that? I remember when she told someone they had bad breath, and they did, and I think that helped them toward better oral hygiene. She told someone else their perfume was too strong, and I think they toned that down a bit after she said it. But you know, not everyone wants to hear that. She wouldn't talk about you behind your back. If she had a beef with you she'd tell you to your face. She complained constantly about grammar and spelling in text messages and even in newspapers. She thought the world was going to hell. But I liked her."

"Thanks, Lisa.   You've been a real wealth of information; you don't realize how much. Have another cup of coffee? Or tea? Another meringue? Wine?"

"No, thank you, Frances. I appreciate it but I've got to get home to start dinner for my husband. You know he builds up an appetite rubbing elbows with the town officials and then comes home to complain to me about them."

Chapter 12 – Allison

After Lisa left I had to sit and absorb some of the things she'd told me. I was filling in the details of this person who met an untimely death and now I wished I'd taken the time to get to know her better.

I wanted to meet with Allison, another close friend of Ellen's. Maybe I'd invite her to the Harp and see if we could score one of those high-backed booths that seemed so cozy and private. Or I could make her lunch. I knew Haggarty would be coming back in a few days and I wanted to see what he knew, and he might just give me more information if I had something to give him.

Allison lived with her husband and teenage sons on Plains Road, right next to St. Paul's. I sent her an email, hoping that planning lunch together would allow her time to visit before she had to make dinner for her crew.

I thought I should also talk to Shelly, maybe even before Allison. After all, Shelly didn't seem to like Ellen very much and might be an even better source of information. I sent Shelly an email too, also inviting her to lunch. I knew Shelly rented from Joyce, who had some rental apartments. Rather than live alone in a big old house it is nice to have others living there to make it feel safer and less lonely, and certainly the money doesn't hurt. Several people in town had rooms they let, often to UConn grad students.

Both of them got back to me. Allison said she could visit me the next day. I'd offered her chicken curry with fresh vegetables. I knew she didn't eat very much beef, so chicken might be just the thing.

I told Shelly I'd take her out to lunch. I thought she might like Mexican and suggested that, or lunch at the Brewery if Mexican didn't appeal to her. She chose the Brewery. I thought in the next few days I'd be getting not only too many leftovers but also, I hoped, some good information.

Allison and I hit it off. I knew she was handy because we'd chatted at social gatherings. Someone had told her I had a drill press, and she needed some holes drilled in a board for a loom she was repairing. Most people, even those with good workshops, don't keep drill presses, which need to be fastened down and are just in the way unless you need them, but when you do they're invaluable. So we'd swapped shop talk. In her free time she was a weaver. In the barn out behind her house she had a large floor loom she'd shown me a while ago. It was quite impressive. I didn't know very much about weaving, and she took the time to show me how the loom worked and how some fairly complex weaving is done. I'd had no idea and was very impressed. She made beautiful scarves, towels, and lap robes, and she said sometimes she'd even do larger pieces. Occasionally she had to do minor repairs to the loom, which was an older one. I'd met her husband, also talented, who made metal sculptures. I was surprised that someone working in metal didn't have a drill press, but they said they were considering getting one. He did welding and cut the metal with a heavy-duty saw much like a jigsaw with a hacksaw blade. They both fascinated me and I was glad of the opportunity to visit with Allison.

I was at the stove finishing up my curried chicken when she arrived. It was one o'clock and I thought if I offered her a lighter white wine it might be fine with the curry. I set her up with a glass and cheese and cracker snacks so she could settle in before lunch.

"So, I heard you're asking about Ellen." She looked at me from the table, slicing the sharp cheddar thinly to get the most flavor.

"You heard right. Do you mind?" Of course I had expected it would get around.

"No, I don't mind. I doubt I have any information worth your chicken curry, but I'd love to visit." She gave me a wry smile.

"I know you were friends. What did you like about her? I'm hearing things about her that I didn't know, and they're making me wish I'd gotten to know her better."

"I liked her a lot. She was no nonsense, you know? Sensible. In our meetings at the historical commission she was practical, not going into a long explanation if a simple one would do, not breaking the rules but evaluating them to see if some of them were perhaps outdated or too restrictive. She was like that, someone you would want to deal with, not someone who tried to be bossy or wield power just to serve her ego. She was a breath of fresh air." Allison paused to have another slice of cheese. "On the other hand, if she felt strongly about something it was hard to get her to budge; she'd stand her ground against anyone.

But she would also listen and if she thought she was wrong she was willing to change. I'll really miss her."

"Do you think there were people who didn't like her?"

"Oh, yeah. But you can be sure they won't tell you that. I mean, she's dead so who's going to talk bad about her now? There were a couple of guys on the commission who were always butting heads with her, and I think she especially like twisting their tails. She was always so sensible and sometimes made them look foolish. They were usually polite but you could see their faces getting red, and you knew they were pissed off. I wouldn't be surprised if Stanley had a dart board in his garage with her face on it and he and Mike took turns throwing; they were aligned in their love of detail and complexity."

"Really. I hadn't heard about that. Good to know. Thanks." I carried the pot of curry and pan of rice to the table.

"Ooooh, looks wonderful. If it's as good as it looks can I get the recipe?"

"Of course. I share all my recipes."

"What's in it?"

"Start with chopped onions and a generous dose of olive oil, then the chopped up chicken, and the curry – I use this canned red curry – makes it just hot enough, then carrots and squash cut up, broccoli florets and a can of coconut milk and white raisins." We spooned out the rice and ladled the curry onto it.

"Oh, this is delish! Spicy, but delish."

"Anything else spicy about Ellen that you can dish to me?" She chuckled and took another bite.

"I know there were a few more people she had trouble getting along with, but most of us loved her. I will miss her a lot."

Chapter 13 – Shelly

I had more leftovers than I could manage and considered who else might be willing to visit within the next few days. But next I was taking Shelly to the Brewery.

I picked her up in front of Joyce's and headed into town. I was grateful the dining room wasn't too crowded during lunch hour and we could find a seat in the corner that gave us a little privacy.

Shelly was what my mother would have called prickly, that is, easy to rile and take offense, but she had a good sense of humor and was quick to laugh, even at herself. So it wasn't hard to talk to her, especially after a couple of the brewery's hazy IPAs.

She knew exactly why I'd asked her to lunch.

"So, what's new in the Ellen Richardson investigation?" She smiled as she took another sip of the brew. I wasn't surprised she opened the conversation that way. We'd chatted about the weather and the house decorations as we drove into Willi, avoiding the obvious subject. Up to this point Shelly and I had not spent much time together. I liked her well enough but she was a griper, one of those people who easily found fault and complained openly about it. When gripers met up with each other they could spend a whole evening whining about everything, especially those things they really had no control over and so no responsibility to change.

I once had a lieutenant say to me, "Don't bring your complaints to me unless you are also bringing a solution.

Otherwise I don't want to hear them." That attitude changed my way of thinking about everything. Who cares who's making the laws or who's in government unless we're willing to work toward changing them? Who cares about climate change unless we're willing to do our little part, recycle, save a tree, whatever is needed. If you're not willing to try to fix it, don't complain about it.

Shelly's complaints frequently fell on deaf ears but she made changes when she could, often ruffling feathers when she did – the easier-to-make-apologies-than-get-permission type, making changes without getting authorization, without talking to anyone, and letting the chips fall where they would. She was the one most expected to show up for a demonstration, or at a town hall meeting about a controversial topic in town. Often her point of view was spot on, but her way of couching it riled people; much too often she'd point out the problem and the person she held responsible. That did not go over big, even when she was right. She was a thorn, but maybe one that each town needed, someone not afraid to confront.

Really, I thought, if anyone was going to be murdered, I would not have been surprised if it was her. In retrospect I probably should have begun my queries about Ellen with Shelly, who might give me something to bring up with other people.

"Well, I haven't heard back from the investigators so I don't really know what's going on with that. I hope to talk to at least one of them in the next week."

The waitress came and asked about our meal. We'd both ordered a Reuben, which is particularly good at Willi

Brew, and the two of us mumbled with our mouths full that they were delicious.

I continued, "I didn't really know Ellen very well, but everyone I've talked to seemed to really like her, and that made me wish I'd gotten to know her better."

Shelly patted her mouth with the napkin. "Actually, I wanted to like her too. I thought she was honest and straightforward and generally not afraid to air her opinions. That's not something I see a lot of in this town, where everyone seems busy trying to tiptoe around some people and some issues. But she was arrogant, and damn, I just hate arrogance. I'm thinking of one particular time when she interrupted me in a meeting and when I tried to finish she shushed me. I felt I was back in grade school with my teacher telling me to quiet down. It was humiliating. Everyone looked at me, I guess knowing I'm really not one to be shushed. I was mortified. I didn't say anything until later. I approached her, and you know what she said?" I shook my head. "'You should have known better than to talk about something you don't know anything about.' That's what she said. Well, no matter whether I knew something about it or not, that was just rude. That's what I thought and I lost it. So I used the 'F' word. I asked her who the 'F' she thought she was and said I thought she was just a conceited old fart. She replied that my comment didn't surprise her as I was only trailer trash." Shelly took a gulp of the IPA. "That hurt, but more, it pissed me off. I just avoided her after that, and when we were in meetings together I made sure I knew what I was talking about, a little timidly at first, but I wasn't going to have that old bag shut me up."

"Oh, goodness, that must have been hard. I know it would have gotten to me."

"Yeah. I've never forgotten it."

"Do you think there are other people who feel the same way?"

"You mean angry enough to kill her? Good question. I don't think I ever heard her directly insult anyone else. But yes, there were people she might cut short in a meeting or might directly contradict, but not in quite so demeaning a way. I bet there are students who hated her... and, well, she's not married anymore..."

We had almost finished our Reubens.

"Are you interested in dessert?"

"Sure. I wonder if they have ice cream."

"Let's ask."

We not only had dessert but also nice tall bottomless cups of coffee, for which I was glad. I couldn't help but support Ellen a little. "I bet Ellen was a good teacher, but I imagine you'd have to be a good student too. If you were a slacker she'd probably be hard on you."

"Yeah. When did she quit teaching? Like ten, fifteen years ago? I wonder if there are any students who had her living in town."

"Oh, I never thought of that. I should ask around. She was a professor at UConn so some students of hers must still live near here. You know it's funny the way people go to school far from home and end up staying in the area. Don't you think that's odd? Maybe some of those people are from small towns that seem dull after going to a big school."

"I guess, but I think UConn has a rep as a party school." I sensed she was ready to move on.

"How about those Huskies?" She laughed.

Chapter 14 – Should I?

Shelly gave me something to think about: What if a student of hers from years ago was still harboring a grudge? I put that in my notes. What if….

What if they were poorly performing students? Once upon a time students were given real grades, reflecting their actual work or lack of it. From what I was hearing, this wasn't true anymore. Teachers and professors could not give failing grades because the administration no longer allowed it. So below average kids were passing, and who knew what kind of learning actually happened. Anyhow, many of them, believing they knew better than their teachers or elders, just did things their way, not following directions or understanding the knowledge behind the teaching. How much cheating was going on in the era of computers and artificial intelligence? Fifteen years ago, when Ellen was still teaching, did some of her students get failing grades? Or were they stung by her acerbic tongue? I was getting the sense she might have had favorites, and if you have favorites you might also have less than favorites, for whom it would be difficult. I wondered if I still had any connections at UConn and if I could see old records of her students and their grades. That might be interesting. I wondered if she might still have of her students' records. Would she have kept them, and where? I decided to call Barbara. Maybe she would know something.

"Hi, Barbara, it's Frances."

"Yeah, I recognized your voice. What's up?"

"Did Ellen ever talk about school, you know, when she was teaching, anything negative?"

"Yes, once in a while. She compared what students and classes were like when she was younger to what they were later on when she was about ready to retire. She didn't have much good to say about it."

"Really? Do you remember anything specific?"

"No, not really. Sometimes she'd bring up this occasion or that, when there was a particularly difficult encounter, but never any names."

"Do you think she kept anything from when she was teaching? Graded papers or anything like that?"

"I don't know. She may have. She had a desk in the back of her bedroom, an older oak one, nice, with several filing-sized drawers built into it–at least that's what I think I remember. I suppose she could have things tucked away there. But you know how fastidious she was, so if there is anything, I'm sure it would be filed alphabetically." She chuckled. "But she was discreet, and professional. If she had something I'm sure she wouldn't want to have just anyone see it."

"Thanks, Barbara." I paused. "You don't think there's anyone who would…" Another pause.

"What? You think someone killed her? One of her students? Someone in the neighborhood?"

"I don't know."

"That's crazy. No one in this town would do that. What are you thinking, Frances?"

"I don't know. Maybe I'm getting senile." We both laughed. "Or maybe…"

"Oh, stop. That's silly. Just stop. You'll have us all looking over our shoulders, imagining which of our neighbors are murderers."

"Okay, but do you know anyone in the neighborhood who went to UConn between fifteen and twenty or more years ago?"

"Let me think about that. I'll talk to Allison. She might know a few people. She went to UConn ages ago."

"Really. I didn't know that. When did she graduate?"

"Oh, maybe twenty, twenty-five years ago."

"Hmmm. Good to know."

It was a real long shot, a student or faculty member harboring a grudge for so many years and with such ferocity they might be willing to kill. It did seem hard to fathom. But who else? I doubted Ellen had insulted anyone in town so badly they would want to hurt her. Even Shelly, who still remembered the sting of Ellen's tongue, had bad things to say but would never act on them.

Detective Haggarty called and left a message on my machine. He wanted to visit and wondered when I might have some time. This was just what I was hoping for. I called back and we arranged to visit on Monday, giving me the opportunity to do some more digging over the weekend.

I called Allison and invited her to share some holiday eggnog. Everyone knew what I was about by now and would either say yes because they were willing to talk about it, or no because they were tired of what they might think was rehashing the same old stuff. But I knew that rehashing was a great investigative tool too. Often new things came up or a change in someone's story revealed what had been forgotten. Frequently rehashing was how criminals were caught, as stories changed and changed again until they enmeshed themselves in a spiderweb of lies that when scrutinized revealed the truth.

I had to find a way to lure these people who were already tired of my prying to open up willingly and not feel they were being morbid.

The holidays were hard upon us and people were busy and stressed. Those having company were cleaning and cooking and perhaps changing bed clothes in the spare room. Gift shopping was stressful because the stores were full of grouchy people rushing about, parking in jammed lots and shopping in crowded aisles. Somehow the spirit of Christmas seemed lost in the bustle. All the while I plotted a way to get more information about the characters in our little village.

I knew I'd be seeing Haggarty soon, but what if I got a peek at any files Ellen might have stashed away in her desk? How would I get in? I could crawl under the crime scene tape without damaging it, but I didn't have a key and I knew Sue had given hers to Haggarty. Sue had said several people exchanged keys so they could care for each other's apartments in case they weren't home, so who else might have a key? Would Sue be suspicious if I asked? Apartment two was directly across the hall from Sue's apartment on the first floor, and below Ellen's. I knew that Jim and Nancy lived there in retirement. I wondered how close they were to Ellen. They must have been friends. The people above her weren't too social so my gut said Jim and Nancy might have a second key. I didn't see any way of getting it. Sue, Jim, and Nancy all knew Ellen's apartment was still sealed off and would likely be unwilling to support my clandestine activities. Would someone who shared her apartment key with two other people in the building perhaps have hidden a key in case she lost hers? Could I look for it? Could I go into the inn and up the stairs without arousing the suspicion of others in the building? When would be the best time? Sunday. Half the people would be at church and maybe the others would be out for breakfast or shopping. I would be watching. I lived close enough to see their cars go by, and strolling casually past would not be suspicious. I decided Sunday morning between nine and ten would be ideal. I waited.

Chapter 15 – UConn

In the meantime I contacted the records department at UConn. Having been a detective sometimes opened doors that were often closed to many.

Once I got them on the phone I was transferred to an administrative assistant who told me it might be much faster to submit the request online. The paperwork, as it might be in any corporate or academic structure, was loaded with fill-ins and lots of questions about the requested documents. What, I wondered, would be too broad? Could I just ask for all Professor Ellen Richardson's students? How would I delve into that to find who might have liked or not liked her? Then I thought of yearbooks. Might some students have made comments critical of her? That seemed the easiest path. I could visit the Homer Babbidge Library at UConn.

UConn allows the public to go into this fine library and use the computers and study areas, but some things require registration. Looking at yearbooks did not. I went to the library.

I looked at the 1999 Nutmeg, UConn's yearbook, and found nothing in particular, only her photo. Same for 1998. Then I opened the year 2000, over twenty years ago.

The educators were all in the front and there were a number of them, but it looked like only department heads and the tenured had accompanying photos. I poked through Anthropology, Applied Mathematical Sciences, Art History, Biological Sciences, Biophysics, Chemistry,

Classics, Communication Sciences, Ecology and Evolutionary Biology, Economics, and finally came to English. There she was near the top of the page: Ellen Wolfe Richardson, Professor of English Literature. She didn't look bad, though I might not have recognized her. But across her photo, in heavy ballpoint pen, large and underlined, screamed the word BITCH! Obviously someone didn't like her, having taken the time to search out a yearbook open to the public.

I started going through that yearbook, page by page, looking for another comment made with a heavy blue ballpoint pen. I found others, most in the English section. Next to an attractive blonde with long wavy hair and a large bosom was "Ooh, La, La!" By a nebbishy-looking fellow with glasses was "NERD!"; by a plain looking girl was "SUCK-UP". But then on the photo of a good-looking boy was a smiley face. I wrote down his name: Calvin Grusso. I thought it might be worth finding out who he was. I finished paging through the rest of the book with little else to show for it and then looked up Calvin. He was twenty-two at graduation, making him around forty-five now. I used my iPad and the library's internet to search for more about him. All manner of information about people is available on the internet, especially if you're prepared to pay a reasonable fee, and I was prepared.

Calvin lived on Jerusalem Road in Windham Center, just up the road from the center of town. I went to LinkedIn, the database for professionals, where I was hoping to find him. I wanted to know what he was doing now.

Going through two more yearbooks I found a second photo of Ellen defaced with the same fiber tip marker. This one had devil horns, mean eyes and tongue sticking out. All other markings in that book were penned-in comments on several more professors and students. Apparently, when the year was over and students knew they wouldn't fail once that diploma was in their hands, they felt free to comment. That was more than twenty years ago; today they would lodge a complaint with the administration and try to get the professor censured. I wouldn't doubt that some of these complaints were exaggerated and complicit with compatriots who might not have gotten the best of grades or who might have been stung by a professor's sharp tongue.

Now I had to schlep myself halfway across campus to where I'd parked. Walking was so much harder than even just a few years ago, when I wouldn't have thought twice about hiking a couple of miles. Now after half a mile I felt every step, knee and back complaining.

I decided not to attempt to get into Ellen's apartment and hoped that when I told Haggarty my theory he would support looking into her file drawers and sharing what he found.

I headed home to see what more I could find out about Calvin Grusso, even driving up Jerusalem Road to look for his house. About a mile up I saw what I thought was his winding driveway snaking into the woods, a garage barely visible at the end. It didn't say Grusso on the mailbox, only the number.

Chapter 16 – Sheila

I had a hard time settling myself down while I waited to talk to Haggarty. I wanted to see if Ellen had any files, to know who Grusso was and if he remembered her, and to talk to Allison to see what she remembered of her UConn days.

Instead I called Sheila, who lived next door to the firehouse in the sweet little cottage with lots of windows. She and her husband lived there for several years, and when he ran off she stayed on. When I invited her to my house for dinner she readily accepted, knowing my soups were rich and hearty.

I should have thought to call her sooner, as she was a curious combination of discretion and candor; when she felt safe and had a few glasses of Cabernet, she could be something of a gossip.

I'd made a pepperoni, bean and rice soup with onions, tomatoes, carrots and finely chopped kale. Paired with some Jarlsberg and crackers it was perfect for a chilly evening.

I knew she had crossed the green and was coming down the gravel walk when my terrier started barking wildly.

"Shush, Sherlock. Calm down. You know Sheila." When she came in he ran up to her, his whole body wiggling. Sheila bent down, petted him and gave him an air kiss.

"Hello, Sherlock. I've got a treat for you." She took a dog biscuit from her pocket and made him sit before she gave it to him. She slung her carryall on the table. "I've got something for us too." The loaf of French bread was still warm.

"Just made. I'm so glad you called; I was just going to have a couple of scrambled eggs." She also pulled out a bottle of red wine.

"Perfect. Thank you! I love your bread." She smiled. I set out the corkscrew and glasses.

"Come on into the dining room. It's a little more comfortable than the kitchen." I brought the soup and cutting board, bread knife and butter out to my already set table. Sheila poured and we savored the warm bread and soup, chatting about the unusually warm weather before moving on to the subject I was most interested in.

A small town can be populated with very private people and outgoing people, with perpetually cheerful and grouchy people, and with people drawn together because of their common interests or just personalities that draw others to them. Friendships develop that last decades, and occasionally dislikes develop but they don't usually interfere with gatherings. People help and support each other, dog-sitting, child-sitting or elder-sitting when needed, making the customary casserole when someone in the family is ailing, giving baby showers, birthday parties and even after-funeral buffets. This was our village, but I would say it had more than the usual number of people who were involved with the community.

Sheila was caring, more than commonly intuitive, very astute and socially aware. Perceiving small often overlooked nuances in a conversation, she understood deeper meanings below the surface of the words. She once told me she thought she was an empath. I didn't know what that was and had to google it. Because of this she knew more about what was going on in town than most. She listened, was quiet about it, and took it all in. If she felt you were discreet enough she might share with you what she'd heard or intuited.

I was hoping she'd be in a talkative mood tonight and plied her with a little more red, partially filling her already empty glass.

"Delish, Frances. You'll have to give me the recipe."

"It's easy and fast if you used canned beans rather than having to soak them overnight and all that." We both took another sip of wine and I cut off a crusty piece of bread and slathered on butter somewhat too liberally.

"So, what a shock about Ellen, right?" Aware I would bring up Ellen she gave me a knowing look, pushing her dull brown scraggly hair behind her ear.

"I guess so. It was a shame, but she was getting up there." She took a sip.

"You know they think it was suspicious, don't you?"

"Yeah, I'd heard that, but that seems somewhat farfetched, don't you think? Couldn't it have been just an accident?"

"The detective doesn't seem to think so. I'll find out more on Monday when I see him. Haggarty, Sargent Inspector Finn Haggarty. Have you ever heard of him?"

"Really? No, never heard of him." She looked into her glass and swirled it.

"What do you know about her?" Determined, I came right to the point.

"What do you want to know?"

Chapter 17 – Who We Are

"Well, anything. Anything and everything you're willing to share." Now I paused. "You know I won't tell anyone. I'm just trying to understand her better and figure out why someone would want to hurt her."

"You're serious. You really think someone did this?"

"It's not beyond the realm of possibility, right?" She chuckled.

"You don't know the half of it." My heart raced. Oh boy, I thought, this is exactly what I was hoping for.

"Okay?"

"Do you know when she moved into town?"

"I think I heard it was like forty years ago–is that right?"

"Yes, that's about right. She and her husband moved into the big old Guilford Smith house, that beautiful Italianate on the corner." I nodded. "Let me set the stage a little. Several families here aren't Yankees, you know what I mean? I see Yankees as kind of rigid, insular, staid, frugal, hardworking, but not overly outgoing. Whereas the people from other parts of the country who have moved here, particularly from the Midwest, are very friendly and outgoing, gracious and very polite. Ellen was a born and bred Yankee, as social as she needed to be as a professor, but not especially outgoing. Things turned around though when a couple moved to town from Wisconsin. She and her husband welcomed them, and they all became the best of friends. Totally un-Ellen. For a few years the two couples spent a lot of time together. Well, somewhere along the line Ellen fell for Allen and they were having their affair right under everyone's noses. It went on for a while but eventually they got caught. It ruined both marriages. George, Ellen's husband, left and took the kids."

"You know, I'd never heard the whole story. I knew something went on with Ellen but I didn't know exactly what, and no one talked about it. Isn't that odd?"

"Not really. We're just too nice and polite to share the seamier side of our town story, or not old enough to remember–you know that was a long time ago. So, Allen and Elizabeth left town and tried to repair their marriage, and Ellen, no longer able to sustain the house by herself, moved into the inn. But you know what? Allen and Elizabeth had left something, an indelible style; the town had become more of a community, more overtly involved with each other, more social. Even though they left under a cloud, the town recovered and became more than it had been. It became what you see today, a real community, all due to Allen and Elizabeth." Sheila took a thoughtful sip of the wine. "I think some people in town never forgave Ellen, some of the old-timers, because she essentially drove Allen and Elizabeth out of town, or at least was a catalyst. You have to realize there are not many people who remember this; it was a long time ago, and mostly we don't talk about it. But I'm surprised you'd never heard of it before. I guess it's one of those scabs we no longer pick." I felt honored that Sheila trusted me enough to share that with me… although if I'd pried enough there may have been others who would have told me, eventually. So, our little village still had secrets.

"Okay, on to dessert." I smiled as I brought out a nice rice pudding with raisins. Sheila smiled back.

Chapter 18 – Ellen

Sheila's talk gave me more to think about. Did Ellen, smart, commanding, once attractive and elegant, have more secrets to divulge? I went over the things I'd discovered and wrote them down.

Ellen Wolfe Richardson
- Eighty-two years old, born Oct. 12, 1941
- Parents: Gardiner and Miriam Wolfe
- Grew up in the area – Columbia
- Once pretty, once well-to-do, classy dresser Loved Katherine Hepburn, who influenced her style (Barb told me)
- Professor of English Lit at UConn
- Originally in Guilford Smith House in 1972
- With husband, George Richardson, Married 1972 (at 32yrs old)
- Two children: Alice born in 1975 (Ellen 34) Gerald born in 1977 (Ellen 36)
- Cheats on George with Allen Fisher (1980)
- George divorces and leaves her, takes the kids (1983)
- Allen Fisher and wife Elizabeth leave town (1983)
- Ellen sells house and moves (1984) to Windham Inn Apartment Four

- Found at the bottom of the stairs on December 5, 2023
- Possible murder
- (Why didn't she ever change her name back to her maiden name?)
- Townies resentful of the scandal?
- Do George and Elizabeth ever visit town?
- Maintain any friendships?
- Some students didn't like her–Calvin Grusso?
- Shelly didn't like her: snobbish?

It was interesting, but was any of this enough to incite murder? Was there more? Who else might know more, and how much could I find out before my Monday visit with Haggarty, just a day away now?

I always found it interesting to investigate a particularly odd murder, one there was no obvious reason for. So you had to do a lot of legwork because the answers were not right there as they were with theft–that was obvious–or a rape/murder, or a domestic case where the motive seemed easy to grasp. But when it's not obvious and you have to dig to find out more about the victim just to get a grip on what might have happened and who did it and why, that was a challenge. It's like creating a biography of the person, what they were like, what their family was like, what their home life was like, how their work life was. Who were their friends? Who were their enemies? What were their likes and dislikes? What circumstances molded this person? Reams of what seemed like minutiae. After a while you had a whole person, like one of those three-dimensional holograms in glass, a person you would never get to meet whether you grew to like them or dislike them–it didn't matter. You felt you knew them. The best part for me was that I no longer had deadlines and a supervisor harassing me. Now it was for sheer love of the investigation.

What else did I know about Ellen? Maybe I needed to look more into her early years: where she grew up, what her parents were like, where she went to school, what her grades were, what kind of student she was. Much of this would be difficult because she was older so getting that kind of information might be almost impossible. If she had siblings still alive they might be able to throw light on her early years.

Perhaps on Monday before my meeting with Haggarty at four I'd go to the Columbia grammar school, Horace Porter, and see if they still had the records. I no longer had access to professional systems that could search for people in-depth, but some fairly good search applications were available online for a fee.

I started with Facebook just in case she had an account, and she did! The photo was dated; she looked ten to fifteen years younger, professional, attractive. I looked through her posts, which were scant; she apparently wasn't that engaged with Facebook. Some of her activity was reposting other people's posts, mostly those with a wicked sense of humor. She hadn't posted in over a month, but friends of hers had. I wanted to go through her old posts and check for comments on them... just maybe.... But before I did that I tried one of the search systems, which found her and wanted payment before releasing the information. I paid and was surprised at how complete a private search company could be.

Yes, she grew up in Columbia as Ellen Wolfe, daughter of Harold and Miriam Wolfe, and had a sister and a brother. She graduated from Horace Porter school with good grades and from Windham High School in Willimantic with good enough grades to get into Central Connecticut College and get her master's and doctorate at the University of New Hampshire.

I wondered why she didn't go to UConn, which was so close.

Having finished her doctorate she applied to UConn and took an associate professorship there until she was granted full tenure. Ex-husband George moved to North Stonington with the two children, Alice and Gerald. Gerald. Could that be the Gerry on her calendar? I carefully collected all this information.

Her sister, Lucy, had passed away ten years ago, but her brother, Bill, was living in Norwich. I hoped to find him and see if he would talk to me and maybe unlock some of the details of her youth.

This is the life of a detective, constant research and chasing down loose ends, often to no avail, but when you do find something useful it's like finding the proverbial golden nugget in the bottom of your pan; it's exciting and gets your heart racing. I felt that finding Gerald might be that something.

I called Attorney Kelly. I assumed Officer Haggarty had contacted him and told him Ellen was dead, so Kelly would file the death certificate and have the coroner probate the will, thus making it public. He confirmed that the will had been filed with probate and would be available at the town hall.

When I retired from the state department I kept a private detective license, which was silly because the fee was rather steep and I rarely needed or used it, but I had hoped I could use it to open a few doors.

Chapter 19 – Barbara

I now had a number of leads to follow but wanted to circle back to Barbara. I thought she was perhaps Ellen's best friend and even though she harbored a grudge I hoped she would fill in some of the blanks.

I instant-messaged Barbara: "Hey, what are you doing? Got a few minutes to have a pastele?"

I knew Barbara had friends in Puerto Rico and had acquired a taste for some of their cuisine. So had I, and I loved pasteles, which were hard to find but during the holidays you could get them at one of the Latino restaurants in Willimantic. It was an indulgence worth waiting for and I thought Barbara might not be able to pass it up. She got back to me almost immediately. It was midafternoon and I knew she wouldn't be cooking until later.

"Yes, yes! I'll be right there."

I dropped the pasteles into boiling water and turned the flame off, allowing them to warm up without agitation.

Sherlock started barking and I knew Barbara had hustled across the green.

"Hey!" She opened the door and Sherlock ran up and recognized her, wigging and wagging his tail as she bent down to pet him and scratch his back.

"Hello, Barbara. I was fortunate enough to get four of them; you know they sell out fast. I think I got the last few that weren't saved for anyone else."

"Oooh, I'm so excited! I haven't had them in years." She rubbed her hands together in anticipation.

I pulled two pasteles out of the water with tongs and put them on her plate along with a fork and pair of scissors to cut the strings wrapping the precious gelatinous mass within.

We started right in, not waiting for them to cool.

"Do you want some Malta to go with them?" She almost screamed.

"Really? Yes! I really miss this delicious cooking."

"Yeah, me too." We were both quiet for a few minutes. "Hey, I've got a few more questions about Ellen. Do you know anything about her family? Her brother lives in Norwich, right?" She almost rolled her eyes.

"Really, still Ellen?" She took another bite. "She never talked that much about her family. Her parents passed years ago. I seem to remember her saying there had been some bad blood in the family, I think over the estate. Her sister moved out of state. I think her brother lives in Norwich but don't quote me. Apparently they thought Ellen got more than her share, especially since her children were no longer dependent upon her so she had no one but herself to use that allotment, and her brother had three or four kids too."

"Huh, that doesn't seem right. I mean, whatever the parents wanted to give was what you got, right?"

"That makes sense to me, but you know how people are when money is involved. They can get squirrely."

"What about her kids? Did she ever mention them?"

"Well, that's another black hole, not exactly black but something she rarely talked about, although I don't think she had a strong maternal instinct. She did miss them, especially her son, but she rarely talked about them. I once saw her choke up over him. She'd been going through some old photos and a few were on the kitchen table. I picked one up to look at it but she grabbed it away rudely, then apologized, then looked at it and shook her head, turned away and sniffed. But she hated to show her emotions like that so I think that was why any talk of her kids was tamped down." I sat quietly for a moment.

"What about a will? Did she ever talk about what she wanted to do with her money? She must have had a fair amount salted away. She took a few vacations abroad and I don't think she was frugal when she went, but she didn't have much to spend her savings on, right?"

"I'm not sure. She did talk about that nonprofit in town, you know, Windham Preservation, Inc., the one that helps save and protect older buildings. I think she was planning to leave some to them. The library too, and probably the Covenant Soup Kitchen and Pantry; she was always giving them something…. Listen, I've got to get home and start dinner. Thanks for the pasteles. That is such a treat and brings back so many pleasant memories." She wiped her mouth with her napkin and patted Sherlock. "I hope something will come of this, your personal investigation, but I can't imagine that anyone would murder her. She really was in her heart a good person."

Barb put on her parka and I saw her wave as she went by the kitchen window.

Who next? Attorney Kelly? Town Hall? Then I thought maybe I should try to get all the ladies together the next time we had a breather – the holidays were so hectic.

Chapter 20 – The Outline

I visited the probate court. The historic 1800 brick Willimantic Town Hall that housed it had once been the county courthouse. As I climbed the worn but well cared for wooden staircase, I imagined the many others who had climbed it. I wasn't surprised to find that Attorney Kelly was also the Probate Judge. I should have known that. I asked his clerk if I could see Ellen Richardson's will, explaining who I was and why I was interested. Although I had no real connection to Ellen the court was required to release records to whoever desired them.

The clerk wrote down my information and went into a back room to search for the will. She returned and pointed to a desk and chair where I could review it but reminded me I had to return it before I left.

I opened it carefully and noted the recorded date of death, remembering that day not so long ago. I used my cellphone to photograph the pages.

Looking through it I was somewhat surprised to see she had amassed a small fortune. The local nonprofits were included as Barbara had described, but also several others: the volunteer fire department in town, the local land trust Joshua's Trust, and the conservation group Community Action Works, known locally for saving a large tract of riverside property from becoming an ash dump. Then I found an addendum, a separate document that changed and updated a section of the will. It gave her daughter only ten thousand dollars, a Clyde Baker fifty thousand, two percent to Leslie Goranson, and her son, Gerald, twenty percent of the whole, which amounted to over four hundred thousand dollars. The addendum had been filed in November. Last month! I jotted down all significant information, larger disbursements, dates. I returned the will to the clerk and rushed home, hoping to compile all the information I'd collected before my visit with Haggarty.

First I listed all the information I'd collected from the people I'd spoken with.

What info I had about Ellen:
Graduated from Central Conn. and from
   University of New Hampshire
   with a Doctorate English Literature
Started at UConn as an associate professor until
   given full tenure.
Sister, Lucy Wolfe (passed 10 years ago out of
   state)
Brother, Bill Wolfe, currently lives in Norwich
Voracious reader, periodicals, classics,
   biographies, contemporary, nature,
   best sellers, science, obscure topics
On several boards & commissions:
   Historic Comm.,
   a local land trust, Rails to Trails group,
   a professional women's group
Personality: Honest to the point of being rude,
   caring, generous, secretive, thrifty but
   not cheap, organized, neat and tidy, liked

good theatre, wry sense of humor.
What did I know about Ellen's friends
and acquaintances?

Barbara, Lisa and Allison went out with her.

Sue Gallen – Apt. 1, Windham Inn –
Friend, helped Sue with cat,
anything else?

Barbara Dixon - lives in Shubael Abbe
House, Good friend but felt slighted
by Ellen.

Lisa – Scotland Road – just up from the P.O.
Described Ellen as fickle, blunt and
outspoken; said people from the university
would recognize Ellen when out and speak to
her. Said Ellen seemed like a recluse, but
would go out if she wanted, but often
preferred to stay home. Thought Ellen had a
journal.

Allison – Friend, Plains Road, attended UConn
20-25 years ago

Shelly – Lives in Joyce's house –
Thinks Ellen is a snob

Joyce – Lives in Eleazar Fitch house –
rents to Shelly
Stanley & Mike Historic Commmission
Butted heads w/Ellen

Calvin Grusso – Student with grudge
(BITCH in yearbook) maybe not a
hot lead - keep on a back burner.

Sheila Fuller – House next to firehouse –

> Shared story about Allen and Ellen's affair. Discussed Yankees vs Midwesterner styles.
> Allen & Elizabeth Fisher (from Wisconsin) – Allen had affair with Ellen – ended up leaving town in 1983.
> George Richardson – ex-husband moved with kids to shore. Remarried.
> Alice Richardson James - Daughter
> Gerald Richardson – Son

All that information seemed to yield little. I wanted more and decided to reach out to Gloria, who lived with her husband in Ellen's old house.

Chapter 21 – Gloria

Gloria and Henry Bishop still lived in the house they purchased from Ellen in 1984. One of the grand homes abutting the green, the Guilford Smith house was an elegant Italianate, the main house built in 1885 and a subsequent addition in 1900. Upgrades to the kitchen made the home a perfect place for entertaining, and it was a favorite on the soup night circuit.

As a prosperous insurance executive, Henry brought some of his special clients and their wives to dinner where his wife might feature her home-grown herb and greens-based cuisine. Gloria specialized in botany and local plants and spoke at local conservation group gatherings. Henry played bass in the town orchestra.

Both accomplished and interesting, they fit into the village as though they'd always been a part of it and had no ill feelings toward Ellen. Gloria had even become very close to her over the years. Ellen had shared some of her experiences in the house such as where she marked her children's heights inside a door jamb, and Gloria never painted over it. When Ellen visited she often sought out that measure and touched it, showing a nostalgic side that few ever witnessed.

Once when Gloria was doing laundry, Ellen helped her change the sheets in the bedroom facing north, giggling about how she and Allen, who lived next door, would signal their plan for an upcoming tryst from their respective bedroom windows, then easily slip from one house to the other behind the hedges, unnoticed by prying eyes. Allen, she said, was a traveling sales and marketing person who was animated and entertaining. Elizabeth worked at the town hall clerking for the building department. They were, like so many couples, as different as night and day.

When I asked Gloria if she wanted to have lunch, she agreed only if I brought some of what she called the best coleslaw in the village, and I was excited when she offered her version of Caprilands herbal rub chicken.

By now of course everyone knew I was conducting my own private investigation into Ellen and her demise, so when the topic came up Gloria told me the story Ellen had told her about the bedroom window signaling and the worn path through the big rhododendrons that hid the trysts. She brought me up to that room so I could see the other window across the way and imagine their signaling. Ellen said she'd open the curtains and hang a handkerchief from the curtain rod, knowing that when he saw it he'd come to the back and enter unannounced. She'd use only a handkerchief, never an undergarment, since she imagined that to be gauche. She said she'd once forgotten to take the handkerchief down and when her husband was readying for bed he'd asked her about it, and she excused it by saying she'd noticed some dust on the sill and it was the closest thing she had to swipe it up.

Gloria explained all this to me with a pleasantly satisfied air of someone who knows they have an interesting and amusing story to relate. At this point she didn't think it would be harmful to share it–who was it going to hurt? And indeed it was a great story.

Who knows what goes on in a little village? We were certainly not a Peyton Place; scandals were reserved for other towns. Or were they?

When I asked about children Gloria said she thought both families not only had children around the same ages but that they regularly played together. Now I wanted to know more about Allen and Elizabeth's kids.

Chapter 22 – The Inn

Haggarty called to ask when he could visit. Of course I wanted to see him as soon as he had a chance. I told him I'd been talking to people around town and would share what I had, although I didn't think it was much.

Murder, unless it is a robbery, is usually personal. Even with a robbery, sometimes the perp knows who the target is or knows of them or has found information about their lives that makes them a desirable target. Many burglars strike while the owners are away, usually at work or sometimes on vacation, but these days, with Covid forcing so many people to work from home and the availability of new technologies like Ring cameras and cellphone tracking, pulling off a burglary is much riskier than it once was, say just ten years ago. But the inn had no surveillance cameras and the owners had never been required by the town or the renters to have any installed. Who would monitor them?

Clyde, the renter who was the more-or-less superintendent and also took care of the mowing, snow shoveling and minor maintenance, lived in one of the smaller apartments in the ell. He was often not available to help unless an appointment was made. The rumor, well substantiated, was that Clyde abused alcohol and often was not seen the whole weekend if he was on a bender. He appeared on Monday to do maintenance work for the schools and municipal buildings and was missing again by Friday evening. The single ladies in the building didn't want to reach out to him for maintenance unless they saw him in the parking lot and he looked sober, and then they'd ask for something like a lightbulb change in the hall. Otherwise he was pretty much left alone. But he knew what was going on in the building and might know if someone had gone up the fire escape to Ellen's that morning.

I made a mental note to try to get in touch with Clyde since both doors into Ellen's apartment had been found open. Would someone have gone up the fire escape stairs, or run down them and disappeared? Why would the other door to the inside staircase be open, as well as the door to the outside at the bottom of the stairs? It might make sense that one was left open, but all of them? I jotted down who lived where at the inn.

> Apartment 1: Sue lives alone, left of front entry.
> Apartment 2: Jim and Nancy, first floor,
>   right of entry, across from Sue.
> Apartment 3: Marie and Paulo Sanchez,
>   above Sue and across from Ellen – they
>   share the same staircase to the front door.
> Apartment 4: Ellen lived alone, above
>   Jim and Nancy.
> Apartment 5: Betsy and her daughters Dylan
>   and Lila live in the ell, above Apartment 7
> Apartment 6: Jake, on the third floor
>   above both the Sanchezes and Ellen,
>   sharing the same staircase to the front door
>   and same fire escape as Ellen.
> Apartment 7: Clyde, the caretaker, in

the ell, below Betsy, Dylan and Lila

Perhaps I should try to talk to everyone to see if they were home on December 5th and noticed anything when Ellen died, or maybe even days before that. I could stop in on the weekend, when most would be home.

Haggarty came by on Friday, setting me up for what would be a busy week.

Chapter 23 – Haggarty

Haggarty came right to my house late Friday afternoon. I thought he might want to talk to Sue, but instead he pulled in with what must have been his personal car, not a state police vehicle with obvious outfitting. Anticipating his visit I had a batch of walnut and raisin scones in the oven.

I watched him from my kitchen window. He was carrying a cardboard box– did he have a lot of evidence already? Excitement ran through me, emotional, even physical, like caffeine. I remembered how I'd felt when I was given a new case. There was a thrill to it: something new, something challenging, something to dive into like a great book you just wanted to immerse yourself in. I tried not to be too obvious but I knew he'd understand.

He knocked and I let him in. "Hello. I'm glad you had the time to see me." He was polite.

"Are you kidding? You are the highlight of my week, maybe my month! Want some coffee?" He chuckled and looked at his watch.

"Sure, I guess it's not too late for coffee. Um, something smells good." I set about grinding fresh beans and setting up the coffee.

"Yeah, I just put in a batch of scones. Hope you can have one. You can put your box on the table."

"Well, if they're anywhere near as good as they smell..."

He set the box down. My kitchen table, which I tried to keep fairly free of clutter, was, I thought, big enough to lay out any files he had that he could share with me. I still couldn't believe my good fortune.

"I hope you don't mind but I went through your records. I didn't feel I could share this stuff, but I talked to Lieutenant Godde and he said I could if I wanted to. He remembers you and sends his regards." He smiled and began unpacking folders from the box. I brought mugs, milk, and sugar to the counter and poured the coffee. He picked up a mug, added a little sugar, and gingerly set it on the table.

"Here, use this." I handed him a saucer so nothing would spill on the files. I set the scones on plates and we sliced them crosswise so the wide sides were open and steaming, applied butter liberally and settled in at the table.

"You know when I was starting out in investigations, I didn't want to share what I'd found. I wanted to solve everything by myself and get all the glory, but I soon realized it was a team sport and not sharing didn't really make you a better investigator, maybe even the opposite. With cutbacks now, I'm thrilled to get help on an investigation. I'm glad to be sharing this with you and hope you can help." He smiled and punctuated his words by popping a piece of scone into his mouth, washing it down with a gulp of coffee.

"Thanks! I can't tell you how excited I am to be involved." He opened the top file and took out the coroner's report and photos of Ellen's naked body with the traditional Y incision from shoulder to sternum to shoulder then sternum to pubic bone, so I assumed the organs had been removed and examined for injury, disease, poisons, or drugs. This involved taking small samples and sending them to the lab for analysis. Then he laid out photographs of her thin left arm, bruised and broken, and two fingers of her left hand, dislocated I thought perhaps in an attempt to stop herself from falling down the stairs. A photo of her hip showed it too had been broken. Her head showed massive bruising, and even with all blood cleaned up it was obvious she'd hit it in several spots and opened up a large gash at her hairline. Next came x-rays showing broken ribs and clavicle, and another of her skull showing the cracked and broken supraorbital ridge region of her brow.

"She certainly took quite a fall."

"Yes, and it may not have been accidental." We exchanged glances and then he looked back to the papers on the table. "She wasn't in the best of health. She had some underlying conditions that would have made her life very difficult in a year or two, and she probably knew that. Not just the normal aging stuff, osteoporosis and diverticulosis and maybe a touch of Alzheimer's where they found some amyloid plaque, but a seriously enlarged heart and weakened blood vessels that could have caused a stroke if she were under much stress. In other words, she was a ticking time bomb, but something else got to her first. They found traces of a narcotic, not one readily available; it was fentanyl. Well, you know sometimes that's prescribed for end-of-life cancer patients to ease pain, but that's not something she had a prescription for. I suppose somehow she could have gotten it or have had it given to her. It might explain the open doors, just being so out of it she'd forgotten to close them, or...? It could explain her falling down the stairs. But how did she get it and how was it administered? After they found it they looked closely for needle marks but there were none."

We had been leaning over the table examining everything, and now we sat down and worked on our scones and coffee as I gingerly lifted photos and x-rays.

"Wow, that's interesting. Why, how, who?" I picked up the ME's report outlining the bruises and broken bones and then the tox screen: Fentanyl.

Chapter 24 – What If

I'd been in detective work for decades so nothing surprised me anymore. I'd seen cases where perfectly respectable people turned out to have secret lives: pastors who were abusing children in their congregation, well-to-do matrons who had a secret drug or alcohol habit, professional men who abused their wives, accountants stealing from their clients–the list goes on and on, almost all of them right under the noses of their friends, family, co-workers and acquaintances. To imagine Ellen had a secret drug habit was not out of the question.

"Wow. Fentanyl. That's surprising."

"We went through her apartment and everything seemed quite ordinary, nothing out of place, almost anally neat. There was no correspondence on her desk, no small tell-tale signs of something off. The only interesting thing was that note on the refrigerator that said "Gerry, don't forget" and the reminder again on her calendar. Nothing else. Nothing odd in the medicine cabinet, just aspirin, Tylenol, antacids. Her fridge had the basics: milk, eggs, butter, a couple of Tupperwares with baked mac and cheese and what looked like part of a leftover grinder. Like everything else, it was very clean – I mean if we were having company my wife would spruce up the house to look the way hers did. Not that we're messy, but it was almost supernaturally clean. Her clothes were neat, all hanging in the same direction, blouse openings to the right – I think that means she was left-handed. Books seemed to be organized according to some kind of method. We were not able to get into her desk, so I still need to see what we can do about that. It was locked and I suppose it could hold some interesting things." He stopped and looked into his cup. "Damn, that was good coffee, but I can't afford to have any more this evening. So how are you? Have you found anything interesting?"

"Well, I have been asking around and doing a little searching myself. Gerry may be her son who lived with her husband at the shore, but I'm sure he's old enough to be out of the house now, married with a family of his own. She seemed to be fairly well liked even though she could be a little too outspoken; she usually felt that she knew what was best for everyone and was not afraid to share it. She had an affair decades ago that caused her divorce and the other couple to leave town. When she was working at UConn she might have been tough on some of her students and made a few enemies over that. She had some friends in town and they went out together. I think she, like so many of the villagers, knew secrets, such as who was maybe on the edge financially, who was maybe struggling with alcohol, who was on what drugs, who was on a diet, who was sick and with what. I know we all have secrets and most of us know some of the ones in our neighborhood, but we're mostly kind and don't want to embarrass anyone or cause discomfort so we keep it to ourselves. We don't rock the boat. But I wonder if maybe there are secrets in that desk of hers, maybe a journal, maybe papers from her UConn years. I don't know, but it would be interesting to find out."

"Thanks. This is good information. I think we'll have to get a locksmith to open that desk, and once we do, I'll give you a call so we can go through it together. You may know more about anything related to the village that she might have stored away in there." I nodded, trying not to show the excitement I was feeling. "Oh, and there were several sets of prints on the doors, both inside and out, several that were not hers and we haven't determined whose they are yet, so we may print some of the neighbors, like Sue, just to compare. I almost wish she wasn't that neat; it's so much easier if we find dust or footprints or stubs of cigarettes in ashtrays, blood-soaked towels or rags with bleach, something to analyze." He shook his head. "We got a copy of the will too. She was leaving a lot to the nonprofits around, but recently had changed it to give Gerry a larger portion. That's important, don't you think? And who's this Leslie?"

"Oh yeah, I picked up a copy at probate too, and yes, I forgot to tell you, I thought that was something worth following up. I think his address is in there. Are you going to contact him? Would it be wildly inappropriate for me to go with you when you do?" Haggarty smiled.

"I think that can be arranged."

"I have one more person in town I want to talk to, another friend of hers. I'll text you if I come up with anything."

He smiled as he picked up the last scone crumbs from his plate and licked his fingers.

"Thanks for the scones and coffee." He put the dishes in the sink. "I'll give you a call when I'm going to visit Gerald. I can pick you up here."

"Okay. And thanks for sharing all this stuff." I watched him pack the papers back into the box. "Wait. Can I get photos of a few of these?" He stopped packing, and I picked out several photos and x-rays and snapped photos with my phone. "Thanks again and hope to see you soon."

Chapter 25 – The Garden

Grace lived in one of the most stunning homes on the green, the Laura Huntington house, a pink two-story Italianate villa. I'd been to soup night there, and for years her lovely gardens were the site of an annual fundraiser for the library, Jazz in the Garden. Her gardens were full of interesting and beautiful plants set in charming beds where paths wound around them like blossoming islands in a sea of green manicured lawns. Grace fussed with them until they were perfect for their special yearly debut. She was not only a private person but perhaps the most discreet person in the neighborhood and everyone knew it, so I was sure she was aware of more of the village secrets than anyone else. She was the local sounding board, the one to whom everyone went to get good advice. Having a problem with your husband or your kids, or a town official? Or a teacher who thought your child was not living up to his or her potential? Something about your love life? Ask Grace, who would give you the best advice and never share your story, and just maybe get a little weeding out of you in the process. I wanted to wait and talk to Grace last, having gathered beforehand as much information from the rest of the village as I could. Not only had she been a professional counselor before she retired, but she also knew most of the people in town and their histories. Should I have spoken with her sooner? Maybe. But she likely wouldn't have told me some of the secrets unless I already knew of them. Would she even tell me now? I didn't know but would soon find out. For this visit I'd picked up a nice pair of kneepads, ones that stayed on your knees and didn't slip down and also felt comfortable and really protected your knees. I also brought a pair of quality clippers, surmising that at this time of year she'd be doing more pruning than kneeling.

I knocked and she called for me to come in. She was heating water in a gigantic kettle.

"Want some tea? I have Earl Grey, English Breakfast or some herbal that I collected from the echinacea and mint blossoms last year, and some elder blow I collected last year too." She pointed at the selection on the counter.

"Oooh, Earl Grey would be just right."

"Great. I have some date-nut balls from my Christmas cookie making if you don't mind leftovers."

"Are you kidding? I love your date-nut balls and your leftovers!" I put the clippers on the counter. "I thought you might be pruning so I brought clippers and can give you a hand if you need it."

"Oh, that's sweet, Frances. I can always use an extra hand in the garden." She poured the water into our teacups as I passed her the tin of cookies, from which she laid a half dozen or so of the white, sugar-covered confections on a plate. "Come on into the sitting room where we can relax." She deftly picked up the tray of tea and cookies, turned to the front room and set it down on a vintage tea cart. We settled in and she sipped her tea. "So, what's up, Frances?" she questioned, knowing the answer perfectly well.

Chapter 26 – Grace

"Ellen?"

She smiled. "Yeah, I wondered when you'd be by." She sipped her tea and bit into the delectable cookie.

"What do you think you can share with me? I mean, she's gone now, so whatever secrets she had can be revealed. You know I'm discreet. I'm working on this with a detective now, and I hope to round out a profile on her, see what I'm missing. You know they're not sure if it was an accident? They found things. I'm just wondering if you might know what else they could find."

"Frances, you know me. You know I don't talk about others." She put her hands palm up and shrugged her shoulders as if to reinforce her words. Crumbs of buttery sugar clung to fingers and a speck lingered on her mouth.

"You're covered in evidence, Grace." I pointed to her hand and she laughed. "I understand, but she is gone now, and if someone did assault her wouldn't you want to help us find out more?" She nodded. "Had she talked to you at all lately? Is there anything you can tell me?"

"I can tell you something was going on with her family, but she wouldn't talk to me about it." Another sip of tea and nibble of cookie. "Did you know she was having health issues?"

"Hmmm, yes, well, the detective, Finn Haggarty, did say she had some issues, some of which would probably be life-threatening."

"Yeah, she was in a lot of pain. I think it was arthritis or osteoporosis or a combination of those. You know she was pretty stoic, so if she complained to me about pain it had to be pretty bad. I think she said she tried to get a prescription from her doctor for it, but apparently they have seriously clamped down on pain meds because of abuse, so now everyone has to suffer more."

"Huh. I didn't know that." I thought I probably shouldn't mention the fentanyl at this point. "What about her friends? Anything going on there?" Grace looked up from her tea, her long brown hair rustling against the back of her down vest. She wore it pulled back in a ponytail, gathered at the nape of her neck. Her old and slightly soiled vest looked stained where her hands went into the pockets. Many of us in this village of older homes wore extra clothes to keep warm, having set our thermostats low enough to afford our heating bills. Seeing people threading their way across the green to the post office or library wearing ratty old wool sweaters or stained down vests or fleece jogging pants was more common than not.

"I would say nothing out of the ordinary. She was brusque, and that sometimes rubbed people the wrong way, but more often than not people liked and respected her. She put a lot of time into the local nonprofits and boards and I think she'll be sorely missed by the people in this town." Grace inspected her fingernails, pulled out a pocketknife and began cleaning them. "No matter what time of year, I can't seem to keep my fingernails clean. If I'm not in the garden I'm repotting or starting seedlings indoors." She shook her head and laughed. "You wouldn't believe I was the homecoming queen." Her smile was bright and charming as she ducked her head for another sip of tea.

"Actually, I would believe that." I lifted my cup toward her. "Will you be mother?" The quaint British phrase was a request for more tea. She smiled.

"Of course." She filled my teacup.

"Can you think of anything else that might help?"

"Someone said she was having family issues, or something like that. It was pretty vague. I'm not even sure if it was issues, but something about family, and I'm not sure which family member. I think it was Barbara who told me that. Now, realize this is all in confidence. If people find out I'm blabbing they won't trust me, and it's very important to me that they trust me and it's important to them to have someone they can trust. So this is what you might call confidential; you'll have to uncover it for yourself. Use what I've given you and do your searching and let everyone think you discovered it on your own. I shouldn't really be saying anything at all. You understand." I nodded.

"Yes. I'll be very careful. I really appreciate whatever you can give me." I finished my tea. "So, can I help you prune a little? Then I won't have to lie about why I'm here..." She chuckled.

"Sure, the apple would love some attention. Have you ever pruned before? Do you get the rationale behind it?"

I told her I had pruned a bit but I'd more than welcome any tips she could offer. We bundled up and headed out to her now-dormant backyard garden.

When we finished up the apple tree I walked across the green to my house, fully aware that anyone and everyone could see me and assume I was pumping Grace for information. So I had to convince some of the group that my visit to Grace was to help her prune, and hopefully they'd believe me and word would get around.

Chapter 27 – Squirrel

Arriving at my driveway I was surprised to find a dead squirrel lying right in the middle of it. I didn't remember seeing it when I'd left for Grace's. I thought it odd. I didn't see any obvious signs of injury. I gingerly picked it up by the end of its tail, walked to the back of my property and flung it over the wall, far enough, I hoped, that Sherlock wouldn't find it and drag it around like the prize I knew he would consider it.

I warmed up some leftover Cajun chicken I'd made a few days before. It was still delicious even after sitting in my fridge for a while.

I thought about Ellen suffering through what was likely a very painful ordeal. Having lately seen my doctor for pain in my joints that was diagnosed as arthritis, I knew what pain was, and as I aged it seemed to get more acute. I remember that when I was a kid things seemed to hurt more, the little scrapes and knocks being quite painful, but in my middle years they didn't seem as bad. Now as I aged, things seemed to hurt as they had in childhood. Whacking my elbow was really painful now. I didn't like this aging stuff.

Sherlock came in as my dinner was heating and I fed him some of his favorite, if boring, canned food. I was amazed at his vocabulary; when I told him I hoped he wouldn't find the squirrel, his ears perked up and he looked toward the door in expectation of going out to chase something. But that was not going to happen in the dark, unless he breached his electric fence and got that dead one. After I thought about that I decided I should go back out there and pick it up – what if it was poisoned? I didn't want any predators to be poisoned by a squirrel cadaver. I put on my headlamp, grabbed a plastic grocery bag and gloves and went in search of the squirrel.

My backyard light needed replacing so when I stepped out the door and was startled by someone running off I didn't get a look, but I knew it wasn't an animal. Someone must have been just outside my kitchen window. But why? I wanted to imagine a kid out there, being nosy or horsing around; it wasn't out of the question. I headed out to where I thought I'd tossed the squirrel and in the circle of my headlamp I saw it and heard another critter amble off. I picked up the carcass with my gloved hands, bagged it and put it in the trash where nothing could get at it.

I thought about the prowler. It wasn't totally unusual for people to be sneaking about, usually just kids looking in windows hoping to find something not intended for their eyes. We'd had a rash of burglaries a few years before, mostly breaking into sheds and garages to steal bikes or tools, anything that could be sold. At least that's what the neighbors thought, probably someone looking for quick drug money. There were repeated burglaries in Willimantic at the Railroad Museum, which was far enough off the beaten path to be a target. That was particularly sad since their budget was so low and volunteers scarcer than ever.

I was on North Road, the main drag between Windham Center and Willimantic, a very busy route with a rustic gravel sidewalk along it from the school all the way to the green. The sidewalk was well-traveled and many people wanted it extended, but those with road frontage didn't want the foot traffic in front of their homes. People in Lebanon had a very fine walking path all along the perimeter of their mile-long green. Our little walk was just enough for the families in the center to get to the school or library or post office. It wasn't unusual for neighbors to visit along our path. I wasn't really concerned about what was a probably a kid's prank.

Chapter 28– What Was Missed?

So far I was disappointed in how little I'd gotten from the villagers. I thought they were being honest, and maybe some were more discreet than others. Were they all protecting each other, or were they protecting one particular person? I supposed it wasn't out of the question, but if they knew something why would they, perhaps all of them, want to protect that person? Really, that could make them an accessory to a crime. Just the thought of being prosecuted for obstruction of justice made my skin crawl. Who would possibly know the most about other people in the village and who and why would they want to keep it quiet? People tend to open up to people they trust, but also to people they think are sympathetic

I decided to go back over Haggarty's coroner's report to see if anything stood out. I printed out the photos and x-rays and then my own photos of Ellen as she lay at the bottom of the stairs. I realized how morbid some people would find this occupation, and how I just dug into it with a certain relish. The coroner's report had the standard line drawing outline of a naked person, front and back, with areas circled where the body was damaged, and next to the pictures a detailed description of the injuries. I looked more closely at the x-rays, trying to associate the description on the autopsy report with the images. Then I looked at my photos, trying to match the mangled body parts to the x-rays and the report. Did the coroner miss anything? Occasionally that happened. Coroners, or more commonly their assistants, might speed through a case, especially if it wasn't high profile or didn't seem suspicious. Often an autopsy is required if the death occurred at home. It was what I considered a "just in case" effort, just in case a question came up later, such as someone getting a big insurance payout or large disbursement from a will, which always raised red flags. Was there a love triangle behind it, perhaps a husband with a new love who didn't want a messy divorce where he might end up having to give up half his savings, income or estate? Or occasionally a wife who didn't want to share her children, maybe because of abuse? Maybe a kid was no longer willing to shoulder the burden of caring for an elderly parent. There were so many reasons a home death is scrutinized more carefully. Sometimes it raised red flags at the office immediately and everyone got engaged, and sometimes it was just a routine, natural home death that might be put on the back burner, not pushed through the system in a timely manner, not garnering much attention– just get it done, send it through, sign off and move on to the more interesting, more exciting, more attractive cases. In truth, the younger you were the more you were interested. First of all, it might seem like a more "untimely" death, and that was a challenge. If drugs were involved it was fairly standard: take tissue samples and do a tox screen. But if violence was involved it was a challenge to put all the pieces together like a puzzle. Many in the coroner's office found that very satisfying. If the person was young and the body supple it was easier to find bruising and damage. I'm sure sometimes there was a certain perverse desire to examine the corpse of a younger person, although most of the workers would be loath to admit to that. The bottom line was that the work was still work and at times it was just routine, and some things might be rushed through because it was just a job and a beer or glass of wine was waiting at the bar once you were done for the day.

So could something have been missed on Ellen's autopsy? Why not? It was possible.

OFFICE OF THE CHIEF MEDICAL EXAMINER
State of Connecticut
University of Connecticut Health Center
Farmington, Connectiut

REPORT OF INVESTIGATION BY CHIEF MEDICAL EXAMINER

Date: 12/08/2023 Time 14:22 Date and time of death 12/05/23 -11:03
Decedent: Ellen Wolfe Richardson Race: CA__ Sex: Fe AGE: __82
Address: 1 Windham Center Road, Apartment 4, Windham Center, CT
Occupation: __Retired Professor__
Type of Death: Violent ☐ Casualty ☐ Suicide ☐ Found Dead ☐ In Prison ☐
Suddenly when in apparent health ☐ Suspicious, unusual or unnatural ☑
Comment __Arrived via ambulance where she died in route to hospital__
If Motor Vehicle Accident Check One: Driver ☐ Passenger ☐ Pedestrian ☐ Unknown ☐
Notification by _State Police_
Address ____Colchester____
Investigating Agency _Conn State Police. Sgt. Finn Haggarty_

Description of Body: Clothed ☑ Unclothed ☐ Partially Clothed ☐
Eyes _Blue___ Hair_Grey_____ Mustache _-__ Beard _-__
Weight (Pounds)_120_ Length (Feet Inches) _5'4"_ Body Temp (F)_72_
Rigor: Yes ☐ No ☑ Liver Color _brown_ Fixed ☑ Non-Fixed ☐

Multiple signs of perimortem bruising. Premortem bruising to right upper arm may have been sustained prior to fall that caused her death. Broken and dislocated right phalanges likely sustained during fall.
Tissue harvested and sent to lab for analysis. Some of the injuries were likely caused by the fall.

Probable Cause of Death	Manner of Death	Recommendation
Blunt cranial trauma causing stroke and intracranial bleeding	Sustained Fall	Further investigation may not be necessary

I hereby declare that after receiving notice of the death described herein, I took charge of the body and made inquiries regarding the cause of death in accordance with the laws of the State of Connecticut and that the information contained herein regarding such death is true and correct to the best of my knowledge and belief.

Date	Place of Investigation	Coroner
12/08/2023	UConn, Farmington	Thomas Joseph Kirzan

Chapter 29 – Autopsy

Could those premortem bruises to her arm be a sign she was struggling with someone?

I studied my phone photos from that day. The bulkiness of the thick wool coat made it hard to determine just where body parts were, but careful analysis made it clearer.

She lay face down, half on the stairs with her head on the landing facing Jim and Nancy's door. It looked like both of her legs were still on the stairs, although one was out in an odd angle due I thought to the broken hip. One of her arms was near her head and the other bent underneath her. The broken fingers I surmised were caused by her attempt to grab the railing or something else before she fell. I wondered if they had swabbed her hands for chemical or DNA analysis. I wondered how carefully they'd gone over her clothing for hair or stray fibers. I wondered how thorough a job they'd done. Ellen died December 5th, and her body was transported to Farmington and the autopsy done December 8th, which seemed like a pretty fast turnaround. I bet it was because of the impending holidays, when no one wanted a lot of work piling up before they got a few days off to relax. Sometimes these autopsies didn't happen for months. Maybe there was a new policy or new staff. A particularly suspicious death would certainly take longer to go over more thoroughly, and imminent indictment of a suspect might help expedite it. We'd like to believe every autopsy would be thorough but many elderly were pushed through quickly because the state required an autopsy for any death that was in-home and not under the auspices of hospice. Sometimes insurance requirements necessitated an autopsy. Most of these were just natural deaths due to aging, no hanky-panky involved, no heirs trying to collect. So a routine autopsy would be done: Nothing abnormal, check; no bruising, check; no unusual wounds, check, check, check, done.

I wondered if the body was still available for further analysis, for DNA and anything else. I texted Haggarty.

"HEY! Do you think the body is still there? Can you get them to check for DNA on her bruised arm and fingers and fingernails?"

After a few minutes he replied.

"Let me check. If it's there, I'll ask them to do it."

I knew they'd found other fingerprints on the doorknobs besides Ellen's and hoped they would follow up and get prints from the neighbors to match against them. Then I thought about her desk and what might be in it. At the risk of becoming a pest I texted him again.

"...and what about that desk? Don't you want to get into it and see if there's anything interesting in it? If you can squeeze out some time this week, I'd love to work with you."

I waited, and sure enough he texted right back.

"I'll be over in a couple of days. I'll call before I come."

Sweet, I thought, and put on my jacket to walk to the post office. I'd ordered a lock picking tool set and expected it today. When I worked for the state I'd had lots of tools at my disposal: lock-picking set, fingerprint-lifting kits, boot and shoe print-collecting set, and really fine cameras, some with special filters... so much left behind when I left. Walking past Gloria and Henry's house I looked up at the window where Ellen had signaled Allen. I thought I saw the curtain flutter, just for a moment, and I looked away, trying to appear a casual viewer of the cars and homes, but I'm sure I saw it. I decided I should have any further meetings in a restaurant, out of town.

Chapter 30 – Number 2

I left the post office and walked the gravel sidewalk around town, past the Congregational church and Grace's and Sheila's. At the firehouse I crossed the road and went up the short street, Webb Hill, past Sandons on the corner and to the upper green onto Weir Court, then past Barbara's, past the green and the library, then up Plains Road past Allison's. I turned around at St. Paul's, went back down past Gloria and Henry's, then past what was the Fishers' old home, past the inn across the street, and finally past Attorney Kelly's before arriving back home. I wanted people to see me and to know I was there, watching. I had a sense there were still things to learn about these fine people, perhaps some secrets not yet revealed. A few people were on the street and waved to me. One person I knew beeped his horn and waved as he drove by.

When I got home I opened my package. The lock-picking kit included not only instructions but also several sample locks with plastic viewing windows so you could see what you were doing when you poked the pick in to move rotors, springs and cylinders.

I played with it for an hour to refresh my skills and test my technique. I enjoyed these kinds of puzzles, testing myself to see how sharp and dexterous I still was, and saw my skills were intact so maybe, if necessary, I could help Haggarty open that desk drawer.

I wanted to talk to Grace again and hoped that in the couple of days since I'd seen her someone else had visited her and maybe revealed more. I knew there were secrets and they weren't being shared with me. I'd have to see if she'd agree to go to lunch or dinner in Willimantic. I would suggest the Harp since I hadn't been there lately and missed their Hangar Steak.

Getting hungry, I surveyed my fridge. My leftovers were finally either past their prime or were goners, so I put Sherlock in the car and headed to the IGA. I couldn't decide between their hot bar, with some yummy-looking pernile with a side of rice and beans, or a six-pack of their tasty, store-made Italian sausage to add to a pot of pasta that would last a few days. I settled on the sausage and picked up a soup bone for Sherlock.

I pulled into my driveway and slammed on the brakes in front of a dead squirrel. Deja vu. It had not snowed in days so when I got out and looked for evidence of who might have left it, chances were slim I would find anything. Although the gravel "sidewalk" path was well-used, it wasn't muddy and unlikely to show any telltale footprints. I had no doubt this was not an accident. It was fairly harmless, not like a horse's head in my bed, and if I weren't being such a busybody I would chalk it up to a childhood prank, and yet there was a hint of menace to it.

This time I picked up the cadaver with a plastic bag and put it in my freezer. I might talk to Haggarty about it, and if it happened again I might want to have it analyzed; as before, there were no visible signs of the cause of its demise.

Looking forward to a good meal, I managed to make a fine dinner of sausage and spaghetti with veggies, with a bone for Sherlock.

In addition to my cellphone I still had an old landline with remote phones I could pick up in several of my rooms, upstairs and down. I noticed a message light blinking. Few people called on that old phone now and I wasn't even sure I needed it and had thought many times of getting rid of it. But they say old habits die hard and this one wasn't dead yet.

Like all of us I enjoyed the convenience of being able to contact anyone anytime, anywhere, whether they were home or not, so I wasn't going to ditch my cell either. I was in limbo between two centuries, still hanging onto many habits from the twentieth. Occasionally I got messages on the old phone, mostly from my physician–for some reason I'd insisted on giving him my landline number. I didn't get too many solicitations because the screen I'd put on the number worked fairly well, so when I saw the blinking message light it gave me a little pause. No one with any common sense would leave an incriminating message on a line that would be recorded. Was it my doctor? All this flashed through my mind before I grabbed my compact voice recorder to get a second copy of whatever it was before it could disappear; I knew the message wouldn't just go away but I was getting a little paranoid. This is a tactic some crime syndicates use to intimidate: small, barely noticeable threats that the targeted person understands the meaning of. Some political groups use it too but not as subtly, outrightly threatening their target crudely and bluntly though usually not following through.

I turned on my recorder and played the message.

Nothing–just twenty seconds of silence, then the dial tone. That was effective. I was getting the meaning. I wrote down the number of the caller, which I did not recognize.

Even living alone as I did, I'd never feared for myself. Neighbors were close and caring. If I ever needed anything I'd just run next door or across the street. I'd always felt safe here and never imagined I'd want a camera installed. Sherlock always let me know if someone was coming up the driveway. Now, for the first time since living here, I felt a twinge of fear.

Chapter 31 – Number 3

I looked online for wireless cameras. I found both doorbell cameras and small wireless ones and ordered what I thought would be adequate for my needs: two doorbell cameras, one for the front and one for the back, and four very small remote cameras. I felt that anyone aware of the doorbell cameras and careful when approaching them might not notice the smaller, easily hidden second and third cameras. I expected them to arrive in two days.

I was startled out of my internet browsing by a loud banging on the kitchen door, the one I customarily used and most neighbors came to. Sherlock, who usually noticed people in the yard, started up from his warm cushion by the radiator and barked loudly enough to wake the dead. Even he had a curious straight-tailed look. I opened the vestibule door and saw Sue.

"Hey, come on in. It's too chilly to dally out there." Sue entered and put a satchel on the table.

"Hi, Frances. How are you?" Without pausing for a reply she continued, "I had something really weird happen and I want to know what you think." She pointed to the bag on the counter. I had a hunch what it was. I gingerly opened the flap and inside was a plastic shopping bag. "It was hanging on my doorknob."

"Did you touch it?"

"Yes, I took it off the knob and opened it. It's a dead squirrel." I knew it. Really, I thought, are there that many squirrels in the neighborhood? I put on my gloves and removed the plastic bag from the satchel and peeked inside.

"What do you think of that?" I asked. I didn't want to tell her about my squirrels.

"I don't know. Don't you think it's weird? Who would do that? Some kids maybe. Do they really think that's funny?"

"Did you hear or see anyone?"

"No, I haven't been out since this morning when I went to the post office and it wasn't there then. I brought it in and put it on my kitchen counter before I opened it. Eewww, gross. Harold jumped up and started sniffing at it. Then I looked in and almost fell over. Poor thing. Who would do that?"

"Huh. So, you just looked in the bag and touched the handles and near the opening?" Sue nodded. "Good. I'll take care of this. Don't worry. It's probably just some childhood prank." I gingerly took the bag and put it inside another bag. I hoped it would have fingerprints. Someone may have made a mistake. I put the bag out in my vestibule, which was very cold. "Want a cup of tea? How about a little sweet potato pie? Sit down, Sue. Take a load off." I saw her alarm and wanted to help her dial it back a little. "Remember last year when those kids were shooting peas at our windows in the evening? Those little brats. I can't believe you can still get pea shooters. Who was that, the Beardsley kids, and Lanskys'?" I poured the boiling water over the tea bags. "I bet they really got tanned. It certainly stopped fast once they were caught."

Sue laughed. "Oh yeah, I remember." I cut a generous piece of pie, shook the whipped cream and hissed it onto her slice and then mine. "Oh geez, Fran, your pie is the best!"

Chapter 32 – News?

Sue chatted on for a while: news of who had Covid, who had the flu they couldn't shake, who was away visiting relatives during the holidays and who had relatives visiting, and on and on. I wished she would leave; I was dying to call Haggarty and tell him what was going on and find out if he wanted to or could test the squirrels for cause of death and for fingerprints on Sue's bag and maybe any possible DNA, a hair or something. I knew the DNA was unlikely, but this was interesting: three silly squirrel cadavers left to intimidate us and a blank message on my machine. It really seemed like kid stuff, I thought, and that's what anyone caught doing it could claim, just a prank. But why would they prank Sue, who was basically an innocent bystander? Finally, after her third cup of tea and second thinner slice of pie and all village talk exhausted, Sue decided it was time to get home to Harold. I followed her into the vestibule on the way out and grabbed the bagged squirrel to put in the freezer beside number two. I knew I'd remember which was which because squirrel number three was in a bag from Walmart, where I rarely went.

"You okay going home in the dark?"

"Oh yeah. It's just across the street and I have my headlamp." She took it from her coat pocket and put it on, tucking it under the earflaps of her knitted sherpa-style hat. She waved and I watched her disappear into the dark as Sherlock stood, front legs up in the window, barking his brains out at the alien-looking Sue.

I texted Haggarty.

"HEY! I've got some new developments. Anything new with you? When can you stop by?"

I waited. I knew it was getting late; at seven p.m., most people would be sitting in front of their TVs watching the news or some talking heads. A text message pinged.

"I'll come by tomorrow. Will you be around? Anything important?"

I was tingling with the excitement that new levels of investigations brought.

"Yes, I'll be here. Nothing important, just a few things of interest."

"Okay, see you tomorrow."

I practiced some more on my lock-picking skills, knowing I was too keyed up to fall asleep. Then I read through yesterday's newspaper, trying to finish the crossword more quickly than the previous day's, then worked on the sudoku, then read today's paper. I was one of the few who still got a printed copy of the paper; one of my guilty pleasures was a crisp (hopefully not saturated with snow or rain) paper to open and a hot cup of coffee. But it could be frustrating because newspapers were being swallowed up by larger conglomerate papers who dictated their news policy, either with a more conservative or more liberal bent, and staff got thinner and thinner to maximize profits so local news suffered. Mostly there were the same stories, shared across the country in every paper owned by that larger company, trying to influence anyone who was still willing to read them instead of the crazy online alternate sources. The world had gone mad with "fake news" and lies and conspiracy theories perpetrated by these whackos. No one knew what to believe anymore.

Chapter 33 – Saint?

With the sun shining across the yard I excitedly opened the morning paper and spread it out on the kitchen table. Sherlock had gone out, my oatmeal was in the microwave, and I sipped my first cup of black coffee. All seemed right with the world. I was trying to stay busy to keep my mind off Haggarty's visit. Then I got a call from Grace.

"Frances? Hey, how are you?"

"Good. What's up, Grace? Everything okay?" I knew she might have news because she didn't usually call me. As with many of us, lunch and dinner plans were often made casually, during a meeting or gathering.

"Well, no, not exactly. It's not that big of a deal, but I just thought you should know."

"Yeah, okay." I waited.

"Do you have a little while to talk? Can I come over?"

"Well, I have a little while right now, but maybe we can talk about it on the phone. What do you think?" I didn't want her crossing the green for everyone to see.

"Okay. Well, I was having dinner with a few people last night, you know, the Sandons and Sheila, and a person on the town committee, Gary."

"Yeah."

"Well, talk turned to Ellen, and to you. People have been talking, others that weren't there last night, and I guess some people don't like you doing what they called 'nosing around'."

"Really?"

"Yeah. They said some pretty uncomplimentary things about you."

"Really."

"Yeah, things I'd never heard before. Things about your work in the department. I don't know where they got that information or why they would want to spread it. But is it true?"

"I don't know what you mean, Grace. What did they say?" I knew exactly what was going around, but I wondered why they had dug it up and were using it to discredit me.

"Well, something about an investigation by one of your co-workers. Someone who messed up and you protected? Someone you were having an affair with?"

"Really? Did they give you a name?"

"Yeah." She hesitated. "Yeah, a Sarah Philips."

"Well, I guess the cat's out of the bag, huh, Grace?"

"So it's true?"

"Yes, but there's a lot more to it than what you may have heard. She made a mistake and tried to cover it up. I tried to help her and was implicated as being something of an accomplice, even though it was after the fact. She shouldn't have done it and I shouldn't have supported her."

"Oh, it sounded so much more lurid than that. So, you weren't lovers?"

"Oh yes," I sighed, "We were lovers. When she first started on the force, she attached herself to me, I mentored her, and, well, one thing led to another. Neither of us were married or otherwise attached, but having inter-departmental affairs was discouraged, and at that time having homosexual affairs was definitely a no-no. We kept our private lives away from work, but it got out."

"Wow, Fran, I had no idea."

"What? I know people think I'm a saint, but do they think I'm a nun?" She laughed. "Who brought that up? Can you tell me?"

"Neil Sandon."

"What else did they say? Anything about Ellen?"

Chapter 34 – Buttinsky

Grace hesitated. "No, not really. Well, Neil said he thought Ellen was 'losing it'. He thought she wasn't as sharp as she used to be, and kind of unsteady on her feet. He noticed it in one of the historic commission meetings. He said he wasn't surprised she fell down the stairs, said she shouldn't have been living on the second floor, and he didn't understand why there was an investigation."

"I guess you did cover some ground."

"It was just an opinion; it didn't seem important to me." Grace seemed apologetic.

"I understand. I'm grateful you're sharing this with me. Thanks. I really appreciate it, and I just want you to know that this does help. Every little bit helps, even if it's just people's attitudes. It gives insight into everyone's mindset and that is just as important as a fingerprint." I exaggerated a little, but I didn't want her to feel bad about telling me or to think what she told me was unimportant.

"So, do you think there was more talk about me?" There was a pause on the line.

"I can't know what is behind it, but yes, I think there was more talk about you. Maybe they just resent you digging around, maybe they don't think it's your job since you're retired, or maybe they don't think you're qualified. I don't remember the conversation word for word, but I think all those things came up, mostly I think about you digging around."

"I see. Thanks. I get it." As we were talking a text message came in from Haggarty.

"Are you busy? Coming by in an hour. I hope to get into Ellen's."

"Thanks for calling, Grace. Again, I really appreciate it. Do you think we can get together for breakfast soon? I hear there is a delicious special at that breakfast place."

"Yeah, I'd love to! Give me a call." We hung up and I replied to Haggarty. I couldn't wait for him to arrive and asked him to stop at my house before going to the inn. I didn't tell him I had a couple of cadavers for him. I expected him to be using his police cruiser and really wished he would park at the inn and not in my driveway, knowing it would just stir up those who were annoyed at my involvement.

He arrived and of course drove into my driveway.

"I've got some coffee if you need any." I invited him in and wanted him to feel comfortable.

"No thanks, I'm on the clock. What's up?"

"I've had a couple of weird things happen." I told him about the squirrels in my driveway and at Sue's and that two of them were in my freezer and I wondered if he wanted to check them out. I told him about the phone hang-up and about people talking about my being a buttinsky. I asked him not to park at my house when he was in his cruiser, even when he was here just to see me. He listened carefully and nodded at it all. I offered to show him the squirrels.

"Well, this little town is turning out to be more interesting than I'd ever imagined it would be." He smiled. "I'm not sure if we need to investigate the squirrels yet, but if more events like this happen we may want to, so if you don't mind, please hold onto them for now, okay?" I thought that was fair. I grabbed my lock-picking kit and we headed to the inn.

The first thing we noted was that the remaining paper crime scene notice was stuck to the door and the jamb had been torn as though someone had used a key to score it and open the door.

Haggarty paused, looked back and forth between the breached door and me, then took out his phone and photographed it.

"Huh. The plot thickens." He opened the door. The place was warm, the thermostat probably set where Ellen liked it. It smelled stale but not like something was rotten, although there was a slight scent of dead rodent. We entered slowly. The living room looked as it had, but a few pillows seemed out of place. The kitchen was the room where the rodent smell was strongest, and when Haggarty opened the cabinet below the sink a desiccated mouse in a snap trap revealed the source. He picked up the trap and dropped it into the garbage, mouse still attached. He opened the refrigerator and removed the old milk carton and other things that were spoiling, then pulled the garbage bag out and handed it to me. We walked through to the front room she'd used as a study, the large oak desk in front of the east window giving her a view of the post office and the comings and goings there as long as the big maple in between wasn't leafed out. The room looked much as I'd remembered it, but several books were now on the floor instead of on the bookshelf. Peeking into her bedroom, we saw little that looked suspicious, just a drawer that seemed to have been opened and not pushed all the way back in. A quick look into the closet revealed no disarray. We went back to the study.

I noticed the chair was pulled out and knew Ellen would have pushed it in, not left it like that. Inspecting the desk I saw pry marks and small pieces of oak where the drawer had been attacked. Someone had tried to get in and I thought hadn't succeeded. Whoever did this was a very polite burglar, and/or maybe afraid to wake anyone or attract any attention.

Chapter 35 – Lollipops

Haggarty tried the center drawer but the lock held fast. "Well, do you have a key?" Haggarty was hopeful.

"I didn't even have a key to her apartment, so no, I don't have a key." I tried not to sound snarky. "But..." I paused for dramatic effect. "I do have a lock-pick set and I've been practicing." I produced it from my pocket like a magician revealing a trick.

"Good. Get to work." He smiled. I opened the kit on the top of the desk, which was bare except for the closed desk calendar. I sat down and bent to inspect the lock to see which tools I'd need to pick it. Pulling out three of the most likely ones, I worked the cylinders, gently turning and poking the tools around. After about five minutes I'd breached the lock and Haggarty leaned over me as I slowly opened the drawer.

He motioned me to move. "Can I sit there for a minute?" Everything was as I had expected: fountain pens, pencils and highlighters in the pen tray in front, a pink eraser, a box of paper clips, stapler, scissors, a couple of thumb drives, but also some things I didn't recognize. Haggarty made a low whistle.

"What?"

"Do you know what those are?" He obviously did.

"No. What?"

"Those are fentanyl lozenges, 'lollipops'." He held one in his rubber gloves and inspected it. "Wow, twelve hundred micrograms. These are seriously dangerous."

I leaned over to get a look at them. There were about half a dozen. He picked up another and looked closely at it, one of two that had a different color label on the end. "Well, she's got a couple of eight hundred micrograms too." He took them all. "Any paper around?" I noticed a piece peeking out from under her blotter and pulled it out. It had numbers on it, an obvious tabulation. Haggarty photographed the notations and then flipped it to the blank side to line up the "lollipops" and take several photos. "This investigation just got a whole lot more interesting."

He took a bag from his pocket and wrote on it the date, time, and case number (which was easy to remember as it was Ellen's date of death followed by a hyphen and a short number), then put the fentanyl lozenges into the bag and sealed it with the attached tape that was impossible to open without damaging the bag. "Okay, let's see what else we can find." The next drawer on the right was half height and it too had a lock. The file-size bottom drawer wouldn't open so I set about picking the lock on the half height drawer, assuming once that opened the bottom one would too.

Fentanyl lollipops. I couldn't help thinking about them. Were they for pain? How did she get them?

I heard the last cylinder click and pulled the top drawer open, revealing several bottles of ink, an old rubber stamp with her return address, a small tin containing an old watch and a couple of rings, a roll of postage stamps, a small address book, a small plastic container of rubber bands and, tucked on the inside edge, a business size envelope, which Haggarty pulled out. It looked well-worn and had several lists of numbers on it, most starting with a thousand, with amounts subtracted and new totals, the final one being $720. He photographed it and opened it, pulling out the cash and laying it on the paper in piles of twenties, tens, and fives, each pile fanned out to show how many were in it. He snapped another photo.

Another evidence bag appeared, which he meticulously labeled, put the cash into, and sealed. I watched the process, understanding how important evidence was.

He took a quick look through her address book, stopping at G to take a photo: Gerald 860-564-5909, with an address in North Stonington. He scanned a few more pages and made out another evidence bag.

"If you find anything interesting will you send me photos?" I was hoping to get my hands on some of this, but the fentanyl had pushed the case to a different level, which probably entailed more caution with the evidence.

"Of course." Then he opened the bottom drawer. Behind several composition books in the front were files, one labeled Health, which he pulled out. She knew she was in trouble. A scan showed brittle bones and advanced arthritis. She must have been experiencing a lot of pain. There were prescriptions for special calcium supplements, for sinus pills and an asthma inhaler. Nothing for fentanyl. Was she getting her drugs on the street? Really?

"Where's the fentanyl scrip?" We looked at each other, knowing she had to be getting it somewhere. "Well, here's her doctor's name so we can find out what he prescribed and what he thought about her health." He bagged it all, then opened one of the composition books, revealing beautiful long-hand probably written with a fountain pen. Someone had said she was keeping a journal, so might these books be a key to her thoughts, the key to everything?

Chapter 36 – Journals

Other files contained receipts, and one was labeled UConn. This was going to be a treasure trove.

"I'd really like to get a look at this stuff, the journals and the UConn folder. Could you give me a pair of gloves?" We both knew this was slightly unethical. Although he'd gotten the okay for me to help him, the boundaries of that were not well defined and probably only meant for me to see what I could stir up in the village and have him bounce ideas off me. Could I poke through evidence, even with gloves on? Could I go to the station and look through it there? Ideally for me I'd love to bring it home and slowly work my way through it. He was looking at me thoughtfully.

"Geez, I don't know, Frances. You're putting me in a bind." He pondered a bit, then said, "Here, take these, and look through quickly for anything interesting, and if you find something maybe I can get permission for you to come down to the station." I put on the gloves he'd given me and sat at the desk as he continued to root through the other files.

First I opened the UConn file and as I expected found copies of student papers. Some she'd made notations on: 'Exceptional! A++', then, 'What Were You Thinking? D-', clearly a shot at the underperforming student. I looked for the name: C. Grusso. Just as I thought. She really had no love for this guy. I read through the paper, which compared Shakespeare to Bob Dylan and probably could have been interesting if it weren't so poorly done, going off on tangents about topics that had nothing to do with poetry, writing or creativity. It was actually bizarre. He may have imagined he was clever or an original thinker or a great writer, but the reality was he was just using up paper to get the word count that the assignment required.

She could be both an amazingly encouraging teacher and a wickedly hard one. But would anyone hurt her for that? I didn't think so, but you never know. I paged through a few more papers, mostly praise with encouraging notations.

Haggarty continued to pull out folders: taxes, banking, bills, Historic Commission, Museum, Library, all the committees and boards she'd worked on.

I moved on to the journals, plain black and white cardboard-covered composition books. I opened the first one and noted the date, 1970, likely during her UConn and marriage years, and the second one, dated 1985, after her affair and marriage breakup. The third, dated 2002, was probably after she retired and would have notes about her village life. I went for that one. It opened with her focusing on town events she attended in the community. Right from the start she recorded everything, almost like a play. The setting is described, the warmth of the afternoon sun at an outdoor barbeque and potluck that also included a planning meeting agenda for a local park project. The food is noted; the hosts' grilled sausages she judged outstanding. Most people brought delectable side dishes and desserts, while occasionally someone might be caught short and bring something store-made, but, she explained, we all understood how busy lives made it hard to always bring something special as most people tried to do. Then she broke down the interactions, the personal dynamics in the group: who was focused, who was grandstanding, who didn't really care about what they were there for but just wanted to be part of it, who might have a bone to pick, who was a hard worker, who was less disciplined but well-intended, and who was only supporting a spouse. It was interesting seeing the village interactions from her point of view, and more often than not I found her on target. I recognized most of the players, although some had left town or passed away.

I flipped in about thirty pages, finding much of the same documentation of village social life but this time with more of an angry edge to it. At about sixty pages it seemed pointedly harsh toward some of the group, not vulgar but edging toward that. What had happened to Ellen?

I'd always heard she was kind and very generous but occasionally could be egocentric and what some called bossy. I'd heard stories of how she mentored some of the less able students and got them into schools they might not have been able to attend without her efforts. But a mysterious woman lurked behind that and all the other things I'd heard, or at least that was my view. As much as I heard about her, I still felt I didn't know or understand her any better. And for some reason I wanted to know her better, to find out what made her tick. It probably seems like a silly endeavor, getting to know a person who is dead, although volumes are written about people who have passed and volumes are read about them.

I looked around her study and thought about what I'd seen in her other rooms. No photos, no photographs of her, no photos of anyone and yet her home was pleasant and comfortable, not barren or spare. Her several original oil paintings, mostly by local artists, were landscapes, still lifes and village scenes. But no photos. Was there something in her past she was burying?

Chapter 37 - Plus

"Finn, I really want to go through these. Is there any chance I can come down to the station and read them? I know you can't let me have them..."

"Geez, Frances, I don't know. Let me ask and see, but they may just let you if you come down." He continued to root through the drawer. "Or maybe I can get them photocopied?"

"Photocopies would work. Are you finding anything interesting?"

"Not yet. Other than the fentanyl, not much. Actually pretty sparse, like everything she did, neat, clean, no extra stuff hanging around."

"Sort of like Swedish death cleaning?"

"What? What the hell is that?"

"You've never heard of that? I guess it's a practice in Sweden, maybe everywhere. Older people do it so their kids, or whoever, don't have to go through mounds of their possessions after they pass away, so their children aren't burdened with getting rid of it or deciding what to do with it all. Really, it makes your life easier. You know, we just collect too much stuff, some of it important only to us. And kids these days don't seem to want our old stuff, even what we would have considered heirlooms when we were younger, the china, the silver the crystal. Nowadays they're just not interested. Times have really changed."

"Where did you ever hear of that? Swedish death cleaning– really?"

"Aw, I've just read some articles about it. It's a real thing."

"Well, yes, I guess she subscribed to that–what would you call it–lifestyle?"

"Yeah, I guess so." I looked down at the journals as Haggarty continued to go through the drawer.

"Hey, have you seen any photos of her?"

"Funny you should ask. I've hardly seen any photos; the only one I remember was on her license, when I went through her purse the day she died. I had no idea what she looked like. I mean her face that day was not something to remember her by; it probably didn't look as she did when she was alive. What was she, like five foot six or seven?"

"Yes, she was maybe above average height for a woman, but very thin, and kind of bent over; maybe that was the osteoporosis. I'd always seen her in later years with short white hair, spiked. For someone I would consider more classical the spiked look seemed out of place, but maybe it was because it was easy and her hair was thinning. I think when she was younger her hair was dark. She usually wore "cheater" half glasses that she put low on her nose and looked over. It must have given her students pause if she looked at them over those glasses. I don't remember what color her eyes were but I think brown. You know as you get older they seem to get like 'milky', you know what I mean? To me she seemed graceful, to have a nice way of walking, almost like a dancer, but in the last few years when I saw her she was much slower and even used a cane sometimes." We'd stopped looking through her possessions.

"Hey, let's see if we can finish up this drawer and then have a coffee and discuss what we've found."

"Okay." I opened the journal again, then asked, "What's going to happen to all her stuff? Did you get a peek at the will? Will someone from her family come and go through all this?"

"Yeah, I think so. I think the son, Gerald, is getting some cash from her estate, and I would imagine that once we release it he'd be the one to dispose of her possessions."

"Do you think there is anywhere else you should look? Should you go through her closet or dresser or anything? I've heard that people even stash stuff in their freezer."

"The crew did go over the apartment. The records show they went through everything except this locked desk."

"Can I poke around then, since they've already been through it?"

"I suppose it won't hurt."

"Cool." I went into her bathroom, opened the medicine cabinet and found nothing of interest, but I did open an aspirin bottle and examined the contents. Just aspirin. A small closet held only towels and cleaning supplies. I went into her bedroom and opened her closet. Cool, I thought, old round hat boxes. In one I found a fine felt feminine-style fedora in a soft mousy grey. I wanted to try it on but put it back. The other hat box held a very old-style fascinator with a fine net veil and I wondered why she'd kept it and how old it was. In the back of them was a smaller old Olympia typewriter, but nothing more of interest.

Her bedside table had a drawer and a shelf, the drawer holding only cough drops and kleenex and a couple of bookmarks. On the shelf was a hardbound worn-looking copy of "The French Lieutenant's Woman" by John Fowles.

As I lifted her pillow to look underneath I noticed the pillowcase was very heavy. When I picked it up a handgun fell to the floor with a heavy thud.

"Hey, what's going on in there? You trying to wake up the dead?"

"Shit, Finn, it's a gun!"

Chapter 38 – .22

"What? You're kidding!" He came rushing in. "Why didn't my guys find that?"

"It was in her pillowcase. I was lifting it to look underneath and it felt heavy. When I picked up the pillow the gun fell to the floor."

"Holy cows!" He gingerly used his pen to pick up the weapon by the trigger guard and inspect it. "It's a Ruger .22 revolver." He still had his gloves on so he popped the cylinder to see inside. "Eight shot–that's unusual. Most are six or even five. And it's loaded. You're lucky it didn't go off and blow a little hole in you. Small as a .22 is, it can still do a lot of damage; those slugs tumble once they hit the body, and..." He paused, looking it over carefully. "There is no safety. You live a charmed life."

"I know. I am lucky," I said, still feeling a little shaken.

"Of course you are." He stood there, gun in one hand, scratching his head with the pen in his other hand, and repeated, "Why didn't my guys find this?"

"Just want you to know there's a typewriter in her closet too, but I don't think that's important."

"I want to wrap this up for today. Did you see the other notebook from the drawer?"

"I saw three journals, dated 1970, 1985 and 2002. Right now I'm most interested in the 2002 if you can get me copies."

"Well, there's one more book that looks more like poetry or something, not a diary."

"Oh, let me see it." That was kind of exciting. Even though she was an English Lit professor, somehow I didn't see her as a person who would write poetry. It gave me a little more insight into this woman.

We went back to the study and Haggarty pointed to the fourth book on the desk, which I started to look through as he bagged the additional evidence. The poetry was not flowery rhyming stuff, but more like haiku and short stanzas about nature and life.

"Okay, I have to bag these too, but I'll see what they think about my copying them for you. I'm pretty sure they'll let me." I handed them over and one after another he bagged and tagged the four of them.

"Do you have time to come over for coffee and leftover meat loaf?"

"Oh yeah, I can be persuaded." He put all the bags into a larger one and locked the door as we left. "Let's see if anyone is going to be back. I've got a little remote camera. Before I return to the station I'll come back and put it up just inside the door. I want to see if anyone drops in again." He locked the evidence bags into his trunk and pulled out the box with the camera and found some batteries to set it up. "I'll be back in a few minutes." He headed for the inn.

"What's your next step?" I asked, working my way through the meatloaf and baked potato.

"Probably contact Gerald and try to talk to him. He should know there is an investigation, and I want to know what he's planning to do with her apartment and possessions. What about you? What are you doing?"

"Now that I've put out feelers in town and have gotten some 'feedback' I may just wait and see what else pops up. I'm looking forward to reading through those journals too. They could be very revealing." He smiled.

"I'll try to get copies to you ASAP."

Chapter 39 – Laptop?

That evening I walked my now routine loop through the village, from my house to the school, back past the inn, up to the firehouse, to the upper green, to the lower green, to St. Paul's and back home. I wanted people to see me and know my routine. Anyone paying attention would be reminded of my interest and know when I was around and when I wasn't home–just in case someone wanted to drop by and talk or leave another squirrel.

I realized I'd overlooked an obvious detail and wanted to ask Haggarty about it. Did Ellen have a computer? Maybe a laptop? And if so, where was it? A person who taught, even twenty years ago, should have some new technology and not use a fountain pen to write in longhand and a typewriter that was up on a shelf in her closet. It didn't make sense. We hadn't seen anything in her files that looked like she photocopied or printed anything at home. Of course, the library, just a stone's throw across the green, was almost always open and had a very nice PC available to the public. She did have an iPad, and I suppose it might be all she required for her computing needs. The modem and router I'd seen in the living room tucked on a little table next to the couch told me she had to be reaching out to the world on the internet. But I wondered about her computer needs and planned to visit the library, thinking they kept a record of who used their computer. Of course if I were doing something I wanted to hide I might avoid my local library and use one in another town. People notice and people talk, and if she used our library people would notice, and the librarian, although professional and discreet, might offer help, or in wiping out the records on the computer for that day might see something on the search engine like street addresses or email addresses. Anyone not technologically astute might not realize that very little that has been done on a computer is ever lost. You can delete things but they are not gone; you can wipe a disk but a good technician can get it back. The only way to really destroy information is to take the disk out and smash the crap out of it with a sledgehammer. If you've done a search, a record of it remains there. I know this doesn't help people who lost files they were working on and didn't save. It's all maddening. But sometimes the right tech person can restore files. Those hackers from home and abroad can be traced and caught if you have the resources, which most of us do not, but if they do enough damage, especially if it involves utilities or commerce, governments can track them down.

I texted Haggarty.

"Hey, I was just thinking, did Ellen have a laptop? Did your guys bring it back to crack it? If not, do you think she might have used a public computer? Like a library computer? Just thinking..."

He got right back to me.

"No. No computer. Yeah, that's odd. Yes, libraries might be an interesting direction to search. We do have her iPad; haven't cracked it yet."

Okay, maybe that's another place to look. Then another text came in from Haggarty.

"P.S. I got the okay to copy the journals and someone is doing that right now. Will drop them off as soon as they are done."

Woohoo! That made my day. I might start by visiting the local library, just in case.

Then I thought about who was going to be responsible for her possessions and opened the folder containing her will.

Chapter 40 – Who?

In addition to Ellen's bequests to nonprofits, she had left her son, Gerald Richardson, what I considered a goodly sum. A meager ten thousand was left to her daughter, Alice Richardson-James. I wondered what was behind that and how I could reach her. Fifty thousand went to Clyde Baker, and two percent to someone I didn't recognize, Leslie Goranson. I'd have to find out more about that, and I wondered why Haggarty hadn't brought it up. Leslie Goranson?

She seemed to have given some thought to her physical assets. A beautiful painting of the library by a prominent local artist went to the library. A set of leatherbound books went to Shelly, an unlikely gift in my opinion since Shelly didn't seem to like Ellen and judged her a snob. Was it a peace offering? What was behind that? A small collection of gold broaches, which I hadn't seen in the bedroom although there were photos of them in the will, went to Grace. An elegant silver-tipped cane went to Sheila, and a very expensive designer bag to Barbara. Likely realizing Susan would not only inherit Harold but could use the money, Ellen left her five thousand dollars. I was surprised and touched to find she left me a lovely sculpted alabaster lamp of a young half-naked woman holding up a torch. I had once mentioned to her that I thought it pretty. It was obvious to me she had given a lot of thought to the things she was handing out posthumously.

I puzzled over how she allotted her monetary assets. Other than the nonprofits, the cash handed out to her family was bizarre, and who was Leslie, and why was Leslie getting more than her daughter Alice, and who was Clyde Baker? Could it be the drunken caretaker? Wondering if Grace would have any answers I sent her an email asking her to dinner the next day. A couple hours later she got back to me and said yes.

I was very excited to be going to the Harp on Church, a favorite of mine, and I knew Grace liked it too.

I sat in one of the old-fashioned looking high-backed booths facing the door, so I saw her when she came in.

"Hey, thanks for meeting me."

"No problem. I was going to the co-op anyway and this is so conveniently close. I haven't been here in a while. Have their specials changed?"

"Well, one of my favorite thin crust pizzas with chicken, basil and balsamic vinegar is no longer on the menu. I'll miss that." The Harp was owned by an Irish family and had the feel of a pub from the old country. It was a small and very popular watering hole in Willimantic. Their meals were usually hearty and filling, and their drafts a perfect accompaniment.

"So what's up, Frances?" Grace wasn't beating around the bush.

"Well, I've been looking at Ellen's will and had some questions I thought I'd pass by you." She nodded, taking a good gulp of the just-delivered dark brew that still had a thick, creamy head. "Her son, Gerald, is getting a generous amount from her estate, but her daughter is getting hardly anything, and then there is this person I've never heard of who is getting fifty thousand. My question is, why is her daughter, Alice Richardson-James, getting so little, and who is this Clyde Baker, who is getting fifty thousand?" I didn't know the caretaker's last name but had to find out if it was him. "And who is this other person, Leslie Goranson? Have you ever heard of her? " At this Grace almost snorted the foam off the top of the glass she had up to her mouth. She must know something.

"What? Leslie Goranson?"

Chapter 41 – Cat

"Yeah. You know her?"

"Well, sort of. I think I recognize the name. I think it's one of the kids staying at Allison and John's. You know they have two boys. Well, a little while back they took in another, whose name is Leslie. I don't know that much about the circumstances, but that name sort of sticks in my head."

"You're kidding." For a second everything in my mind stopped, and then thoughts flew around like dislodged bats. Someone in Ellen's will is living in town? A younger person, probably a teenager? The "bats" settled down into a puzzle that was coming together. "How? Why?"

"I'm really not sure, Frances. I do know they have taken in foster children, but I'm not sure if he is a foster. I really don't know anything about it. I just sort of remember that name; I guess it stuck in my mind because Leslie is not a common name for a boy." My thoughts chattered how? when? who? so fast I had to slow them down to ask her.

"What did Allison tell you?"

"Well, it was sort of in passing. Maybe a month and a half ago, around Thanksgiving, perhaps? The three kids were leaving, each grabbing a cookie on the way out, one yelling they'd be back later. Allison hollered, "Mr. Goranson?" He stopped and she said, 'Mr. Goranson, don't forget your hat.' And he grabbed one from the rack by the door, smiled at her and rushed out after the other boys.

Allison said something about Leslie living with them for a while. No details, just that."

"Wow. That's interesting. He's in Ellen's will. Weird, huh?" I took another sip of the amber I'd ordered.

"Are you sure?"

"Yeah, I saw the will. How is he related to Ellen, if he is? It must be him. It's such an uncommon name it would be too much of a coincidence for it to be anyone else."

She shook her head and picked up half of her Irish Reuben as I dug into my shepherd's pie.

"And if he's related to Ellen why isn't he staying with her?" I managed between mouthfuls.

"I wonder if Allison even knows they're related. She probably would have said something if she knew, at least I think she would have." Grace's fork speared a couple of pickle pieces to follow up her bite of the Reuben. "Man, this is so good. Thanks for inviting me out, Frances. I miss this place." I smiled and took another bite.

We moved on to what Grace was planning for her garden this year, what seedlings she would start in a few weeks, and how she'd just about finished her pruning.

When I drove into my driveway it was dark, but I could see an animal lying there. When I got out my headlights revealed a cat. It was dead and, in the cold, very stiff. I brought it to my back door so I could pull my car in. This whole business with the dead animals was now freaking me out. I'm not someone easily shaken, but I'd also never been targeted before. Granted, it was only dead animals, and small ones at that, but still, someone was aware of when I was away and did this then. Why did my mind go straight to Leslie Goranson? Because it sounded like he was a youngster and kids do things like this for fun, for effect, and maybe to frighten. Should I go over to Allison and John's this evening? Maybe explain to them what had been happening and find out if they or their kids knew something?

I bagged the cat and put it in the upright freezer I had in the basement, then thought for a while about my next step.

Chapter 42 – Allison & John

I walked over to Allison and John's.

The kitchen and living room were lit up. When I knocked at the back door it took a little while for Allison to answer it.

"Oh. Hi, Frances! We just finished up dinner and were settling in to watch the news. Everything okay? Come on in. Want a cup of tea?" She went to the kitchen and filled the electric kettle. "Or how about a glass of wine?" A bottle of red was on the counter. "Can I get you a glass?"

"You know, I would like that." Allison reached for the glasses.

"So, how are you, Frances? What's up? Want a snack?" She busied herself while she talked, putting cheese and crackers on a board. "Come on in. John's already relaxing." She put three glasses on a tray with the food and led the way into the living room. "Hey John, Frances stopped by." John stood up and shook my hand.

"Hey, Frances. I haven't seen you in a little while. How are you?"

"I'm pretty good. How are you?" I noticed a bandage on his hand and pointed toward it. "One of your sculptures bite you?" He laughed.

"As a matter of fact, yeah, I had a little slip up with a tricky piece and didn't have my gloves on. Just a stupid accident, but no stitches. I'll be right as rain in a few days."

"Good to hear. Your work is beautiful. I'd like to pick up one of your pieces if I can afford it." He chuckled. I sipped the wine, a nice one. "You know I've been helping the detective do some work on Ellen, right?" I dove right into it, watching them. They both paused, wine glasses in hand, and looked at each other.

"Yeah, we've heard you're asking around, but we don't know anything." John replied.

"I understand. It's just that weird things have been happening to me." They again looked from me to each other. "In the past three weeks dead animals have been showing up in my driveway. Isn't that weird?" They seemed concerned.

"Yeah, yeah, that is weird. Who do you think is doing that? Do you think it has something to do with the investigation?" Allison put a strange inflection on 'investigation'.

"I don't know, but it never happened to me before."

"So you don't think it's a coincidence? You think it's deliberate? How often has it happened?"

"Well, I don't really know, but I've had two squirrels and just tonight a dead cat. And Sue had a squirrel at her house. What the heck, right?" They looked at each other.

"I can tell you it wouldn't be our kids. They wouldn't do anything like that."

"I know, your kids are really nice." I sipped the wine. "Do you have someone else staying with you?" Again they looked at me and then at each other.

"Yeah." Allison sounded pleased. "We do have a young man staying with us. His family is away on a getaway, a long one in Europe, and he wanted to stay here instead of traveling so he didn't miss any school. He's a good kid. How many kids want to stay back and go to school rather than travel?" She smiled.

"Nice! What's his name?"

"Leslie. Leslie Goranson."

"How do you know him?"

Chapter 43 – Leslie

John looked at me funny and tried to joke. "What, Frances? Is this an inquest?" He picked up a piece of cheese and layered it on a cracker.

"Oh, John, if this were an inquest, I'd be dressed more formally." I smiled and sipped the wine.

"He's a friend of the boys, someone they know from school." Allison stepped in to defuse the tension. "He asked our permission to stay for a few months. He's a nice boy, very polite, and our kids like him. I think they said they were going down to the pizza place – you know, Jimmy has his license now and they take off. I told them it's okay as long as they don't go too far and always keep their phones on. I have one of those trackers in the car too, so if I'm worried I can see where they are without making them feel I'm checking up on them."

I wanted to know more. How did this come about? Was he going to Windham High when they met him? So many questions, but I could feel the tension and just decided to leave it at that and see what Haggarty and I could find out. I sipped the wine and complimented it, and we watched a little of the news before I thanked them and headed back home. The whole thing was weird. Leslie didn't share a surname with any of the relatives in the will. Who was he?

When I went home I checked the cameras I'd set up. None of them were aimed at the area where the cat had been so I tried to reposition one of them.

Wondering if Haggarty had gotten those journals copied, I texted him.

"How's it going? Did you have any luck with the journals? I've got a few things of interest."

He texted back almost immediately.

"Good news–they're on my desk. Can I stop by?"

It wasn't that late and I was excited to get my eyes on them, and I had some weird stuff to chat about.

"Tonight? Absolutely."

I knew he was busy with other cases and I was grateful he was spending so much time on this one. I fed Sherlock and wrote down what I wanted to talk about:

Now an additional cadaver in my freezer.

I'd put up some cameras but didn't catch the cat killer.

Records at the library in the center showed Ellen had never used it. Next step: check South Windham Library, then maybe Franklin and Willimantic?

Had he done any looking into Ellen's son and daughter?

Who was Leslie Goranson, the kid currently living with Allison and John?

About a half hour later Haggarty drove into my driveway in his personal car.

First I told him about the cat, and that didn't meet with much concern. We spent a few minutes repositioning the cameras again and he said I might need an additional one pointing at the street. I told him about the libraries.

He said he'd checked everywhere and there were no prescriptions for fentanyl lollipops for her. Then he told me she didn't have a license for the gun I'd found, and he thought she possibly had it prior to the Connecticut law passed in 1995 that required licenses and background checks.

Last I told him that Leslie, the mysterious person in the will, was now living in town, just a stone's throw from Ellen's apartment. He was obviously as puzzled about this as I was and actually scratched his head, making me laugh.

Chapter 44 – Haiku

Then he gave me a fat envelope with the copied journals. I was in heaven.

I opened the envelope and the four journals flopped onto my kitchen table. Haggarty had had them copied on both sides and stapled in the left margin, book style. Perfect, I thought. Although I wanted to dive right into the one that began in 2002, I opened the poetry journal first.

So beautiful, so
Dangerous the towering
Trees along my path.

"Wow, Finn, did you get a look at these? She was a poet– these are haiku. Who knew?" Now it was his turn to laugh.

Curled stiffened fingers
Of resentment choke the breath
From my compassion.

I couldn't wait to read more but knew I had to focus on the investigation so I decided I'd save the poetry for later when I could relax and enjoy it.

Haggarty left and I made myself a cup of chamomile tea, and after Sherlock did his business we headed up to the bedroom where I could get warm under the covers and sink my teeth into this journal. During the winter I was perpetually chilly. Like many other homes in the village, mine was not well-insulated and the older windows approved by the historic commission leaked pitifully, so we kept our thermostats low. We often competed and took pride in waiting as long we could–who would be first to turn on the heat in the late fall or early winter? I had an oil furnace with old radiators (I was grateful to have something to hang my wet mittens on) that helped humidify the house, and even though the window panes often frosted, it kept enough moisture in the air and helped my sinuses.

As I expected, the latest entries in the 2002 journal were dated just a month ago. I hoped to find recent clues to what was going on in her life.

In my excitement I'd forgotten to fully close the second-floor bedroom's heavy curtains, which helped keep the warmth in and the cold out.

I sat propped up in my bed against several pillows, covered as much as possible while leaving my hands free. On the blankets I'd set a pad, pencil, highlighter and my iPad within reach. Sherlock was curled at my feet. I began reading the last entry.

November, 15, 2023 – Tired today and full of pain, but still able to walk to the post office and the library. Took out the latest NYT best seller I'd ordered and been waiting on. Grace came over to share some hollyhock

seeds – it's so hard to find those old single blossom seeds.
She had some pink and some so dark they looked black.
She told me she had to resign as Secretary of the

Abruptly Sherlock sat up, ears perked and face toward the window. He growled low, then barked. I heard a low hum, which grew louder. My automatic response was to sit more upright and pull the covers up tighter. Outside my second story window I saw a red light blinking through the crack between the curtains I'd forgotten to fully close.

For a second I froze, my only thought Holy shit, what is that? Then I realized it was a drone. I watched it and it watched me through my window. Even in my shock and panic I thought quickly enough to grab my iPad and take a video of it looking in at me, blinking and humming loudly. Sherlock jumped off the bed and ran to the window barking. The thing seemed to wobble up and down, and if I didn't know it was mechanical and not conscious, I'd have said it was laughing. I felt assaulted, invaded, attacked. I ran to the window. It wobbled sideways back and forth a few times. I tried to open the window but it stuck and by the time I succeeded the thing had gone up over the top of the house, the hum and the light disappearing with it.

I threw on my robe, freezing and shivering not just from the cold but from nervous fear and excitement. I really doubted I would be able to target the source, the person operating it, and I didn't want to go out into the cold in my robe to confront someone. I also didn't want to send

Sherlock outside for fear of what a person with this much chutzpah might do to him.

I checked my iPad photos, which had caught a small shaky video of the thing in the window that looked like only a red blinking light. The audio caught Sherlock's barking and also a faint hum.

I didn't want to be annoying, but I texted Haggarty and attached the video.

"At my second story bedroom window. What do you think? Does the plot thicken now?"

Perhaps a little dig because he wasn't very concerned about the squirrels.

Chapter 45 – Missing?

My adrenaline was so spiked I didn't think I'd be able to sleep for hours. I closed the curtains, which also served as light blockers so I could sleep later in the morning. The early light always woke me and was great when I worked, but now I'd need to sleep even later if I could. It was late now, yet Haggarty still got back to me.

"You've got my attention now. Do you feel safe?"

"Yeah, I think so, shook, but safe."

"Are you armed?"

"Yes."

"Good. Of course you know this, but still I must tell you, only use it if your life is threatened. We'll talk in the morning."

"Okay."

I changed into regular clothes; as silly as it seemed, I felt safer with my clothes on, clothes I could run out of the house in if I needed to. I got back into bed, still shaking. Sherlock could sense my unease and snuggled right up close. I wanted to read more of Ellen's journals but was too frazzled to focus. Instead I opened my iPad and looked through my streaming services for a mindless series I could binge watch to take my thoughts off the drone and the awful feeling of being violated. I often watched true crime series and so settled on Dateline, letting Keith Morrison's iconic voice lend some odd comfort to the very queer evening.

After a couple of episodes I did indeed feel more relaxed and started to doze off a few times before I paused it and turned off the light.

I slept a little later than usual before a knock at my door woke me. I jumped up and remembered why I was wearing my regular clothes and not my nightgown. Sherlock barked as I tried to smooth the wrinkles out of the slept-in clothes and ran my fingers through my hair.

"Just a minute, just a minute, I'm coming," I hollered loud enough to be heard at the back door. Sherlock wouldn't stop barking until I opened the door to the vestibule.

"Hello, Allison. Everything okay?" Allison looked as disheveled as I felt. "Come on in and I'll make some coffee." She sat down at the kitchen table as I ground the beans and brewed a little extra. "What's up?"

"Leslie. He disappeared."

"What?"

"He disappeared." She looked blankly at me, unfocused, and I could tell she wasn't even seeing me. She shook her head as though shaking the cobwebs out. "Last night the boys came home, had a snack, watched a show and then went to bed. Nothing unusual. This morning when the boys got up he was gone. Nothing. No clothes, no iPhone, no anything that was his. All gone.

"I don't know why I'm coming to see you. What would you know? But it was just so odd that you came by last night and this morning he's gone. I didn't tell John yet; he was off to work before the boys got up. You know since Covid he can work from home now and then but still must commute into Hartford fairly often."

I poured the coffee and found some day-old Danish that I popped into the toaster oven.

"Holy cow! Really? What did the boys think?"

"They seemed confused. They couldn't understand it either."

"Where did they go last night?"

"That pizza place on 32, just to get something quick. You know how these kids eat. It seems they're always hungry."

"Yeah, I've heard they can eat you out of... you know, house and home." We chuckled.

"Why did you really come over last night?" She took a sip of coffee and a bite of Danish, and another sip of coffee. "Was it really about the squirrels?"

Could I tell her? Should I tell her?

"How did your kids meet Leslie?"

"They said at school."

"Did you talk to his parents? See what they thought about him visiting for what, a month? More?"

"You know, I trust my kids. They're good kids, they don't get into trouble, they have good grades, and as far as I know they don't do drugs – I do watch for signs of that and talk to them about drugs. The friends they bring home are all polite and well-groomed. We think about our kids, worry about them, but so far I think they're doing fine so we don't monitor their every move. We want to give them some autonomy. If they messed up it would be different..."

"Yeah, but... what do you know about Leslie?"

"You know, home life isn't how it was when we were kids. People don't sit down for a proper dinner every night and talk about their day. We do have dinners on occasion, don't get me wrong, but generally we eat on the fly, go out for quick fast food or pick up a pizza and eat in front of the TV, or sit and look at our cellphones while we eat. It's not anywhere near how you and I grew up, so no, we don't communicate as well as we might. We try to get to their ball games so we stay somewhat involved. I think we're an average home now. Do I know every detail of their personal lives? No. Once in a while they talk about a girlfriend, and sometimes bring one home. But so far girlfriends haven't become the obsession I imagine they will be someday."

I watched her. She was defensive because I was questioning her. Mama wolf was protecting her family.

Chapter 46 – Fishing

"Allison, I have no doubt you two are some of the finest parents in town. You give your kids just about everything they want, and you give them freedom, freedom to make mistakes and learn from them, and that is one of the greatest gifts you can give them before they leave home. You are wonderful parents, so don't think I'm being critical of you." I weighed my words carefully as I tried to decide what to tell her. "It's just that..." I paused. "Allison, if I tell you something do you think you can keep it to yourself? Just something between you and John, but not the kids or others in the neighborhood?" She looked at me, alarmed.

"What do you mean? What is this about?"

"I need your assurance."

"Yes, I'll keep it between John and me."

"Leslie is in Ellen's will. We don't know how he's related or even if he is. He's going to get a nice little sum. But we don't know anything about him, and we're just starting to look. So if I seem intrusive, it's because we're trying to find out more about him."

"Oh for goodness sake! Really?"

"Yeah. Don't you think it's odd that this youngster just dropped into your lives? Has come to stay for an indeterminate amount of time? You don't know him or his family. Where does he say he's from?"

"Geez, Frances, now that you put it that way it seems like we're questionable parents. I thought we were just trying to be easy-going when it seemed like it wouldn't do any harm. I mean we do lay down the law when we think it's appropriate, but it's such a fine line between permissive and overbearing. We vowed never to be so strict or rigid that the kids wouldn't take our warnings seriously, you know what I mean?"

"Yeah, I know what you mean, and I think doing that makes for a better relationship with them. Do they confide in you? I know life isn't what it once was, but do you manage to have meaningful exchanges?"

"I think so. It's weird. When I'm out in the barn weaving one or the other will come out and really open up. I'm focused on the weaving, the rhythm of that shuttle passing back and forth, the treadles, the beater–somehow they must find it a comfortable environment for sharing things. Once Brian opened up about some boys bullying a gay kid and how he supported the kid and then the bullies started picking on him too; it all worked out because he's got some tight friends. But they talk to me." She sounded like she was trying to understand if there was enough communication.

"You both must have great relationships with them. I think they will grow into fine men."

"We hope so."

"So do you think you can talk to them about Leslie? I don't mean give them the third degree but see if you can get them to open up about him, how they met him, where he's from, you know, things you'd like to know about someone who's spending time with your kids."

"Yeah, I get it. I guess we dropped the ball on this one." I poured more coffee.

"Want another cup?" She nodded.

A good investigator casts her net far and wide, sifting through information and letting the loose ends dangle until they either produce something or get dropped. Sometimes hot leads go nowhere and you feel too much time was wasted chasing them. Sometimes you focus too much on something you imagine is going somewhere and you try hard to find and develop information that supports your theory, and that's when some edgy detectives go wrong and manufacture evidence where none really exists. That can be a difficult pitfall to avoid, especially if a subject is maybe not just unlikable but you know is also dishonest and probably should be in jail, and not just for the crime you're investigating.

So I cast my net wide. I hoped the whole village could give me feedback on Ellen, something, some crumb or some nibble. (I always found that fishing tropes fit investigating well.) Or maybe UConn, or even more likely her family, whom I had yet to look into very deeply. I was hoping Haggarty would do that with the vast array of tools at his disposal. Now finally it appeared this line would pay off, but I couldn't ignore some of the rest just in case there was more I might miss. Working on a case when it's fresh is best. People remember more, there is some buzz, some adrenaline not only for the detective but also for anyone involved. Too many guilty parties do too much investigating on their own, trying to find out what the investigators know. A lot of that can be traced, and generally an innocent person might show some interest but after a while lose that interest. But guilty parties never lose interest. They want to know how the investigation is going, even sometimes insinuating themselves into it, sometimes doing such morbid things as searching for a missing person when they know perfectly well where that person, likely dead, is. I had put bait out in the neighborhood and a few people had come back to me. I had a good lead now, and just had to chase it down and wait to see if anyone else had something to share.

I thought about a memorial service for Ellen, which might be just the thing to rekindle interest. Who would be the best person to organize that since Ellen wasn't affiliated with any church? Sue? Barbara? Someone at UConn? How sad not to have anyone to organize a memorial service in your honor.

Chapter 47 – Sue

I texted Haggarty.

"You must be so tired of hearing from me... but... You know I told you about Leslie Goranson living in town, staying with Allison and John Bailey, just a few houses down Plains Road?"

He didn't get right back to me so I continued.

"I went to their house last night, thought I'd just fish around, stir it up a bit, and I certainly must have because Allison just came by to say Leslie went missing this morning."

To me it was clear something was going on involving Leslie. I wasn't sure what it was, but I guessed he felt threatened by me and was the source of the dead critters and probably even the drone. Now he's missing. A text came in from Haggarty.

"Yeah, you're a pain, but a good one. I can't get free right now. I am working on the case and will drop by tonight if that's okay."

I couldn't wait. What was I going to do until then? I went back to Ellen's 2002 journal. The last entry, on November 15, was only about Grace and her gyrations over leaving as secretary of the garden club.

The entry a few days earlier also concerned Grace. Ellen was talking about her sometimes rocky friendship with Barbara, who didn't understand why once in a while Ellen had to cancel with her. Barbara didn't like that and Ellen felt she couldn't explain since it was private. She thought such a good friend as Barbara should trust her enough even if she couldn't open up about it. But she could talk to Grace about the situation. Grace should have been making money with all the off-the-books counseling she was doing in town.

I read several more journal entries in which Ellen sounded off, trying to process interpersonal issues, mostly with other villagers.

My clock struck ten and I decided to take my walk through the town. Maybe I'd do it twice today, once now and once when people were home from work. Sherlock was getting used to this daily routine and when I took the leash off the hook he danced around like a ballerina on a jewelry box top. We headed first to the school, then back up North Road to the post office, where I picked up a bill and some junk mail, past the Congregational Church, down to Webb Hill, up to the upper green and Weir Court. There I paused and surveyed the sweet village, encrusted in snow, just as J. Alden Weir must have viewed and painted it almost a hundred fifty years ago. Still charming, still idyllic. Then we walked on past the library, up Plains Road to the Episcopal church and back down. I stopped at the inn and knocked on Sue's door, thinking about what I'd witnessed there only a few short weeks ago. I heard her chair scrape against the floor.

"Just a minute." Some sounds of shuffling before she opened the door. "Frances, good to see you. Oh! You've got Sherlock with you. Hold on a second while I shut Harold in the bedroom." I glimpsed the cat, back arched and hair standing on end. She shooed him into the bedroom with a broom and I heard her close the door. "Harold is just not good with dogs and I bet Sherlock would love to chase him around." She bent down and petted my little wiggling terrier.

"So, you working?" I had noticed a bunch of wood blocks, carving equipment and shavings on her kitchen table.

"Yes, the sun today is just perfect for fine work." The table fairly glowed in the window light. "Here, look at these new cuts of Harold. Isn't he just the best subject for a card?" She showed me a block of the cat lounging in the window with his paws rolled inward in front of him, resembling the Egyptian Sphinx. "I swear I don't know how they can bend in the ways they do, like little rubber dolls." She smiled. "Want a cup of tea?"

"Yes, thank you." She filled the electric kettle and turned it on. "Weird. Remember the last time I asked you if you wanted tea and instead we had sherry? Funny how our minds work, isn't it? Some days I can't remember my name, but that day... everything is etched in me like stone."

"I know. I feel the same way. How are you doing?"

"Oh, pretty well. You know Harold is a blessing."

"I get it. Any other news around town?"

"Not really, not that I'd know. Same comings and goings at the post office. That's one of the bonuses of living here. I get to see everyone go by and they wave to me. Helps me feel less lonely." She poured the tea from the full pot she'd made–I guess I was going to stay a while. "Hey, I've got a little banana bread left over. Want some? I'll toast it up and butter it...."

"Absolutely; sounds perfect." She moved off to cut the loaf and stuff slices into the toaster.

"So, not much going on?"

"No, not really, but you know that Detective Haggarty came by a couple weeks ago and went through Ellen's again."

"Yeah, I heard. I wonder what's going to happen to her apartment. I'm sure the owners will want to get it cleaned out and rented again."

"Yeah, I imagine so. Speaking of that, do you have contact information for them?"

"Yup, let me get that for you." She poured tea and took the warm bread from the toaster, slathered on butter and put it on a plate for me.

"Now let me see..." She shuffled through a pile of papers and envelopes on the counter and found her address book at the bottom. "Here, let me copy it down for you." She made some notations on a used envelope and passed it to me.

"Thanks, Sue." We sat sipping our tea. "Do you ever see Allison and John? Did you know they had a kid staying with them?" Sue gave me a look it seemed everyone was giving me these days, side-eyed and suspicious.

"No, I rarely see them, mostly at soup night and some of the meetings. I forgot to tell you–here's some news: Jim and Nancy went away a couple of weeks ago, to Mexico, I think. They should be back next week. Nancy hates the cold."

"I was thinking we should have a memorial service for Ellen. What do you think? I can find out what's going on from Haggarty, if she's going to be cremated or what.

Don't you think we should do something to honor her? I know she rubbed some people the wrong way, but she was a good person and we should do something, you know, so we can have some closure."

"You know what would give me closure? Finding out what happened to her. That would give me some closure." She looked hard at me. "I know Haggarty and you are trying to find something, but how could this be so complicated? Really? An old lady gets pushed down the stairs. Come on." I was taken aback. Sue was rarely so harsh.

Just then Sherlock started scratching at the bottom of the bedroom door.

"Sherlock, stop." I grabbed the leash, hooked him up and pulled him over to the table.

"He's as nosy as you are." Sue widened her eyes, then innocently fluttered her eyelashes and smiled.

"It's a curse." I smiled back. "Really, though, if you hear or see anything, give me a ring, okay? We've got to shuffle on. Maybe you can come over for lunch soon?" She nodded.

"Love to."

Chapter 48 – Three Blind...

Sherlock and I headed home as I puzzled over what I was going to do for the rest of the day before Haggarty came.

Then, there they were. In my driveway. Lined up like soldiers. Three mice. Three mice deader than door nails. I made a mental note to google "deader than door nails" –where did that saying originate? Then I thought how oddly our minds work, that even in my shock at finding my driveway decorated by three dead mice my mind went to idioms. Sherlock went fairly mad and if I hadn't had a tight rein on him he would have had all three of them down his gullet in a flash.

Holding him tight on the leash I sidestepped them to go inside, grab my iPad that had been charging, and return to photograph the sad little trio.

The snow had melted and only a bit of ice remained in the driveway, nothing that would hold footprints. They were curiously laid out like small cadavers on slabs, on their backs, petite paws curled up, tails out straight, miniature incisors peeking from tiny jaws. No obvious signs of trauma. I took photos and then used a stick to roll them over – I wanted to see their eyes. Were they blind? It would be the mark of a twisted and somewhat humorous mind to blind them, but their eyes were closed peacefully.

Now I was baffled. Leslie was the one I would have pinned this on but as far as I knew he had left town.

Then I remembered my new camera system and hoped I knew enough about it to review what it must have just captured. I had tucked some rubber gloves into my pocket and now I gently scooped up each little critter and put it into a plastic bag to join the two squirrels and the cat in my freezer.

I now had quite a collection from my driveway. I wasn't sure whether I should feel threatened or pleased I was getting so much attention or angry for the wanton murder of more or less innocent creatures.... but are squirrels and mice really innocent?

I read the instructions for the cameras, which were somewhat cryptic and probably useful for a techie, which I was not, even though I was proud of being somewhat ahead of most of the seniors in the village. But I was sure kids these days were way ahead of most of us. I spent too much time just looking up what the latest online abbreviations stood for, many of them off color.

Finally I was able to install the new camera app on my iPad so I could access the cameras. It involved finding camera makes and models and plugging them into the app, then getting my Bluetooth (who came up with that name?) turned on and connected to them and then going back to the app and fiddling around some more. Then, viola! One of the damned little screens popped up on the app. I could see down the driveway but it was live, so I had to somehow get it to rewind or show an earlier time. So much finagling. I saw on the menu that I could pick a day and then fast-forward or go backward though the video. I was nervous because I didn't want to accidentally erase what was recorded in the last few hours. I had to pause the current video and restart it so I could view the one that began at midnight and ran until I'd just stopped it. The menu listed the videos by day. Fortunately the dates were correct and I chose the one starting at midnight.

Finally I was able to access it and I fast forwarded through until, there! Someone was walking up the driveway to the front porch where Haggarty had suggested we put the additional camera. Someone in a hoodie, with the hood up. A UConn hoodie. Average height, not tall, not short, on the slim side, with a bag. The person disappeared onto the porch, then went to the driveway, removed the mice from a bag and carefully laid them just so. The whole thing couldn't have taken more than a minute. He (or she, but it looked more like a he) didn't look around nervously. No cars were passing by. He didn't look toward the back breezeway where this camera was positioned. His face was too hidden and far away for me to see.

Hoping to get a better look at his face I fussed to get the camera on the front porch connected. When I succeeded I saw him approach the camera but he was off to the side, barely visible, and then a large hand came up toward the camera and the picture went blank.

I rushed back outside to the front porch camera, and there it was, a piece of gum stuck over the lens. This was GOLD. As smart as he was he wasn't thinking about DNA. Finally, I thought, a good break.

I was so excited I almost fell off the porch. I didn't remove the gum, leaving it for Haggarty. What a tale I'd have to tell him! Maybe now I could get the cadavers out of my freezer. I headed to the garage for my spare cooler.

I realized I was hungry and went through the fridge to salvage the leftovers, whistling "We're in the Money" and giving Sherlock an extra treat.

Okay, I thought, it must be Leslie, or who else? The person was young, a man or boy who looked fit. UConn hoodie? That could be anyone. If it was Leslie, where was he now? Where would he be staying tonight? Where did he get all the dead critters? How could I possibly be a threat to someone I didn't even know existed until just a few weeks ago? What if it were someone else? But that didn't make sense.

Ding! The microwave went off and I downed my three-day-old rice and beans.

Chapter 49 – Gum?

I fussed with the third camera that was inside the breezeway pointed at my back door, not down the driveway.

I reviewed the videos of the back door and found nothing, only Sherlock and I going in and out and in and out.

A text came in.

"Leaving a little early. Do you have time now?"

I was thrilled.

"You betcha! Coffee will be on shortly."

He drove in and parked his personal vehicle next to mine. He brought in the usual briefcase. I had already made room for it on the kitchen table.

"So, I had another visitor… well, actually three." I handed him a mug of coffee as he gave me a puzzled look. "I strolled around town yesterday, and these greeted me on the driveway when I got home." I showed him the photo of the three mice so carefully lined up. He laughed.

"These are some serious threats you're getting."

"Yes, but I got some video of the Mouse King." I sound self-satisfied. "I figured out that confounding camera and video app." I opened the app and showed him the UConn hoodie perp. He watched with focused interest. "Not only that one, look at this." I switched to the front porch video that went blank. "The best part?" He looked up from the video. "He blacked out that camera with what looks like... CHEWING GUM!" His eyes got big.

"You're kidding!"

"No. Get your evidence bags out. I left it on the camera." He reached into his pocket for rubber gloves and opened the briefcase to pull out a plastic evidence bag.

"Let's go!" On the front porch he examined the camera. It had been attached to the door trim with a little screw that he unscrewed using the small phillips screwdriver on his knife. We brought it into the house. "I may just take it all with me. I don't want to tamper with the evidence. It will leave you without a camera for a day or so before we can get another to put up." He busied himself filling out the tag on the evidence bag.

"Okay, no problem. We may need a couple more; this guy is pretty wily. I wonder if we can put one or two where he can't see them."

"Hmm. Might be a good idea."

"So, I have a cooler here and a bunch of critters in my freezer that now may be more than just a joke."

"Okay, you're right. I'll take them. We've got some new forensic guys just getting their feet wet. I'll have them take a look, see if there's anything suspicious." I packed some ice into the cooler around the six bagged critters. "The squirrel in the Walmart bag came from Sue's – remember when I told you someone hung it on her door? The Walmart bag was handled by Sue and by whoever left it, and I carefully bagged it inside another. It may not be important, but it could be. The three mice are in here." I pointed to a sandwich bag.

"I suppose these will be okay overnight in my car since it's freezing out." He took the cooler. "I'm not squeamish, but my wife might not be so understanding. As it is I think she's getting jealous of this Frances lady who's texting me in the middle of the night."

"Tell her not to worry. I'm taken, right, Sherlock?" I pointed to the dog lying under the table, who seemed to understand what I'd said, lifted his head and wagged his tail.

"Actually I've got some news for you. I was able to get ahold of Gerald. Gerald Richardson." He smiled.

Chapter 50 – Evening

"You're kidding!" I was bowled over. This was a big key to several leads we were trying to chase down. Ellen's son, in the will. He might have all kinds of information.

"Yes, and I have an appointment to see him tomorrow." I looked hopefully at him. "Are you busy?"

"Tomorrow? Let me check my calendar." I opened up my iPad, feigning a look at my calendar, which I never used; I prefer an old-fashioned desk calendar. "Yeah, I guess I'm free. I thought you'd never ask." We chuckled. "So it won't be a problem for me to tag along?"

"Nope. The boss thinks we're a good team. I've had a lot stricter guys over me. This guy can be a stickler for protocol, but not crazy. As long as we're honest and upfront he's pretty good. He's not one of the ones who just want to throw their weight around to let you know who's boss. I like him a lot. Everyone does and we all work hard for him."

We sat down for coffee and a sweet pastry from the co-op. "I just don't get it. If Leslie ran away from Allison and John's why is he still around dropping mice at my door? It doesn't make sense."

"I agree. If it is him he's either still in town or maybe it's a parting shot. Perhaps Allison and John's kids are hiding him, helping him, or maybe all these warnings are from a disgruntled neighbor who doesn't like your prying, who maybe has something to hide and just wants you to stop."

"Well, most of the people in town know me well enough to understand I'm both persistent and not easily intimidated. But I can't help thinking this is something a kid would do, you know?" Haggarty nodded. "And how many adults have drones to play with and the expertise to peek in my window and then disappear? I think that takes some practice. Drones aren't that easy to manipulate. Who's got the time to play with them and get good at it? Mostly kids, right?"

"Yeah, yeah, I guess so. I just know, as you do, that it's often not the most obvious explanation and can be a more complex one. Just keep an open mind, that's all I'm saying." He tipped up his coffee, finished it off and walked the mug to the sink. I liked that he felt comfortable enough to do that. "I have to head out. See you tomorrow? We have the appointment for 11 a.m. in New London where his office is. I'll pick you up around 10." He hoisted the cooler and headed for the door, saying over his shoulder, "Thanks for the stiffs." I laughed and closed the door after him.

I sat down and thought about tomorrow. Things were finally moving along. "Come on, Sherlock, let's go for our evening constitutional." The dog knew exactly what that meant and came out from the cozy spot by the radiator under the table, wriggling with excitement. I leashed him, slipped on my jacket and one of Barbara's hats and her warm mittens, and put a flashlight in my pocket just in case I underestimated the fading light, which I thought might actually give us a nice sunset.

We traced our now usual route to the school, back to the post office across the street and the main drag to the fire station before crossing and going up Webb Hill to Weir Court, past the library, where I paused for a second to look around the green at the cozy houses. People were arriving home and windows lit up as the inhabitants started their evening. It was my favorite time of day, the twilight; there was something magical about it that I couldn't explain. Everything quieted. If there were birds they got quiet, and usually even the breeze stopped. All was still. We stood there for a moment. I breathed deeply and let the stillness soothe me, but I could feel Sherlock stir as dusk fell and critters started to move about. Ready to resume our walk, I made one last visual sweep of the vista, and something caught my eye at the inn. A light, at least I thought I saw a light, just a quick flash. What the?? I was standing by the scion of the Charter Oak, in front of the library, close enough to it that in the lowering light we might not be visible, but I could see others if they were in the light. But this wasn't a person; it was just a small flash of light, now gone. In Ellen's bedroom. Did I imagine it? I stood and watched for a minute, maybe two. Nothing more. Maybe it was my eyes. I had floaters and every once in a while little flashes, so it could have been my eyes. Now I was hypervigilant. If I stepped away from the tree the streetlight would make me visible. It was chilly and I wasn't going to stand here forever, so I gave Sherlock a little jerk to signal we'd be moving on. At the corner I took the usual left onto Plains Road and tried not to be too obvious as I passed Allison and John's lit-up windows, where I could see cable news on their big screen TV. Then to the church, where I turned around and went back, but slowly, and when I got to the four corners I looked hard at the windows where Ellen once lived, but viewed from such a sharp angle they were hard to see, and I noticed nothing more.

Would I find cadavers in my driveway upon my return? I saw few people outside, just Sheila putting her recycling and garbage receptacles out; she didn't have a jacket on and waved and quickly rushed back in. Someone else got out of his car at the post office to drop a letter into the outside box. Several people were arriving at the fire station, likely for a meeting. No one else. No shadows skulking around and no critter bodies on my driveway. Sherlock paused to pee and put his nose up to sample the air. Nothing of interest here.

Chapter 51 – Secret?

I was so excited about the next day I thought I'd never get to sleep. I picked up Ellen's journal.

Sept. 27, 2023

Damn. What am I going to do. I'm so damned confused. Gerry called me and we made a plan for him to visit. I am so conflicted about this. He's reached out to me several times in the last couple months. He's got a problem and hoped I could help, but I don't know if I can. What to do, what to do?

I almost jumped out of bed. So her son was in touch! Why weren't there more entries in the journal? Was there another journal? I grabbed one of the 3x5 cards I keep at my bedside and wrote a reminder to ask Haggarty to search the papers he'd removed. Maybe there was another journal. The final entry in this 2020 journal was last November, 2023. Shouldn't there be more if Gerry or Gerald was in touch with her? Obviously he was listed in her calendar, so why wouldn't she be including that in her journal, especially since she seemed conflicted over it? She sounded like this was a real concern, something she needed to process.

I went off on one of my tangents. Process—what a weird word that meant "think about." When did that become part of our vocabulary, like so many other words that have changed meaning in the last few decades?

If Ellen were really troubled or had angst over seeing her son, wouldn't she have worked through that in her journal? Or maybe she talked to someone. Grace? But would Grace want to keep that from me after Ellen was gone? Was Grace hiding something? If so, what was it?

I thought I should ask Haggarty whether his guys had gone through the papers, and if so had they found anything interesting in them? And perhaps I'd talk to Grace, intimating that I knew Ellen was in touch with Gerry, that he'd reached out and they met, and what did she know? I was pretty sure she knew more than she was telling me, but why would she be evasive now? I knew she had never married but she had a son who was a big wheel in aerospace or something like that, something technical. Connecticut, for a small state, has quite a large slice of the defense and aeronautical industry. But I couldn't remember what she said he did. Could there be a connection that way? I intuitively understood that even though we were a very social community, not everyone wanted to share everything about their lives. Most of us were caring and would go out of our way to help and protect one another, but some were, let's say, a little more vindictive than others, especially if there had been a spat. I might not trust everyone equally, being a little cautious about telling my personal life to some. Most of us were secure, well-grounded adults who wouldn't be either threatened by or overly impressed with another's accomplishments; most likely we'd be encouraging. I must say I have a sixth sense about these things. Intuition is in my opinion a large part of investigative work and I always wondered why more women didn't enter that field, since I think we have a more highly developed intuitive sense.

Because of this I thought Grace knew more than she was telling, that Gerald was involved, that Leslie was involved, and Leslie was responsible for the dead animals and the drone and he hadn't left town and might even be staying in Ellen's.

Chapter 52 – Gerald

Now that I was retired I rarely used an alarm, but today I wanted to get an early start. After our morning routine of coffee to jumpstart me and a walk to jumpstart Sherlock's digestion, I had oatmeal and showered.

I was trying to collect my thoughts. What did I want to know? What would be appropriate to ask about? I knew it was Haggarty's show and I shouldn't be saying anything, but I also knew Haggarty valued my opinion and after we talked to Gerald he would ask if I had any questions, or at least I assumed he would do that. I had a sense this would be a very weird interview.

Haggarty arrived just as I expected, right at ten. I had let Sherlock out and then blocked him into the kitchen so no plants would get eaten or firewood chomped leaving clumps of sticky chewed bark all over the oriental rug.

"Are you nervous? Excited?" Haggarty made small talk while driving.

"Yeah, probably both. You know people in town seemed to think Ellen was pretty much estranged from her family, certainly from her husband. I'd never heard talk about any kind of reconciliation, about her being in touch with either of her kids. So I hope this will give us some good leads."

"I agree."

"Last night I read a little more of her latest journal and it mentioned Gerald, mentioned he'd reached out to her in the last few months. That entry was in November. She seemed very conflicted about it, like she didn't know what to do. What I don't understand is why after that one entry she wrote no more about it. You know? She went on to write about other things, but no more about him. I didn't go earlier in that book, but there may have been more." I paused.

"Really? Did you bring that with you?"

"Well, yes, I just so happened to do that. But what about the other papers you have? Was there another journal hidden in there? Or notes, or anything that might indicate something about seeing Gerald?"

"No, I don't think so. I looked through some and another guy looked through some and there didn't seem to be much, mostly legal docs, some committee notes, a few things about her days at UConn, a couple of certificates of achievement that honored her, but not much else."

"I'm getting a feeling we've missed something. Here, let me read her entry about Gerald and tell me what you think." I read it.

"Hmmm. That is interesting. She does sound conflicted, and what is the problem he has that she's worried about?"

"Right. So, however this goes today you have something to maybe bring up. Is this the first time you've talked to him?"

"Yeah. The coroner called him to tell him about her passing and I think Attorney Kelly said he called him to discuss the distribution of her property, but this is the first face to face. I'm hoping it will give us something." We were on Route 32 in New London, headed into the downtown area. We parked on the street, found our way to the newspaper lobby, and asked the receptionist for Gerald. She said he expected us and told us to take the elevator upstairs, giving us directions to his office. He was in their technology department and had an office just outside the computer room. We found him, head down, looking through some papers. At our knock he motioned us in.

"Hello, Mr. Richardson. My name is Finn Haggarty. I'm the detective in charge of your mother's case. This is Frances O'Connor. She's helping out." Haggarty reached across and shook Gerald's hand, and I did too.

Gerald was middle-aged and looked in pretty good shape except for a little paunch starting. His brown hair, thinning a bit, was cut in a conservative fashion, shortish on the sides and, although not too long on the top, combed back. He was clean-shaven and wore half glasses over his piercing hazel eyes. His expression was serious, but he smiled when he greeted us.

"First, I want to express our sincere condolences to you and your family." Haggarty wanted him to know we respected his grief, if he had any. "I believe the coroner and Attorney Kelly have been in touch with you, right?"

"Yes, Detective Haggarty, they have, and thank you." He moved all the papers in front of him off to the side, turned off the computer screen and motioned for us to sit. "I can't say it's a big surprise she passed away. She wasn't in the best of health." Haggarty studied him, and I knew he was trying to decide what to say next.

"Perhaps the coroner didn't tell you." Haggarty paused. "But we don't think this was a natural death. We think it was caused by someone." Gerald looked at him expressionless.

"Really? I thought she'd fallen down the stairs."

"Yes, she did, but we think someone may have pushed her or there may have been a struggle at the top of the stairs. So there is an investigation. You understand."

"Oh, I guess I didn't understand that. What does that mean?" His face was still expressionless.

"Well, we're trying to find out who might have wanted to..." Haggarty paused again. I knew he didn't want to say "kill her." That is a hard message, suggesting violence, nefarious intentions, an ugliness that no elder should endure. "...harm her, and why." Gerald still showed no expression.

"What does that have to do with me?" This is the most common question someone who is a peripheral suspect would ask. I was sorry I hadn't asked to record the interview.

"Well, we're investigating this and you understand we need to get as much information as possible. We've already interviewed several people in town, we've swiped the area for DNA and picked up fingerprints. Of course, relatives are always suspects; you're a newspaperman so you know that." Haggarty smiled, greasing the skids. "So we need to just ask you a few questions." Now Gerald smiled.

"Of course. Ask away." Didn't Jeffrey Dahmer once say that? Haggarty pulled out a small notepad, knowing that asking to record would be a step too far even though we both wanted to. Gerald watched his every move.

"Your mother is Ellen Richardson, correct?" Gerald nodded. If we'd been recording this he would be asked to answer out loud. Haggarty wrote something down. "When was the last time you saw your mother?" Gerald looked up toward the ceiling like he was thinking.

"I don't know, years I think. I haven't seen her in years, but I don't know how many." Haggarty didn't blink and wrote something more in his notebook. I was electric, sure Haggarty could feel sparks coming off me. I was positive Gerald was lying.

"I see. When was the last time you talked to her or had any communication with her?" I held my breath.

"Hmmm…. I haven't seen or heard from her in years. I'm guessing more than ten, maybe fifteen years."

"Do you remember what you discussed the last time you talked to her? Why and what it was about?"

Chapter 53 – Lying?

Why was he lying? Only guilty people lied.

"When we had our firstborn we wanted her to know. My wife thought we should tell her. You know we'd been estranged and so we had no contact with her, but my wife thought the arrival of a grandchild would be something important to tell a grandmother." This seemed genuine.

"And how did that go? Was she pleased?"

"I think so. I think she was really surprised to hear from us after so many years, so, yes, pleased but taken aback."

"Was that her first grandchild?"

"Yes, Gerald. We named him after me, Gerald junior."

"I see. Did you know you were in her will?"

"Yes. Attorney Kelly contacted me, maybe a month ago, and sent me a copy." Again a straight face, but I felt he was suppressing something, maybe resentment.

"Can you tell me if you think your mother had any enemies? You know, people who would wish to harm her?"

"Well, I'm not sure. I guess she wasn't the easiest person to get along with." He half smiled. "But you know I haven't seen her in years and don't know any of the people in her town or people who worked with her, or even any of her friends, so, no, I don't know who might want to hurt her."

"Do you know a Leslie Goranson, who's in your mother's will?" His blank face became quizzical as though he were thinking, then he shook his head and muttered, "No."

"How is your father, George?" At last Gerald showed a gleam of emotion.

"He's not very good. He's got dementia. He's still home and his wife, my stepmom, is taking care of him, but I don't know how long she'll be able to do that. He may have to go into a home soon."

"I'm sorry to hear that." Haggarty wrote more in his notepad, then closed it. "You wouldn't mind giving us a sample of your DNA, would you? Just a little swab..." Haggarty reached into his pockets for rubber gloves and a small DNA kit. Gerald stiffened. "It's just routine, nothing to worry about, we have to do this with all family members. You don't mind, do you?" Oh, that Haggarty! I almost wanted to kiss him.

"Ah..." Gerald hesitated. I could see the wheels turning. If he didn't it would be suspicious, so he had to, but he was struggling internally. All this happened in a second. "Ah, no, that's all right." Haggarty went around the side of the desk and broke open the swab and tube. Gerald opened his mouth and Haggarty swabbed carefully, then put the swab in the tube and labeled it with his pen.

"Thank you for your time, Mr. Richardson. We really appreciate it." He reached over and shook Gerald's hand again. I smiled and said goodbye as we left his office and found our way to the front desk to leave our visitors badges. Out on the street I took a deep breath.

"Wow, that was interesting." Haggarty looked at me.

"What do you think?"

"I think he's lying. But why?" Haggarty nodded.

"Yeah, me too, but you're right–why?"

"I want to know more about this family. His father has dementia? His mother, or stepmom, is taking care of him? What about his wife and his son? Does he have more than one child? Do we have his contact information, email or phone to text with him in case we have more questions?"

"Yeah, we do, and you know how investigations go. If we wait a few days and contact him again, it's more effective. Those callbacks scare the heebie-jeebies out of the guilty ones, and that's when their story changes and we nail them."

Chapter 54 – "Screwed"

On the way home we analyzed every second of the interview. His expressions, his denials, his response when Haggarty asked for DNA.

"You are a smooth operator, Finn. The way you slid that DNA in at the last minute–that was great." He smiled.

"You liked that, did you? I wanted to surprise you, a little gift. It would not be anywhere near as satisfying if I didn't think he was lying." He glanced at the clock on the dash. "Say, do you want to pick something up from Paul's Pasta? I know it means crossing the river, but my wife would love it and you could get something to go for dinner."

I knew Paul's, a small well-established eatery that made their own scrumptious pasta.

"I'd love that."

It was on the way home, as I was nibbling on one of Paul's breadsticks, that it occurred to me. "Damn, why didn't we ask if he had plans to meet her before she died, or on the day she died? We know there was that notation on her calendar, 'Gerry.' It had to be him, right? Or maybe his son? I would like to hear him lie about that. It would be the final confirmation that he's hiding something."

"You're right. This could be one of those 'follow-up' things I can ask that make a perp nervous." We drove along on Route 395, both of us, I'm sure, going over the interview in our minds. "Those critters you gave me and the bags, they've been sent to analysis for testing. We're looking at cause of death for the animals, DNA or fingerprints on the bag from Sue's and possibly on the animals. I'm hoping something will show up and it's not just dead ends." I groaned and he chuckled. "Sorry about the pun."

As we pulled into my driveway I could see something scattered on the ground.

"Stop!" I put my arm out across his chest, an automatic response like someone protecting a child in case of a sudden stop. He had partially pulled in, straddling the gravel sidewalk. We both got out. What looked like dozens of screws and nails were thrown across my driveway. No dead critters this time. Was this more threatening, meant to frighten?

"Wait here. I've got a cleanup magnet in my shop." I went into the garage and got my long-handled shop magnet and a plastic jar, then returned to sweep the area. Haggarty had been picking up pieces with his fingers and he put them in the plastic jar. In about ten minutes we had all the pieces we could find, about fifty or sixty screws, nails, tacks and miscellaneous things I would expect to find in a hardware drawer. Haggarty pulled his car into the driveway.

"Let's go in and see what your cameras caught." Reviewing the recordings we saw the same UConn hoodie. It took only seconds for him to empty the can full of junk onto my driveway, but the last frame pushed my buttons. After tossing the stuff he faced the breezeway camera and saluted with two fingers of his right hand. He knew where the cameras were so none of them showed his face; the hoodie was pulled too far forward for that. He showed no fear, no concern about being caught. When he left he headed toward the center, toward the inn. We watched for a few more minutes as several cars went by in both directions. Nothing more.

"Okay, my car is in the driveway so how does he know I'm not home? Would he be bold enough to do this while I'm home, when I could be looking live at the camera?" We looked at each other.

"You know I brought a couple more cameras to install so we could get more coverage, but I didn't have time before we left. Let's go do that now." From his car Haggarty got tools and two compact cameras. We went out to the cherry tree we both thought was the best vantage point, and there, attached to the tree, was a small camera. "Did you put this up?" Haggarty's eyebrows were arched. I was dumbfounded.

"No. You didn't put it up?" The little red LED on the device blinked at us, almost laughing. When Haggarty stepped out of view of the lens I understood and did likewise. With his always-handy rubber gloves he gently removed the little device, which wasn't even screwed on, but Velcroed and wire-tied. "So he's watching me as I'm watching him. Smart little bugger. I wonder if there are any others around." I was getting paranoid.

"How far do these remote cameras operate from? Isn't the distance limited? Like maybe five hundred feet or so?" I knew there was a limit.

"That's a good question. If it's similar to a trail camera, which just takes pictures and stores them locally to the device, videoing only if it detects motion, it doesn't matter. The person who set it up would come by every few days or so and take out the memory card to review what's on it. But if it's actually transmitting in real time that's a whole different ball game; it's got to be fairly powerful battery-wise and it's got to be within a certain distance of a cellphone or router or whatever is being used to connect to. So yes, depending on the sophistication of the device, it does have a certain range." We looked at each other, realizing this was a transmitting device.

Chapter 55 – Camera

Haggarty looked right into the lens of the camera and smiled evilly, then dropped it into an evidence bag and put up his own camera in its place. Whoever was watching would be seeing the inside of the bag–that was clear. Haggarty made a note on the bag and put it in his trunk.

"Let's go in and have a look at your router to see if we can find the device on it." We went in and I logged into my router and opened to see my devices: TV, Roku, iPad, cellphone, and all four of the cameras we now had up outside. Then at the bottom one more popped up: LX-24064A. I didn't know what it was.

"That must be it."

"Drill down to see if you can get any more info." I was amazed to get tons of it: the serial number of the Sunyo device, the MAC address, the unique identifier, the IP address. I took a screen shot and emailed it to Haggarty.

"If it was Bluetooth the range would be short, less than a hundred feet or so, but some of the remote cameras these days can go three hundred and some even five hundred feet. Basically whoever is using this can't be too far away, not in another town, that is, unless they have a booster or are using your router."

"Could it be using my router?"

"Probably not without your password to set it up."

"Now I'm starting to get really paranoid. I don't give my password out, but could someone break into my house, hack my laptop or router and manipulate it? Use it?"

"You don't have any home security, do you?"

"Not other than Sherlock and my sidearm."

"Well, it may be time to invest in something that can't be hacked and maybe even hire a security company who can monitor the house when you're not around or when you're sleeping or out for a walk, or whatever."

"Geez, I never thought I'd have to do that."

"What about your neighbors? You said you have a tight community and you watch out for each other, right?"

"Yeah, but people might not notice someone skulking around. Burglars and sneak thieves are masters at being invisible, and sometimes that means hiding in plain sight, looking like maintenance men or whatever. You know what I mean? And there are lots of people walking around town, on this sidewalk, so obvious we might not notice them."

"Okay. I'll give the camera and the stats you emailed me to our IT guys and see what they can find out, maybe even check for fingerprints and DNA."

"I wonder if there are any others." I thought about Mr. UConn holed up at the inn, or maybe even back at Allison and John's, possibly without their knowledge. I think their house is within 500 feet, and certainly the inn is. For some reason I didn't tell Haggarty about the flash of light I saw at the inn. That was unprofessional, but something held me back. I wanted this for myself, wanted the whole thing to ripen, to see what would come of it, see what his next move would be, Leslie or whoever it was. It was like lighting a fire and smoking out the target. I thought finding his camera would certainly provoke something. I decided to do a sweep of the yard, maybe even the house. Could there be a bug? I know professionals have devices that can detect bugs and other hidden devices. Or could he have broken in? He seemed not only wily but also tech savvy. That could be a dangerous combination.

Chapter 56 – The Ghost

Haggarty left and I did a sweep of my yard. He and I had put up four cameras, one on the front porch, one on the breezeway pointing down the driveway towards the street, one at the back door facing the garage and now the new one on the cherry tree. I did just a simple visual of the yard, trees, porches, breezeway, garage and around the outside of the house.

Then I went inside and did a check there too, clocks, paintings, mantle, in the plants, under tables, even under chairs. Some of the newer cameras were almost invisible, and if he'd gotten in he could have installed one without breaking anything. He could have bought a $30 lock-picking kit like mine, and with a little practice could certainly have broken in – I wasn't particularly security-minded and my locks were cheap. I thought of purchasing better dead bolts, which would be a hassle to install because most required some drilling and chiseling on the door, but still, it might be worth it.

Sherlock sniffed around outside. He knew there was an intruder and had probably smelled him before.

I heated up the Paul's Pasta lobster ravioli with their to-die-for fettuccine alfredo and some of their salad with the dressing that was one of my favorites. I savored every bite knowing that a little later, as the evening closed in, Sherlock and I would do our walk around the village and look for some movement at Ellen's, and then do another camera search.

Dishes done and everything put away, I grabbed my jacket. It was still pretty chilly out although we'd had a little thaw and I was seeing small crocus and daffodil greens starting to poke their way up through the leaves and spotty snow. Sherlock was dancing about. On the sidewalk he pulled a little, but then settled down and walked nicely beside me. I was hyper-aware of my surroundings and as always enjoying the sight of people arriving home and lights coming on and flashes of people working in their kitchens or going into their dining or living rooms. The sunset showed pink in the eastern clouds, and I knew it would be a stunner as the colors crept toward the west. We walked to the school, turned around, passed my house, Kelly's, and Fisher's old house, then crossed the four-way stop and strolled in front of the Congregational church, deliberately in view of the inn so if anyone was surveilling me, I would be easily seen. We went past Grace's, whose front room was lit; past Sheila's, which was lit only toward the back where the kitchen was; past the firehouse where a couple cars were parked and the garage door open to reveal someone polishing the fire engine. Then I crossed over to Webb Hill and where the Sandons TV was flashing a sports program. On to the upper green and Weir Court, where I slowed. The sunset burned red in the west, throwing an eerie pink glow on the village for only a short minute before starting to dim. I was hoping I might, if it darkened a bit more, catch a glimpse of the specter in Ellen's window. I remembered the story of the ghost at the inn, the ghost of a young woman, Elizabeth Shaw, who was hanged for infanticide in November 1774. She'd had a baby out of wedlock and speculation was it might have been her father's child. Legend has it her father turned her in for murdering the baby, she was tried and sentenced to death, and in the dead of winter she rode atop her own coffin in a horse-drawn wagon to her hanging place on Plains Road, a rise with a big oak. Since then there are rumors of her being seen slipping around the halls of the inn, or a ghostly figure in a long white dress walking the streets looking for a kindly face. Of course I didn't believe in ghosts, but still I glanced surreptitiously toward the inn.

Chapter 57 – The Frogs

I thought I saw something but could not be sure—damn my eyes. Dusk had fallen. I walked to the library, where a new bench beckoned me to sit for a few minutes and I did. The evening was warmer, still chilly but not bad. Sherlock hopped up onto the bench. I looked around the village and watched the passing cars. Someone with a flashlight strolled by, pulled by his dog. At the post office he dropped something into the box and turned around. I imagined no one could see me sitting there in the dusk, and Sherlock, sitting next to me, was quiet, watching just as I did. I heard an owl off in the distance, then even further away some coyotes wildly yelping. I realized this little village was in a perfect hollow, where sounds were amplified so you could hear them across the green very clearly, and even those from up on the surrounding hills came down louder than elsewhere. The story of the frogs making such a racket in colonial times in this village made sense when I listened closely to sounds. The legendary battle of the frogs was famous here, when a wild night of rampant amphibian orgy and desperation for water caused so much noise the settlers thought the Native Americans were attacking them and assembled with their muskets in an emergency muster to protect themselves, only to find out it was frogs fighting in a nearby pond. Probably the good-humored wives passed the story on until it grew into the long-lived legend of today. The town seal honors the story with a frog, as do Windham High school class rings, and even the major artery bridge across the Willimantic River sports 12-foot replicas of frogs sitting on spools, the spools symbolizing the cotton thread manufacturing that built the city. These were my thoughts as I sat on the bench in the gathering dark, waiting to see if a light would again flash in Ellen's window. It did not. I finally gave up and walked to Plains Road and toward St. Paul's, passing Allison and John's.

Back home again I did another scan outside, of the yard, trees, and garage. With my flashlight set to wide beam and held next to my head, I scanned all the areas; any camera lens should reflect back at me like a little mirror. Still nothing. Inside I turned the lights off and did the same, looking for a small reflection from a lens, and also found nothing.

I knew Nancy and Jim were coming back from Mexico soon, and I hoped somehow someone would hear or see something. Since they lived directly below Ellen, I thought maybe they would be willing to watch and listen for me. Maybe Sue had noticed something. Tomorrow I'd visit her and find out when they were coming back.

After an evening snack Sherlock and I turned in, making it an early night. We cozied into the down, scrunching low to get warm. I opened Ellen's poetry journal.

Face your fears and talk
To them. Soon they will bore you
And you will move on.

A gentle plink, plink on my window startled us. Sherlock growled. Plink, plink again, like a little stone hitting the window. I sometimes had a flashlight by my bed but not tonight, although my cellphone had a flashlight on it. I picked it up and walked slowly to the window. The curtains were closed this time. I turned the flashlight on and swiftly pulled back the curtain with my free hand. There it was again, the drone, banging up against my window.

Chapter 58 – Gotcha

Drones usually have four propellers, and some have protective plastic bumpers outside the propellers to protect them from damage and getting caught up in things. The bumpers on this drone were banging against my window, scary, insistent, annoying, red eye blinking at me, watching my reaction. I was frightened, but also pissed. I shined the cellphone flashlight at it, probably, I thought blinding it and the person running it. With my free hand I opened the window and made a grab for it.

"Come here, you mother!" It swung just out of my reach. I looked for something to throw at it or whack it with. My room was relatively clean but next to the window was a chair with one of my shirts tossed over it. I grabbed the shirt and threw it at the drone, and somehow, maybe because the person maneuvering it was temporarily blinded, I hit it. It hung for a second and then made a buzzing noise as though something was caught in one of its propellers. I saw it weave and slowly drop. I grabbed my bathrobe and ran down the stairs, Sherlock preceding me.

I turned on the driveway lights and rushed out to the plastic creature sputtering under my shirt. A figure ran up the sidewalk and started up my driveway. I grabbed the thing, still whirring. The figure in the UConn hoodie stood just beyond my driveway spotlights, holding a device that showed his face dimly in its glow, looking back and forth between the device in his hand and me.

"It's mine now," I said with conviction. Sherlock stood next to me, barking wildly but not moving forward.

"You'll be sorry, you bitch." He turned and ran toward the green. I wanted to follow him, but with my bathrobe on and the thing buzzing in my hand, I couldn't.

I went to the end of my driveway and watched him cross the road, headed toward the inn.

Gotcha, I thought.

I went to my door, trying to open and close it with one hand while holding onto the drone with the other. It buzzed. I held it in the center of its body like a lobster, facing the obvious camera lens away from me. It was like an animal trying to escape. First one of the rotors sped up, then another pulled this way and that. I could only imagine what it would do if it got loose: crash into some of the tchotchkes I had sitting about, tear into my plants until they were diced up, terrorize Sherlock, get into my hair. It could be a nightmare scenario. I held on tight and tried to figure out what I could do. If it were not so busy trying to escape I might be able to find an on/off button, or maybe a battery cover. But all I could do was hold on. Then it suddenly went dead. The buzzing stopped, the propellers were still, the blinking red light was off. Still, I needed to find a way to be sure it wouldn't start up again. I flipped it belly up and there was the button, the little round circle with a short line bisecting it. I pressed it. I was relatively confident it would not start up remotely, but where could I put it to ensure it would not escape if somehow it came back to life? The garbage can. I went out to my vestibule and pulled in the 40-gallon can, took out the garbage bag, and after inspecting the inside and finding it pretty clean, I dropped the drone in and locked the lid. I'd keep it in the kitchen and put the garbage bag in the outside bin. Sherlock followed me, sticking close, I'm sure not wanting to seem the nervous nellie he was acting like.

Poor Haggarty, I thought, you're going to get another late-night text. I'd have to invite him and his wife over for dinner to try to make it up to both of them.

Chapter 59 – Broken

I thought about taking a puff of my CBD vape to try to relax and get to sleep, but first I texted Haggarty.

"Ready for another fun-filled day? Caught this bouncing on my window. It's sleeping in my garbage can, waiting for you."

I attached a photo of the drone.

It was ten. I knew his phone would probably ping and I felt bad bugging him even though I thought this was a very special catch. I knew I'd have to tell him my suspicion about the inn now, but wished I didn't; the old investigator thrill-of-the-hunt excitement was still coursing through my veins and I wanted to enjoy it longer, especially since I felt we were closing in.

"What world do you come from? Most of my investigators never experience this level of engagement. Be by again tomorrow."

I knew this was out of the ordinary. Usually only the criminals got hooked into an ongoing interaction, a turf war, but here I was trying to match wits with what I imagined was a tech savvy teenager with boundless energy, strength and guile. I was outmatched, but I had some experience in my corner, years of understanding the devious minds of those who are dishonest. What continued to shock me was the number of seemingly honest people who were being dishonest right under our noses, often those in positions of authority who professed to be against the very thing they were doing. Who was this guy and what was he up to? The only reason he would target me, I thought, was because I was investigating Ellen's death. It made sense that he was somehow connected to Ellen. He must know I wasn't the only investigator on this case, but I was certainly the most available to him.

I decided to call Allison tomorrow to see if they'd seen Leslie again or heard from him.

After the vape I was getting drowsy, and the drop in my adrenaline level left me feeling somewhat drained. I tried to run through the things I wanted to do tomorrow, writing by lamplight on one of my 3x5 cards.

Call Allison

Maybe talk to Grace soon and see if she does know more about Gerald, or if Ellen talked to her about him.

Visit Sue to see if she'd seen anyone unfamiliar hanging around.

Visit Nancy and Jim if they were home.

The drone, maybe get a better look in the daylight.

I had taken photos of the drone top and bottom where the serial number was. I should send that to Haggarty too.

CRASH! My woozy mind jerked awake. What the heck was that! It sounded like glass breaking downstairs. Sherlock jumped a foot. I was now shocked into action. I grabbed my bathrobe, located my slippers and sped downstairs where I could hear crashing about in the kitchen. Sherlock trailed after me.

Yikes! I could see from the motion detector light over the kitchen sink that not only was it tripped and on even before I entered the room but the window was smashed and glass was all over the floor. I pushed Sherlock back into the dining room and blocked his path into the kitchen. The cold air from the broken window was jolting. The curtain hung half in and half out of the window. The garbage can sat in the middle of the room, open. I gingerly stepped across the glass and looked in. Empty. That evil little bastard. Now not only did I not have some valuable evidence, but I also had a broken window to mend and glass to clean up. I wiped the glass off a chair, sat down and cried.

Chapter 60 – Letting Go

I was finally realizing my adversary was more dangerous than I had hitherto imagined.

I got the broom and swept up all the broken glass and found the little stone frog statuette that the stinker must have used to break the window. How convenient for him that it was just outside in my garden. I picked it up with a plastic bag on my hand that I inverted over it. More evidence. I dumped the broken glass into the now empty garbage can, not bothering to put in a bag. Then I went searching for some plastic but found a large Amazon box in the basement that I cut to fit the broken window hole, using duct tape to hold it tight in the window frame until I could get it fixed tomorrow. As I was doing it I thought about the break-in. I didn't see any blood so he probably didn't get hurt climbing in and exiting my window, but I'd know better tomorrow when it was light. He most likely had some kind of tracking device on the drone that let him home in on exactly where the thing was. I knew some of our now-everyday devices were very accurate at locating and being located. I wasn't thinking when I hid the drone and had totally underestimated his desperation to retrieve it.

I decided not to text Haggarty until tomorrow because he'd likely feel he should come right over, but at this point there was nothing he could do that he couldn't do tomorrow.

Why was this kid so desperate? Was this bigger than I'd imagined? I'd been thinking it was someone related to Gerald who wanted some of the inheritance. I kept going back to Gerald's son, Gerald Jr., but who was Leslie, the mysterious person in the will? What relationship was he to the whole thing? Haggarty would have to put more pressure on Gerald to find out what he knows. He must know something.

I let Sherlock out. He sniffed around by the window and down the driveway toward the street. He was getting to know this scent. I went out with him, flashlight in hand, looking under the window. How convenient it was to have my kitchen window so low that after breaking it he could easily climb in if he was careful. There under the window was the doormat from my back door, which he must have draped over the broken window frame to protect himself from broken glass. I thought the driveway, which ran right up to the foundation, would not show any footprints, yet still I shone my flashlight around in the hope of finding something. Nothing was obvious in the dark. Maybe in the morning.

Sherlock put his nose up. What was he smelling? Was the perp still around?

We went back in. The kitchen was colder than usual and I hoped I could get the window repaired tomorrow. I did not like feeling cold in my home.

How would we ever get back to sleep? I felt so violated. A rare discomfort hung over me. I went upstairs for my iPad and then dropped into the comfortable recliner in the living room. With several blankets over me and

Sherlock in my lap, I opened the streaming app that had Dateline on it and listened again to the mesmerizing voice of Keith Morrison. This is how some detectives unwind, listening to true crime, knowing that in the end that the good will triumph over the evil. The cops would catch that bad guy. We would win the battle, however hard and long the investigation might be. The bad guy always slips up somewhere. In this case we had to call in the big guns. Finally I had to let go of the reins.

Chapter 61 – Bingo

I awoke stiff and cold in the morning, startled, grabbing at my iPad that sat precariously on my lap. Sherlock must have jumped off in the night and was sitting up looking at me, wagging his tail, a sure signal he needed to go out.

"Okay, give me a minute." We walked into the chilly kitchen and I remembered the excitement of the previous evening. Small shards of glass had eluded my clean-up. I stepped outside with him, still in my bathrobe, not caring if anyone saw me. I inspected the window frame more closely in the brighter light. Ah. A small bit of grey cloth hung on a piece of glass. It could be part of a UConn hoodie. I didn't touch it, leaving it for Haggarty. Sherlock and I had breakfast and coffee and I texted Haggarty while I ate my oatmeal.

"When can you come out? The situation has escalated. Last night he broke in and stole the drone."

Haggarty got right back to me.

"I'll be out right after I talk to my boss."

I started going through the camera footage. It was just as I expected, all of it. The camera was aimed too low to capture the drone at my window but it did get me as I ran out and grabbed it and it got the figure at the end of the driveway. It showed him outside the kitchen window looking at what was probably a cellphone. It got him as he looked into the kitchen, grabbed my doormat, took the frog statue from the garden, smashed the window and threw the mat over the window frame, climbed in and came back out in what seemed like only seconds later. I went out with Sherlock and looked around with my flashlight.

I bet Haggarty will be mad. He will think we might have ended this a few days ago if I'd just told him what I thought I had seen and what I suspected. I guessed he would have gone right into Ellen's just to see if anyone was there. With the neighbors below away, anyone being relatively cautious might use Ellen's as a home base. But why? The same questions kept coming up. Who and why?

I needed to buy window glass. It had been years since I'd fixed a window but I knew a little about glazing. This guy had picked the one window that wasn't four over four. Several years ago, against our Historical Commission rules, I replaced that broken window with a single pane instead of replacing eight panes of glass. I knocked out the mullions between the panes to accommodate a single pane. I caught hell from the Historical Commission but promised at some point to replace it with a historically correct window, which up to now I hadn't done. I considered using plexiglass for now and then hiring someone to put the four over four back in. This sucked.

Haggarty texted he'd be out within the hour. I spent the time carefully vacuuming the kitchen to clean up any remaining shards of glass. Then I measured the window and called Duke, my favorite handyman, who was a genius with older homes. He said he'd come take a look, get some measurements and hopefully have it done in a week or two.

I fidgeted. What could I do in the hour until Haggarty arrived? I took out the will again, trying to understand who Leslie Goranson was. I googled him using the person-searching app White Pages, throwing in unknowns for the town: Windham, North Stonington, Groton, Mystic, all just in case he did have an address in any of those places. Sure enough, a Leslie Goranson came up in two places, Windham and Norwich. Bingo!

Chapter 62 – Sorry

Why hadn't I done that earlier? Of course I understood that many of these apps, especially the free ones, were not dependable, but they were a start and surprisingly this one gave me a hit. Leslie Goranson's Windham address was Ellen's. I slowed my mind down and repeated it. The Windham address was Ellen's. Things were starting to come together in my mind. The fog of evidence was coalescing.

I did a search on Gerald Richardson, Windham. It came up with Gerald Richardson, Junior, addresses in Norwich and Windham. Ellen's address in Windham.

Why were these guys hanging out together? What was the common denominator? Ellen?

So if Leslie is in trouble and making trouble here, where is Gerry junior? Why would Leslie be staying at Allison and John's?

Haggarty drove into the driveway in his cruiser.

"Hey, want some coffee? I've got some things to tell you." He understood from my tone that we needed to sit down before going over any of the previous evening's events. I poured him some coffee and served him day-old carrot cake cupcakes from A Cupcake for Later. He sat down, looking serious.

"So, a few days ago when I was on one of my walks around town, I thought I saw a flash of light in Ellen's apartment. I wasn't sure, but I wanted to wait to tell you, maybe do a little investigating of my own. Well, I've walked around town for a couple of nights since then but haven't seen it, or anything, again. But you know when that kid was dropping off critters he headed back toward the inn when he left. So I'm beginning to think that might be where he's hiding. I'm sorry I didn't tell you sooner." I tried to look as penitent as I felt. He was staring at me with a serious look. "So last night, the drone was whacking at my window and I opened the window and threw my shirt at it and brought it down." Haggarty nodded. "I ran outside and grabbed the thing, which was buzzing around, and the kid ran up to the bottom of the driveway. I hollered at him and he yelled back, 'You'll be sorry, bitch!' And he ran off toward the inn. He remotely stopped its propellors and I powered it off. I took some photos of it, top and bottom, and by the way, these things are hard to hold onto when they're struggling to get free. I put it in my garbage can, feeling pretty good about myself, and went back to bed. I heard a crash when he threw that frog statue"–I pointed at it—"through the window, climbed in, and stole the drone back. I didn't want to text you again; it was late and what good would it have done." When Haggarty shook his head and actually smiled I felt a little relieved.

"So, Frances, is this how you were when you were in the department? Kind of a dickens?"

"Well, maybe once in a while." I opened my iPad. "Here are the photos of the drone. I think I got its serial number on the belly of the beast. I'll send them to you." Haggarty inspected them, enlarging the drone belly shots with his forefinger and thumb. "Want to see the captures from the cameras?" He nodded and I brought up the app and walked through them with him.

"So, what do you think?" He knew but wanted me to say it.

"I think he may be camping out at Ellen's." Haggarty nodded. "I'm sorry I didn't tell you sooner."

"I bet, but you know what payback is..."

"Yeah, payback is a broken window that I've got to fix." I sighed.

"Well, I can't deputize you, but do you want to go over to Ellen's?"

"Let me get my coat!" I did and Sherlock looked at me excitedly. "Sorry, baby, you've got to stay home." He didn't understand. "No. Stay." He understood that and looked dejected. "Do you think we need backup?" I was half joking, but I felt this guy was actually somewhat desperate and liable to act erratically if not dangerously.

"I hope not. Let's walk over. Leave the cruiser here. Did you check for more cameras?"

"Yes, I did, inside and out, and didn't find any, but I suppose I could have missed some. They're so small these days."

"So we can assume he doesn't know I'm here." We put on our coats and Haggarty grabbed his metal case from the car. "Just in case we find evidence."

We crossed the street and went in the front door of the inn, trying to be quiet. Haggarty had the key Sue had given him. We ascended slowly, knowing that even though we were careful, some of the stairs in the old place creaked. If you lived here for years you'd know which ones, but we didn't. A creak. I looked up. There at the edge of the molding was a tiny camera. We heard some thrashing about as we rushed up the remaining stairs. It took Haggarty a few seconds to put the key in the lock and wiggle the old knob to get the door open. By the time we were in, UConn hoodie was out the side door, down the fire escape and gone behind the building.

"I'm too old to chase this guy," I hollered as Haggarty ran as fast as he could down the stairwell we'd just come up. I followed at a slower pace. I watched from the front of the building as he ran out to the street, looked all around, up the street and down, and then walked around the building, meeting me where I stood.

Chapter 63 – Evidence

"He disappeared." Haggarty whistled out a breath and shook his head, soundlessly admitting that he too was not a kid anymore. We headed back up to Ellen's apartment. We'd left the door open and walked in cautiously just in case there was some evidence we wouldn't want to destroy. That door opened into her living room; there was the couch that Harold hid behind. On the couch was the drone, sitting quietly next to its controller box. Ooooh, I thought, he left some valuable property. We looked around and found a treasure trove of evidence.

"I wonder if I should get the guys to come in and go over this," he thought out loud. I'd flicked on the lights, grateful the power hadn't been turned off yet. Haggarty focused his flashlight on things of particular interest. I followed him. Empty cans of soda sat on the kitchen counter along with several empty cans of beer and half-eaten bags of corn chips and potato chips, one rolled up. The fridge Haggarty opened with his gloved hand contained more beer and three Styrofoam containers that we assumed had food in them but didn't check.

On the living room coffee table lay half-smoked joints in a saucer with Bic lighters, kitchen matches and vape pens scattered about, and also a baggie of weed, I thought maybe a half ounce.

"This place is loaded." Haggarty sounded pleased and surprised. "He must have been feeling pretty secure." We continued to look around. In Ellen's bedroom/study all the drawers in the desk were open, one upside down on the floor. The bed looked as though someone had slept on top of the covers, where a blanket lay loose and wrinkled but the sheets were undisturbed. Everything from the top shelf of the closet had been pulled down and left on the floor.

We went back through the living room and kitchen and into the bathroom. The toothbrush on the edge of the sink made me wonder about the hygiene of criminals. And there, on the back of the toilet, was Ellen's ivory hand mirror, smudged with white powder and a razor blade.

"Geez, some hard stuff." I was surprised. "Where is this kid getting his money?" We exchanged glances, the truth hitting home to both of us at the same time. "Dealing."

Haggarty turned his flashlight off and dialed his cellphone. "Hi, Gertie, this is Haggarty. I'm at the inn in Windham Center, the one next to the post office. I need a team out here to process evidence. Send them right away. I'll be here waiting for them. Thanks."

Haggarty handed me a pair of gloves as we went into the kitchen. We pulled out two chairs and sat down.

"I wonder how long he's been here," I mused. Haggarty looked deep in thought.

"Probably since he ran off from the Baileys', Allison and John's." I nodded.

"What, a couple of weeks ago? So how has he been surviving? How's he getting around?"

"Maybe those Bailey kids aren't such goodie-two-shoes as their parents would have us believe."

"Yeah, you're right. It seems they get to use the car whenever they want."

"Maybe after the circus comes we should think about visiting them." I knew he meant the investigative team.

"Yeah, but we have to be careful. We don't want to lose this guy if we move too fast."

Chapter 64 – Pig

"You think he's still in touch with their kids?"

"Yeah, I imagine so. How else would he get all the food and stuff? We should probably get more solid evidence before we approach them."

"I agree. They seem to think their kids are angels. Probably like most parents. Kids are pretty wily. They can show one face to their parents while living in a whole other world. Usually they outgrow it. These kids are maintaining good grades so they can't be too deep into the drugs, maybe just an occasional beer and puff of a joint." Haggarty nodded.

We heard someone pull into the parking lot. His team came in the front door and Haggarty called down to them. They came up, suited up in the hall, and listened to Haggarty's instructions.

"This apartment has already been processed after a death, but since then one or more individuals have been camping out here, so this is what I want you to focus on. First get photos of all the rooms, and then process the areas where it seems like people have been using drugs, here in the living room, the kitchen, the bathroom. Process the drugs and try to get prints, like on the cans in the kitchen, really, just bag the cans. Get the toothbrush in the bathroom–it may have DNA–and the mirror and anything that looks like it's been touched in the last week. I want to know about the drugs, what kind of cannabis, if the coke has been cut. You might poke around for drug stashes because the person who was here ran out in a hurry and may have left stuff behind; there could be a bag of pills tucked into the sofa cushions." They both nodded. "Any questions?"

"No. What should we do when we're finished?"

"Call my cell and I'll come back and lock up, maybe reseal the door, not that I think that will stop them." He put his business card on the coffee table. "I'll be at Ms. O'Connor's, right around the corner, if you need me."

We left and walked back to my house. When we got to my driveway Haggarty yelled, "That Mother!" as he ran his hand over the hood of his cruiser where the word PIG had been carved into the paint. "What the hell! I'm gonna get that MF'er!" He was livid. "Well, don't be surprised if I can't spend as much time with you from now on. I'd bet an additional detective will be assigned to this. Really, what if this kid, who's likely hanging out with some unsavory characters, gets hold of a gun? What then? Entirely possible. Why doesn't he just leave town? I guess he wants the money from the will." Haggarty was thinking out loud, zeroing in on motive.

"If we mess up his home base, where's he going to go? You know, the trail could go cold."

"Well, he seems like a vindictive little shit, so I bet he won't go very far. He'll want to torment you."

"Something to look forward to." We both chuckled. "What's your next step?"

"I think we need to talk to Gerald senior and tell him what we've found and that he should open up to us. Then, Allison and John Bailey and maybe even their kids.

Do you think anyone else in town might have information, someone Ellen might have talked to about this or about anything that worried her?"

"Maybe at least one person I think she opened up to, but she seemed pretty private. I'll visit her and see if she might be more forthcoming if I tell her a little of what's been going on."

Chapter 65 – Tamper-Proof

I had leftover pepperoni and bean soup that I heated up with cornbread. I was pleased that Haggarty was always willing to eat whatever I served.

"Geez, Frances." He made a satisfied sound. "You are a hell of a cook. Even your leftovers are scrumptious."

"Aw, Haggarty, I bet you say that to all of your once-upon-a-time lesbian co-workers." He coughed out some cornbread crumbs.

"Excuse me." He wiped his face. "I'm not sure I knew..."

"Well, I'm not exclusive, but I've had a fling or two. Now I'm just too old to care anymore and I've got Sherlock."

"Okay, O'Conner, this is just TMI."

"Duly noted. So, how about them Mets?" Haggarty laughed. "You know, I've been on cases all over the state, big ones, little ones, most solved, some not, but this is the first one in my town. It's unsettling, especially since I feel like I've gotten myself immersed in it. Ordinarily wouldn't I be taken off the case because I was too close?" He nodded.

"Yeah, likely, but this is pretty rare, a detective, on the force or not, getting embroiled in the case. It is rare and it would seem to give you an edge–the evidence is right there, the perp right there. I wonder if and when we catch this guy if you could be admitted as a witness in the trial or if the defense would be able to claim you tainted evidence or manipulated it in some way. This could be tricky."

"Yeah, I get that, tricky." I ladled out a little more for myself then signaled to him with the ladle to see if he wanted more, but he shook his head. "Is there anything I can do to ensure I don't taint the case?" He frowned.

"I don't know. You're so involved already, probably a mistake on our part to have you on the investigation, but it's too late now. I'll talk to my boss and see if there's any way we can put you on the force as a temp or something like that so there will be some semblance of legality behind this. I know we wouldn't do anything illegal or deliberately taint the case, but the defense can still use it against us if it goes to trial. I'm not sure. We'll talk to our legal department and see what they think."

He finished off his cornbread. "Hey, let me look at the videos you took. Can you send them to me or copy them to a thumb drive? Is there a USB port on those cameras? Maybe a little memory card that the videos are temporarily stored to? We should check. I don't want them written over." I pulled out my iPad where I had been viewing them and we tried to save them so I could send them to him. I logged into each camera and checked the memory. Each still had enough so that nothing would be written over yet, but it would be best to save what we had to ensure against losing it.

We fussed with this long enough for the team at the inn to call Haggarty and say they were done. I followed him over as they explained what they'd collected. Haggarty and I cleaned up anything left, which wasn't much, and he locked the door and sealed it with tape that had a warning on it and would show any tampering.

"He's probably got a key and I think it opens the back door on the fire escape. Want to check? We can seal that one too." We walked around to the fire escape and tested his key, which indeed opened that door, and he sealed that one too with tamper-evident tape. "I'll talk to you tomorrow unless you text first." He smiled.

Chapter 66 – Grace

Feeling antsy, I decided to go to Bob's IGA for whatever I was going to eat for the rest of the week. Maybe Cajun chicken?

When I got home Sherlock and I went for our evening walk before making dinner. I had to work off some of my nervous energy. I'd never felt as threatened as I did now. Usually I worked on cases I wasn't involved in personally. I took my flashlight and a walking stick, and even thought about bringing my revolver but decided against it, thinking I might be overreacting. When we got to Grace's I noticed a light on in her front room and on a whim decided to stop in.

I rang her doorbell. It took a good minute before she came to the door, wrapping her sweater closer around her. She looked pleased to see me, but of course she would.

"Hey, Grace, Sherlock and I were just walking by and saw your light on. How are you?" She stepped to the side and motioned us in.

"Hello, Frances. Come on in. You too, Sherlock." She bent down and tapped him on the head as we went past her.

"I hope you're not busy and we're not interrupting anything."

"Oh no, you're fine. I was just sitting by the fire, having a cup of tea and reading the paper. You know, I don't think many people read the paper anymore, not the actual hard copy anyway." She indicated a chair. "Can I take your coat? Could I get you some tea?" She took my coat and laid it on one of the other chairs.

"No, thank you, no tea."

"How about a little brandy? Wouldn't that be nice on a chilly night?"

"You know, I think that would be nice." Grace went into the kitchen and came back with a tray, brandy snifters, and a bottle of Courvoisier. Lovely, I thought. She poured and I picked up the glass and cradled it. "Did you know Ellen's apartment had been broken into?" I laid it right out. She sucked in a little breath like a gasp.

"You're kidding! What happened?" I watched her carefully as she undid the hair clasp that held up her hair, ran her fingers through as though to neaten it, pulled it back and refastened the clasp. Odd motion, I thought. If it weren't under these circumstances I wouldn't have noticed, but motions, subconscious actions, often hold a meaning. Was she tidying up her psyche? Wrapping it tight and closing it with a clasp?

"Someone's been camping out there." I wondered how much I could or should reveal to her.

"Really? Camping out?" She looked confused.

"Yeah, some kid, making trouble." She just stared at me. Something was cooking. I could see her trying to make sense of what I told her. "Things are actually pretty serious. You know I've been working with a detective on this, right?" She stared into the fire, seemingly mesmerized. What was she thinking? Then she visibly snapped out of it, shaking her head but almost imperceptibly.

"Yeah, I heard that. What have you found?"

"Hard to say, hard to put it together, but we think Ellen had some troubles." I was baiting a hook with loose truths. "Maybe something to do with a kid." I waited. "You don't know anything about that, do you? I mean, she's gone. If she told you anything in confidence... you know, it wouldn't be betraying her. Really." She looked anguished.

"I can't. Talk to her son. Maybe he can help you."

Chapter 67 – It's Back

"Thank you, Grace." I understood that she knew more but just couldn't bring herself to share it. "I might come back. If the investigation doesn't pick up more, they might call you in." Now she looked steely, like her mind was made up.

"Let them." I was speechless at this. If she knew more and was protecting someone, that would be serious. I thought the threat of being interrogated might persuade her, but it was just the opposite. I'd tell Haggarty that Grace thought Gerald knew more and maybe we'd have to bring him in.

Sherlock and I finished our walk around the neighborhood. There was no sign of activity except for one person walking a dog and a few people driving through and lights going on, but no light at Ellen's. With Grace's response on my mind I only wanted to get home, not focus on Ellen's apartment, but when we went by the inn, Sherlock's head went up, noting something of interest; I wondered how much better a detective I might be if I had a dogs sense of smell.

I had just stepped in the door and begun to get Sherlock's dinner when I got a text from Haggarty.
"DNA back."

He was teasing me, so I texted back.
"Yeah, and?"
"From original sweep."
"Yeah, and?"
"This is fun."
"I'm not laughing."
"Male DNA."
"Yeah, anything else?"
"Male DNA related to Ellen."

"You're sh*tting me!"

"Nope."

"I talked to Grace; she knows something, won't say what, says we have to talk to Gerald."

"Can you go tomorrow?"

"You bet."

"See you at 9? I won't even make an appointment."

"Okay."

Great! When you do something like drop in unannounced to question someone, they are often shaken and unprepared, and when you catch them off guard you not only rattle them, but you usually get more than they ever expected to give you. Their demeanor, their body language, all of it a giveaway; they know you know something, and sometimes they just give it up right then so you never have to bring them in for a serious interrogation. So I was excited about talking to Gerald tomorrow. Then I thought about Haggarty's text: male DNA from a relative of Ellen. Whose? Could it be Gerald senior, could it be Gerald junior? Then who was Leslie and why was he involved? And was it even Leslie who left the DNA? Was it really Leslie at Allison and John's? If it was Gerald, why would he change his name? Oh, geez, I had too much buzzing around in my mind; could I ever get to sleep tonight? I doubted the drone would be back. I might sleep with my revolver close by.

I checked the memory on my cameras. Nothing important that I could see, a few people walking by, neighbors going to the post office or walking their dogs, nothing else. I actually thought about sleeping in my front room where I had a guest bedroom set up, just in case another projectile came through my bedroom window. How did I know how crazy and desperate this person or persons might be?

I noted on my 3x5 to-do card to talk to Allison again. I wondered if Haggarty showed up there in his cruiser whether the kids would finally realize they were messing with things that were dangerous, and illegal. Would it cease to be just a joke to them and they would spill? I loved cop slang. Spill. What a great word.

Chapter 67 – Gerald Senior

I dropped into bed beside Sherlock, revolver close, iPad ready to watch true crime until I finally fell asleep. I checked my cameras first. Infrared showed nothing.

The alarm went off at 6:30, good enough sleep and plenty of time to let Sherlock out, feed him and myself, take a shower and be ready to go. I was excited.

Haggarty arrived and I shut poor Sherlock in his room, gave him a special treat and turned on the radio for him. He knew the drill and settled into his bed gnawing on his longer-lasting treat.

"So tell me more about the DNA."

"They pulled it from doorknobs, front and back, and the refrigerator. They got some prints too, most of them partial, but a few of them were pretty good and they isolated them from Ellen's prints and DNA." Haggarty was upbeat this morning. I could tell from his demeanor that he had a positive feeling about this and maybe we were closing in.

"What else are you working on? Got anything hot to keep you busy once this one has been solved?"

"In this area, eastern Connecticut? Yeah, we've got a few, nothing too exciting: a hit and run, burglaries at several Seven–Elevens that seem to be the same perp, a somewhat violent carjacking where a middle-aged woman was injured, and of course drugs–somebody cooking meth in an apartment building and almost lighting up the place."

"Huh. Well, I'll miss working with you. It's been years since I retired but I remember it well, and sort of miss the excitement and the guys there."

"Well, Frances, it's been a pleasure working with you, but let's not get ahead of ourselves. It's not over yet."

He smiled at me. We were at the stoplight close to the newspaper where Gerald worked and were lucky enough to find a convenient parking spot. I grabbed my iPad and my little recording device.

"Can we record this? Can we tell him we're going to record this? It's been years and I don't remember a lot of the regs and if they've changed."

"Well, this is sort of tricky because we're going to his workplace rather than having him come in. If we had him come in we'd be required to record him. I believe if we inform him we'll be recording him and do that while we're recording and get his verbal assent it will be legal. I know you have a recording device, but I'll use mine too, okay?"

"Yeah, I'm ready."

We went in and told the receptionist we were going to visit Gerald Richardson. Haggarty showed his ID and badge and told her not to contact him and that we knew our way up. He wanted to shake Gerry.

We were down the hall and could see his windowed office. His view of us was blocked by the large computer screen he was working on. We walked up to where we could see his face and he looked up at us. He turned white and lifted his fingers from the keyboard and mouse. Haggarty knocked and put his hand on the doorknob as though to open the door and Gerald nodded for us to come in.

"I hope this isn't too much of an intrusion." Haggarty was smooth and civil.

Gerald shifted in his chair.

"Well, I wasn't expecting you. I'm kind of busy." He looked over his shoulder at the windowed computer room behind him.

"We understand. We just have a few more questions. I hope you don't mind. It should only take a few minutes." Haggarty motioned for me to sit down and then he sat and took out his recorder. "You don't mind if we record this, do you?" I pulled out my recorder too.

Gerald looked like he would run if he could get away with it. Targets have a certain expression when they've been caught, a desperate, trapped-animal look, sometimes eyes searching for an escape route but trying not to be obvious about it.

"Is this really necessary?" He wanted to seem in control, as though he might be able to turn the tables. It was awkward for him, in his glass office, at work. What could he do that wouldn't attract attention from his co-workers and associates? He tried to look businesslike.

"Yes. It would be good for you if you just answered our questions truthfully." Not waiting for a reply, Haggarty turned on the recorder. Click. "Thursday, February 6th, 2024. Interview with Sergeant Finn Haggerty, Connecticut, Troop K, and Gerald Richardson of North Stonington. You understand you are being recorded, is that correct?" Gerald let out a long sigh and visibly deflated. His shoulders sagged, his eyes seemed to fill a little, and he put his hands flat on the desk.

"Yes."

"You are Ellen Richardson's son, is that correct?"

"Yes."

"You're aware that Ellen passed away on December fifth under suspicious circumstances, correct?"

"Yes."

"Do you know a person who goes by the name of Leslie Goranson?"

"Yes."

"Who is that person and how do you know him?"

Now Gerald had a trapped animal look, and hesitated. "Do I have to..." He put his elbows on the desk and his head in his hands. "I can't, it could endanger my son..." he choked out under his hands.

Chapter 68 – Spills

Haggarty looked at me and we both looked at Gerald.

"Would it help you to know that we already have some information, and that if you tell us what you know we should be able to protect your son?"

He looked up from his hands, and now his face was red, his hair mussed and palms sweaty even in the air-conditioned office. "If I tell you, can you promise that you can help him, keep him out of further trouble, see that he doesn't get hurt or go to jail?"

"That's a tall order, Mr. Richardson, especially since we don't know the situation or how deep he's in." Haggarty had to be honest. Gerald was on the verge of spilling. "Tell us what you know and we'll do our best to help him."

"Okay." Now Gerald looked relieved. He sighed. "I don't even know when and how it happened. I'll just try to tell you what I know." We nodded.

"Good."

"Well, months ago, like maybe October or November, maybe even before, Gerry was getting combative, his grades were slipping, he just seemed angry. But you know how teenage boys are with all those hormones crashing about, so we didn't think that much about it. Then one day when my wife was putting laundry away she found some joints in his drawer. How stupid was that, putting them there. So we confronted him and he lost it, totally lost it and stormed out of the house. Of course we were worried, but still thought it was just teen stuff and once we'd talked it out and given him a punishment, a probation period, that it would all be over." He paused. "Hey, can I get a soda or something?"

"Yes, we'll pause the tape and continue when you come back." He got up.

"I'm thirsty too. I'm going to get one with you." Haggarty was being cautious; perps have been known to take off when given the chance. He didn't give him a chance to say no and they both walked down the hall to the machines in an alcove. When they got back and poured some soda into cups Haggarty started the tape and reintroduced himself and Gerald.

"So what happened after Gerry junior left?"

"He didn't come home that night and we started to worry. Then the next day when my wife went into his room it looked like he'd come home and taken some things, a few clothes and a few personal items. We knew he had a little cash in an envelope and that was gone. His pocketknife was gone, and his iPad and cellphone." Gerald took a sip. "That's when we freaked out. We didn't know what to do." Another sip. "That evening we got an email from him. It said, 'I'm safe, don't send the cops, don't worry, I'm going to see grandma.' Well, that was weird because we hadn't seen her in years. But he knew who she was and where she lived and the circumstances of her break from the family. We thought it could have been worse."

"Can I interrupt you for a second?" Haggarty broke in. "Do you have that email?"

"Yeah, it's here somewhere." Gerald logged into his computer. "It's on my private email. Give me a second to get into it." We waited, Haggarty and I exchanging looks – this was really, really good. "Here, here it is." Gerald turned the monitor toward us so we could see it. Both Haggarty and I took photos of it.

"Can you forward it to me? Here's my email address." Haggarty gave Gerald his card. "So then what happened?"

"He must have felt safe with my mother because he gave her my email and phone number and she called me. She said she didn't want me to worry, that he was staying with her, but then she said something I didn't expect. She asked about the friend that drove him to her house and what was the deal with him? She said Gerry was sleeping on the daybed in her study and the other guy was sleeping on the couch. I didn't know who the 'other guy' was and asked her and she said someone named Leslie. I told her I didn't know him." Gerald's shoulders went up, and with his palms up and fingers open, he looked like he truly didn't know. "I'd never heard of him before."

"Okay, I see." Haggarty was encouraging him.

"Well, after a few days I guess there was a fight. Ellen was concerned that they weren't signing up for school locally, and she wasn't used to having a couple of teenage boys eating her out of house and home. She tried to get them to enroll in school, maybe get jobs, anything. What happened then was Leslie left. He had a car but left it at the inn. She didn't know where he went, but he'd come back every few days to visit and take the car and disappear for a while. Gerald would disappear too. She thought they were going to school." He took another sip of soda. "Well, one day they showed up and Gerry told my mother that Leslie had something to help the aches and pains she sometimes complained about. He gave her these things and told her to suck on one. Not having very good eyesight, she did, and it helped her, probably too much." Haggarty put his hand up.

"How do you know all this? Did she send you emails or call you?"

"She called me the day after she had the drug and sounded worried. It didn't take her long to figure out what it was and then she didn't know what to do. She wondered how these kids were getting this stuff and how much trouble they might be in."

"What happened then?"

Chapter 69 – Relief

He looked back and forth between us. His eyebrows arched. He shook his head slightly.

"I didn't hear from her. I tried to call her and email her and call and email Gerry, but nothing." He took a deep breath and let it out. "I even thought about going up there. I knew where she was living. I'd driven past it once or twice in the last decade or so, but my father had painted her so badly that I didn't want anything to do with her. My father was a hard one and over the years I sort of learned that my mother wasn't as evil as he'd said, but I never got it together to approach her and ask her the other side. So maybe if things had been different I might have gone up to Windham, but I didn't." He had been fidgeting. He stopped and looked at his hands, now calm. "Then about a week went by, a tortured week. I hadn't told my wife. I let her believe Gerry was at my mother's and going to school. I didn't see any reason to worry her too; it was enough for me to be in hell. Then Attorney Kelly called me and told me she was dead." His voice trembled. "I didn't mean for this to happen. You never think things are going to turn out the way they do..." He took a sip of soda. "Then I got a call from Gerry. He was freaked out. He told me Leslie was threatening him." Someone knocked on the door and Gerald motioned him in. Haggarty and I watched as Gerald addressed the visitor. "Listen, I'm going to take an early lunch. You want to start those backups now?" The person nodded and went past us into the computer room. "Can we do this somewhere else?" Haggarty nodded and addressed the recording device, telling it of the pause, and we both stopped our devices.

"So is there somewhere we can go to talk privately?" Gerald nodded as Haggarty picked up his device and we followed him into a small conference room. Gerald posted a sign on the door saying a meeting was in progress, closed the blinds and motioned us to sit down. We set up the recorders and started again.

"You said that Leslie threatened Gerry?" Haggarty prompted.

"Yeah, somehow they had convinced my mother to change her will and include Leslie in it. Leslie!" He was emphatic. "I mean, who the hell was he?" Gerald looked angry. "Now he wanted that money from the will. Just having her change the will wasn't enough for him to get the cash, but apparently he didn't know that when he did it. I think my mother tricked him so that even though he was in the will for what might have amounted to a goodly sum, he couldn't get at it. Gerry said he was frightened. Leslie was losing it and it sounded like he owed people money. It was all so confusing and hard to fathom. I heard several different stories from him. I told him I'd go pick him up but he said if I did Leslie might kill him. I didn't know what to do. Really, I'd gotten to the point where I didn't know if I could trust him, didn't know if he was in cahoots with Leslie or was really in danger. I just knew he was in trouble." Gerald shook his head again and took another drink of soda. "I lost track of him altogether, no emails, no calls. I didn't know what happened or where he was, or how to reach him. Then you showed up here. I didn't know what to do or what I could tell you. I was shaken. Now I'm sort of relieved. I don't have to be the only one who knows about this." He poured the last of the soda into his cup and finished it off. "Can you help me? Help us? Is he going to be in trouble? Is he safe?"

"Well, we need to find him, and Leslie, and find out what happened. We need to get to the bottom of it."

"Yeah."

"So where was he the last time you talked to him?"

"I think they were staying in my mother's old apartment."

"That would make sense. That's the last place we think Leslie was staying, but he, or maybe both of them, left, and we don't know to where yet." Haggarty seemed to signal that maybe we were done. "Is there anything else you can think of that might help us? Can you give me Gerry's cellphone number and email? Do you know anything about Leslie, where he comes from? How they met? What kind of car he drives?" Gerald sat back in his chair and looked up.

"I think they may have met at a basketball game. Gerry went up with friends to a UConn game and they hung out later and came home late. Other than that I have no idea. I think Leslie may have, like, a BMW maybe? I think Gerry mentioned that once. Something I thought too upscale for a teenager, but I don't even know how old he is."

"Mr. Richardson, I appreciate the time you gave us and for being so open with us. We're going to do everything we can to find them and see that your son is safe." Haggarty signed off on the device and turned it off.

"Do you think Gerry's going to be in trouble?"

"We don't know yet. We don't really know that much about what's going on, but you've just helped us a lot and with a little luck we'll find them and we'll keep Gerry safe." Haggarty was reassuring and yet noncommittal about what the outcome might be. We wrapped up our devices and left Gerald still looking worried. Haggarty looked back. "Don't worry. We're good at this. You've left it in good hands." He wanted to be kind to this mixed-up guy even though he'd lied to us in the last interview and threw the investigation off a week because of it.

Chapter 70 – Cell Trace

"So now what?" were the first words out of my mouth once we were in the car.

"I'll see if I can get the techs to trace the cellphone, find out where it's been, if it moved around and where it is now. They've already looked for a Leslie Goranson but that name turned up nothing, so we have to do some serious electronic searching. I'll have them just look for a Goranson and see if he changed his first name."

"Okay, great." I checked my phone for messages, not that I expected any, but old habits.... "What do you think?" he asked.

"I think he was telling the truth. I just wish he'd told us a week earlier. I think they're both in deep. I'll bet Leslie, or whoever he is, is doing some illegal stuff, seriously illegal if he's got his hands on fentanyl lollipops. But where the hell did they go? Should we visit the Baileys? Shake up their kids? I wonder if they could be hiding them right under their parents' noses."

"Oooh, I like the way you think." Haggarty looked at the clock on his dash. "It's past lunch. Want to eat and then drop in on them?"

"Yes, perfect! Hey, how about that little place in Franklin? What is it? Emely's? It's got great Mexican and all kinds of good stuff at reasonable rates. What do you think?"

"Deal!" We were almost to Route 32, and my stomach was growling.

"You know, it's what, 2:30 now." Haggarty spoke between bites. "If we wait until like 4 we can be sure the kids are home and if I pull in with the cruiser it will likely shake them up more."

"Yeah, I was thinking that. Can you call in the cellphone number and get that search started?" He nodded between bites and wiping his chin.

"Geez, I love this place!"

Back at my house he called in the IT search for the cellphone. "This should be interesting. There are enough towers around to give us a good sense of where his phone is and where it's been. When they have the time they can create a map with times and places if you give them a date and rough timeline. I think I'll have them start with today, see if we can locate it right now and work backward from there."

"Did Gerald say he had a phone number for Leslie? Or does anyone? Can they check the cellphone for calls connected to Gerry's number or do you need a search warrant for something like that?"

"Yeah, we'd need a warrant for that, but if I could convince the judge that a person's life might be in danger I might be able to get it."

"Hmmm..."

"I know, I was thinking the same thing." Haggarty called his office and spoke to someone, telling him he needed a search on phone numbers that called Gerry's cell, and that it was important to get it as soon as possible because a teen's life might be at stake. "You know if you mention that it involves a minor you usually get a higher priority. Let's see how long this takes to get approved."

"So shall we visit Allison and John?"

"Yeah, let's go. We'll use the cruiser and see what that does to stir things up. I'll change into my uniform too." He'd brought his uniform in from the car and went into the bathroom to change. He often came to see me in a suit and not his uniform, but now he wanted to look more official to let the parents and kids know this was serious. He came out in his starched shirt, creased pants, and flat-brimmed grey Stetson, looking intimidating. "How's this? Think we'll get some answers now?"

"You know it, Sarge." He feigned a threatening look and then grinned at me.

Chapter 71 – BMW

We hopped into the cruiser and headed for Plains Road. Haggarty pulled in and parked at the end of the driveway near the road, blocking any other cars from coming in or going out. We saw several cars parked up near the barn in the back of the property.

We walked up to the front door and Haggarty rang the doorbell. It's a lovely older Italianate-style home with a front door, a side door to a covered porch and a back entry into the kitchen. We waited for a few seconds, then heard activity. A light came on in the hall and Allison opened the door. She looked from Haggarty to me, eyes wide.

"Hello, Allison, this is Sargent Haggarty from the State Police. He'd like to talk to you." Haggarty stepped forward offering his hand. Allison hesitated–we really had caught her off guard. Then she shook his hand and stepped back to let us in. Just as she did we heard the back door slam. Allison turned and called to her husband.

"John? John, are you there?" John called back from the living room.

"Yeah, Al, what's up? Where did the kids go?"

Suddenly a car revved its engine hard. Throwing up stone from the driveway, it tore across the side lawn, digging it up, bypassing Haggarty's cruiser. It was just a flash past the window, a silver BMW. Allison looked confused, her eyes going from the speeding car to us.

We heard tires screeching. Apparently the car was tearing up our little town center. Haggarty reacted immediately and ran back to his cruiser, threw it into reverse and sped toward the rotary only a couple hundred feet away.

I followed Haggarty out and Allison followed me as I dashed toward the rotary at the center of Scotland Road, North Road, Windham Center Road and Plains Road, where the post office, the Congregational church, the inn and the green all came together. As we ran we heard tires squealing, and when we reached the crest of the hill and looked down at the rotary, we saw the smoke from the burning tires. The BMW went round and round and then seemed to lose control and headed up toward the green at an amazing rate of speed. Allison and I both panicked, thinking it might hit us, but instead it hit the curb, went airborne and with a terrific crash hit the large stone World War II memorial about twenty feet from the road. The front end of the BMW was totally crushed and the windshield and front windows all smashed. I thought I saw a body hanging out of the driver's window. As we inched closer, the car burst into flames.

Haggarty had parked on the little shortcut by the town Christmas tree, between Plains Road and North Road. He ran toward the car and then back to his car when he saw the flames. Grabbing a fire extinguisher he rushed to put out the fire. He was getting it under control when an explosion blew him back and off his feet. The fire alarm went off. Thank goodness, I thought, someone called this in.

The cars of volunteer firefighters and emergency workers flew by toward the fire department. In what seemed like only seconds a fire truck and emergency vehicle converged on the center. Men with fire extinguishers jumped out while others donned orange vests and directed traffic during what is our little village's rush hour. Cars were backing up and people left them and walked toward the green. The villagers from homes around the green were coming out to find the source of the noise and smoke.

Haggarty had picked himself up and was helping to remove the person from the still smoldering BMW.

As Allison and I got closer we saw the mangled form of Leslie being worked on by emergency personnel. Allison recognized him right away.

"Oh, my goodness! It's Leslie!" She tried to get closer but was kept back. People converged on the area even though emergency workers were trying to keep them away.

Allison and I stood by the library. Barbara joined us, wrapping a sweater around her shoulders. Sue crossed North Street and stood by us. I saw Grace and Sheila hustle across Windham Center Road and come toward us. Joyce and Shelly arrived together, one in a parka, one in a shawl. Gloria and Henry, both in jackets, crossed Plains Road to us. We all watched the spectacle.

People sometimes drove too fast through town, but the four-way stop usually slowed them down enough to keep walkers fairly safe. Once in a while drivers did "burn rubber" and certainly the guys in their "coal burners," as some of them termed their big diesels, revved their engines and showed off their unnecessarily loud mufflers. People "peeled out" or had their woofers pounding ear-splittingly so you could feel the beat. But this was a spectacle that didn't happen often. One of the bystanders uncharitably said he was happy the car hadn't hit the Charter Oak scion planted on the green. But the crash did do some damage to the WWII memorial, and I hoped it could be fixed. The person lying on the ground being given CPR could not. You could tell, just by the expression of the emergency personnel, it was probably a lost cause. No seat belt, someone said. They brought the mobile gurney out and four people loaded him onto it. One of them resumed CPR while a second tried to mask his crushed face to give him oxygen.

Haggarty had his clipboard out, writing notes and gathering information from people.

Allison's sons and husband joined us. Half the village was there. But where was Gerry?

Chapter 72 – CPR

As we all stood there, neighbors discussing the event, I tried to surreptitiously watch Allison, John and their boys. The boys were a shade of white that made me wonder where the hell their blood had gone. Every one of the family looked stunned. Allison's eyes went back and forth between the boys and the scene in front of us. The boys just stared open-mouthed at Leslie, who lay motionless except for the bouncing caused by the rhythmic pressure of the CPR.

It wasn't just the excitement of an accident or the tragedy of a young life probably lost. All the bystanders seemed to understand there was a bigger story here, an underlying mystery, as though they all knew this was connected to something dark. But how did they know? Had someone seen the BMW at the inn the day Ellen died? Had there been chatter about it that was tamped down? Were they shushing each other when I visited?

I had watched as they cut off Leslie's bloody UConn hoodie, thinking to myself, what a waste; the kid was probably one of the smarter ones who just didn't get something he needed and turned to drugs and easy money. But of course that's the easy explanation. It's never that simple.

They continued CPR because it was mandatory, but I didn't think he'd make it to the trauma center. Not that different from Ellen just a few months ago.

People bunched into little groups, talking in low tones, then broke up and met again in other small groups. Barbara announced a quiet invite to those in earshot for "something stiff" at her house and people started to follow her in twos and threes, not that they wanted to drink on a weeknight, but they needed to dispel some of the discomfort.

Emergency workers stayed at the scene after the ambulance pulled away and went down North Street toward Willimantic. Traffic resumed and several people with flashlights continued to direct it around the rotary. I watched Haggarty, still talking to people with clipboard in hand. Allison looked totally deflated and said she'd see us later, then turned and walked back to the house with John and the boys. I wanted to go to Barbara's and just be a fly on the wall, but the problem was I was more likely seen as the spider looking for prey rather than the innocent fly. Still, I signaled to Haggarty, who had looked up, that I was going to Barbara's. He nodded.

Entering by the side door I went into the hall next to the kitchen. People were milling about with glasses in their hands. I heard the quiet pop of a cork being pulled. Everyone was somewhat solemn, but I knew the crowd would soon turn to lighter chatter. Grace walked over and handed me a glass.

"It's cranberry juice." She knew I didn't drink alcohol and was thoughtfully giving me juice in a wine glass.

"Thanks. I appreciate it."

"I'm sorry." She looked down at her glass. I wanted to ask why, but I also wanted to immerse myself in the group and see if there was something, anything, I could pick up.

"Can we talk later?" She nodded, knowing what I was about.

"I think I've seen that guy around town. Has anyone else?" It was Sue, looking around, uncomfortably, eyes still wide.

"Yeah, I think so, I think I've seen that beamer around, maybe at the post office?" It sounded like a question from Lisa.

"What's a kid doing with a car like that? It must be his parents'. They'll be a mess after this." Henry, Gloria's husband, weighed in.

"I think I've seen a kid in a UConn hoodie wandering around. Who does he belong to? Anybody know?" Sheila wanted answers too. People were looking about and slowly, all the eyes that moved around the room landed on me.

Chapter 73 – Spill

"Okay, Frances, spill." Barbara was using my own words on me. Tom, who'd been chatting with Sheila, moved toward me. He set his wine glass down on the table and put an arm over my shoulder in a protective gesture.

"Thanks, Tom." I was fairly sure that Tom, my friend and protector, would share some of what I'd told him, the squirrels, the mice, the cameras and drone. He knew I had been trying not to be overly dramatic or alarmist, but the investigation had now escalated to a whole new level and maybe people would be more willing to come forward if they understood what had been going on.

"Don't pick on Frances. She's been trying to get you guys to talk for weeks." He kissed me on the edge of my forehead. They were all still staring. Just then I was twice saved, as there was a knock at the door. I motioned Haggarty in, and all the eyes went to the tall trooper taking off his hat.

"This is Sargent Haggarty. He's been working on Ellen's case." Silence.

"Hello, all." He smiled grimly. "As you must know, that investigation is still open. Although Ellen Richardson was elderly and somewhat infirm, the circumstances surrounding her death were suspicious. We cannot divulge much more since it is ongoing, but if you think this tragedy today was somehow related you may be correct. If anyone has information about any of this, please contact me." He looked at me. "Or Frances. I'll leave a few cards." He pulled some from his pocket and put them on the edge of the table. "We've got to run, but please contact us." He looked at me and I put my glass down and followed him out the door, relieved.

Haggarty was moving like he was on a mission. "Come on. We've got to get to the Baileys'." We sped off in his cruiser.

We passed the rotary, where the telltale signs of screeching tires would be visible for months. The wreck of the BMW now had crime scene tape stretched around it and was illuminated by large lights on tripods and cones while someone photographed the area. A wrecker was parked in front of the library, but I imagined they wouldn't be loading up the BMW for a while. Then to Allison and John's, whose house was lit up like a Christmas tree.

We knocked. Allison came to the door and invited us in. John and the two boys were sitting at the kitchen table, all looking serious and a bit sick.

Haggarty introduced himself to the kids. "I'm guessing you know why I'm here." They both looked guilty and scared. Jimmy picked at the label on his soda bottle. Eddie kept glancing back and forth from Jimmy to his father, then quickly to Haggarty and back again. I could see these weren't kids who were troublemakers. They looked scared, not belligerent and bratty. They had gotten mixed up in something totally out of their league, maybe just testing the edges of freedom, and found themselves caught up in a situation not of their making.

"We didn't know anything when we first met Leslie." Eddie spoke first. "He was just a buddy, someone to have fun with who needed a place to crash. We thought you wouldn't mind. He didn't seem like trouble at first..." Jimmy looked at him with an expression that was between relief and horror. "We didn't know what he was into. He was just fun. He had a cool car and knew what seemed like cool people." Eddie looked down at his hands, then up at Allison. "I swear we didn't know, but then he pulled out a bottle of wine one day when we were driving around and we didn't think it was that big of a deal. It was only wine–you let us have a little when we have holiday meals…." Eddie looked pleadingly at his father. "We just sort of went along. We knew kids in school who drank. We didn't want to seem like losers."

Jimmy chimed in. "Then he started doing harder stuff. Mostly we didn't have any, just once in a while a taste so we wouldn't seem weird." Their parents looked back and forth between them, not saying anything. "Then when he started smoking pot, we thought we were in too deep to get out. Mostly we watched, but once in a while we took a hit." Jimmy was looking at his soda bottle. I watched his mother's eyes get wide but she said nothing. His father shook his head.

"I only had one puff, once. It made me feel so weird that I got scared and laid down on the back seat. I thought I was going to die. Leslie laughed at me and called me a lightweight." Eddie sniffed.

"We drove all around with him. He stopped and visited with people down Norwich way. He would get out and talk to them, exchange something for money. Sometimes people would just walk up to the car and he'd do it out the window. We figured out what he was up to, but he threatened us, threatened to tell you guys." Jimmy looked up at his parents. "I'm so sorry. We should have told you but we were afraid."

"Then he got scared and moved out. We knew he was staying at Mrs. Richardson's old place. We were just relieved, glad he moved out. But he kept checking in with us, bugging us, trying to get us to harass you, Ms. O'Connor. But we didn't want to. We were afraid."

I was amazed at how composed Allison and John were. I could see they were just about speechless, but not reacting in the way I would have, going ballistic.

"So a couple of weeks ago he came begging to us, said he didn't have anywhere to go. We didn't know what to do. We really didn't want him back here but felt stuck with it and sort of bad for him. I mean we have a pretty good life here and he doesn't seem to have anyone. So we put him up in the fallout shelter. He had light and a heater, and we got a chair, a little table and an old air mattress and some blankets and he was staying there some of the time and was mostly parking behind the post office," Jimmy explained. "We'd sneak him food and stuff. It wasn't luxurious but he had a place to hide out. Sometimes he'd joke that he was a bad guy, on the run. He tried to make it sound adventurous, but it was actually kinda gross. Sometimes he had to use a five-gallon bucket as a toilet." Allison and John's lack of response was succeeding because any silence would shortly be filled by one or the other boy recounting the events of the past months. Haggarty knew this was a productive method. In many cases if you let the conversation die, people feel the need to fill the quiet time, so much so that they often fabricate and refabricate their story so it changes and implicates them even more. We waited, hoping for more and to hear something about Gerry.

"We saw you drive in, Officer Haggarty, and we went out to warn Leslie. He freaked...." Eddie started to cry. "We didn't mean for this to happen. I can't believe it!" He sniffed and got up to get a paper towel to blow his nose.

"We knew he had troubles. Mostly he was just bragging and I knew he wasn't as tough as he sounded. Really I just felt sorry for him and hoped living with us would help him, I don't know, get a grip? Obviously it didn't help." Jimmy folded his arms on the table and put his head on them. We could see his shoulders shaking.

John went to him and rubbed his back and said the only thing he could.

"We love you, son. Both of you. We're proud of you for telling us." He paused and we all knew there was a but coming. "But you must know that this is serious and will affect your privileges for a very long time."

"Yes, sir." In unison.

"I have a few other questions." Haggarty now needed to take the floor. "Do you know anyone called Gerry that Leslie hung out with? It's very important that we find him. We think that he's in danger, and Leslie may have hurt him."

Chapter 74 – Shelter

Both boys looked at him, puzzled, then at each other. Jimmy spoke first. "He sometimes talked about someone but we didn't know who it was and how he knew him, just that it was like someone he was taking care of or who owed him something. He'd just go on about stuff and most of the time we figured he was bragging. He called him Junior, not Gerry. Do you think that's who he meant?" Haggarty and I looked at each other. This was too easy. These kids had opened up and now were giving us the final piece we'd been looking for.

"Yes, I think that's who we mean." Haggarty nodded. "Do you know where he is?" They looked at each other again. Jimmy stared up towards the ceiling, slowly shook his head, and then looked at Eddie, who also shook his head.

"He may have been at Mrs. Richardson's. He never said that when he left, but we know he went there and we thought someone else was staying there too."

"He didn't have him in the fallout shelter?"

"No, I don't think so." Jimmy replied and both of them shook their heads.

"Can we see the fallout shelter?" Haggarty looked at John, then Allison.

"Yes, of course." Allison took her parka from the hook by the door and got a flashlight. John and the boys followed, and we trailed them out the back door.

We walked around the large, terraced grass and garden mound that housed the shelter, to the bulkhead-like door that led us down the cement steps into the cellar-like cement bunker, created in case of nuclear attack as a refuge where a family could shelter until safe from residual radioactive materials. This one was almost luxuriously large, but damp, as are most cement structures. Unshaded electric utility lights attached to the ceiling threw a depressingly harsh glare. The two-room bunker had no real amenities except a table and chair, an air mattress, a pillow and blankets, and a few articles of clothing–socks, t-shirt, stocking hat–all strewn on the unmade bed. The whole place smelled of mold, even with a small fan. The orange five-gallon pail in the corner was covered and had a roll of toilet paper on top. On the table were a couple of plastic water bottles, a partially eaten sandwich on a plate, an ashtray, some disposable lighters, and a drone. Haggarty paused at the table and used his pen to lift the old MAD magazine, revealing a partial joint and a possible crack pipe. No one said a word.

There was no cellphone, and no sign of anyone else having been in either room.

"So was he able to get cell service from in here?" Haggarty asked Jimmy.

"Yes, if you stand in this area." He pointed to the center of the room. Haggarty took out his cell, stood there and made a call. The cell in my pocket rang. I answered it. He nodded.

"Did you tell him when we came to the house?" Both Jimmy and Eddie nodded.

"He was in the barn. He had put his car in there and he was sitting in it. When you came we went out and told him." Now his father spoke up.

"He put his car in the barn?" They both looked down. Then Jimmy looked at his father.

"Yes, sir."

"You never asked if he could do that. What made you think that was okay?"

"I don't know why we said he could. He asked and we didn't know what else to do. We knew you weren't using that part, and probably wouldn't know." He looked beaten down. John shook his head sadly.

"So you have no idea where this other boy, Gerry, who you think Leslie may have known and called Junior, you have no idea where he might be?" Haggarty watched them, trying to gauge if they were telling the truth. "Take your time and think about it for a minute. Did he hint about anything?" They looked at each other.

"Well, one time he took a sandwich and said he knew someone who needed it, and took a water bottle too, and he just walked out, so he probably didn't go far because he didn't walk that much. If he was going somewhere he usually took his car. Sometimes he'd get a call and drive off, saying he had an appointment, but he walked that day." Jimmy was talking and then Eddie spoke up.

"But you know he usually parked behind the post office, so he could have been going to his car. I don't know why he didn't just go out and get a pizza. He was always flashing a wad of cash but I don't think he was really as rich as he'd have us believe. If he was so rich why didn't he get the person who needed the sandwich some good food?" Eddie had obviously lost his respect for Leslie.

"So when he left that day with the sandwich he went toward the inn?" They both nodded. "But you don't know if it was to get his car or meet someone?" Both shook their heads and Eddie's hands went palms up. "Did you ever hear phone calls between him and Junior?" They both shook their heads and shrugged. "Okay then, if you remember anything, anything at all, give me a call. Sometimes the smallest detail will be the clue that unlocks the mystery. Leslie's friend Junior could be in serious danger. Please understand that your help could save his life." Haggarty looked at them and they nodded. He gave each of them a card. "Thank you for your help." Both looked at the card but only Eddie spoke.

"Sorry."

Chapter 75 – Jim and Nancy

Haggarty left cards with Allison and John too, and we got into his cruiser.

"I know it's late. Do you need to get home?"

"No. What are you thinking?"

"I want to stop by Ellen's and see if anyone has been there or anything has been tampered with."

"Great." We passed the tire-marked traffic circle and parked in the lot between the inn and the post office. Haggarty had his flashlight out and aimed it at Ellen's fire escape. The door was closed and looked as though it hadn't been used. I imagined he might go up later and inspect it. We went inside and up the staircase to her front door. The crime scene door seal tape had been cut. Haggarty put on his rubber gloves and cautiously opened the door, flicking the lights on. It smelled stale as though no one had been in there for a while. We did a slow walk through, but it didn't seem to have been disturbed since the last time we'd been there.

As we were going out Haggarty noticed that the apartment below, Nancy and Jim's, had lights on. "Should we stop in and ask them if they've seen anything unusual?" I nodded. I thought I remembered seeing them at Barbara's earlier in the evening after the burnout in front of the inn and the crash on the green. We knocked and could hear their voices. Jim slowly opened the door and looked Haggarty up and down, then noticed me off to the side.

"Hello, Jim. Have you met Sargent Haggarty? He's investigating Ellen's case. Can we talk to you for a minute?" Jim nodded in recognition and stepped back to let us in. I saw Nancy sitting on the couch in front of the TV.

"Hi, Frances. Well, what a thing right out here in front of our house! We couldn't believe it, and what a noise! It was frightening. Lucky only that poor fella got hurt and nobody else. That's a busy circle." He was walking more slowly than I'd seen him move before. He went into the kitchen as Nancy pushed herself up from the couch.

"Hello, Frances. Come on in." Nancy smiled and turned off the TV, motioning us toward the easy chairs near the fireplace. The small fire they had going felt good. "We're still rattled by that crazy car going around and around. What the heck was that about?" I introduced Haggarty to Nancy.

"Well, Mrs. Morris, we're investigating that very thing." I loved that Haggarty remembered people's names; it's a skill that can help you in almost any field. "Apparently that boy somehow knew Ellen, but we don't yet know how. We think he's been hanging around the neighborhood. You may have seen him. He wears a grey UConn hoodie and drives that BMW he smashed up on the green. We think he often parks it at the post office. Have you seen it parked there, or seen him in the neighborhood?"

Jim came out from the kitchen with a cup of tea that he placed on the table next to Nancy. "Can I get you folks anything? Some tea? Sherry?"

"No thank you, Mr. Morris. I was just asking your wife about that boy who smashed his car up. Have you seen him?"

"Well, we just got back from Mexico. We get away as often as we can in the winter, so we don't see that much."

"But Jim, I've seen that car parked out behind the post office a lot. Remember, we talked about it, whose it could be. Nobody in the inn owns one of those. We thought it might be someone's guest, but it was there so much, maybe on and off for the last month or two. Even though we haven't been home too much of the time, you remember things like that."

"Oh yeah, some kids driving it around; we weren't sure who they belonged to. You know, we get only one space for each of our apartments, so whoever had them as a guest was being pretty cagey." Haggarty's ears perked up at that.

"Some kids driving it around? Did you notice what they looked like?"

"I don't know, both looked like teens, maybe eighteen or so, hard to say. Average. Blue jeans, one in a UConn jacket, smoking." He shook his head. "Smoking."

"Did they seem like friends, like they got along?"

"Yeah, I think so. One was a little bigger than the other. He was the one driving. He kind of shoved the other one, kind of rough. I mostly remember because I could hear him cussing loudly, using, you know, the 'F' word. If there's not too much traffic noise you can hear pretty well. These aren't the best windows." He got up and placed another log on the fire, using the poker to deftly position it to catch quickly from the fire below. "I tell you, that car flying around really shook us. What the heck was he thinking? I can still hear the noise."

"Do you remember anything else about either of them? Anything at all?"

"Oh yeah, the bigger one called the other one 'Junior', like they were brothers or something."

"Anything else? Did you see where they came from? Did either of them come from the inn?"

"I don't know. There are some kids coming and going. You don't notice everyone and I don't want to seem like a busybody. Maybe Sue might have noticed."

"Okay, thank you, Mr. and Mrs. Morris. Here's my card if you think of anything else." Haggarty must have given out a dozen cards in the last few days.

Haggarty dropped me off and I leashed little Sherlock, who desperately needed to go out. We walked up to the green, Sherlock with his nose down. The car and crime scene tape was still up. We didn't get too close; I didn't want him to cut his paws on anything. We crossed over to the inn. He didn't sniff the burnt rubber closely, but as we passed by the parking lot between the inn and the post office, he seemed drawn to the back of the inn, nose down, pulling hard.

Chapter 76 – Clyde

"What's up, Sherlock?" I was tired and didn't want to be pulled into a wild goose chase. I had my headlamp on and decided to let him explore since he'd been in for so long. He pulled me into the parking lot toward the back of the inn. There on the right side was a low half door, access I assumed to the basement. Sherlock went right for it, drawn by animal instinct and an amazing olfactory system. He scratched at the door and the dirt. The door was padlocked. I knew that Clyde the caretaker lived directly above and was likely home, but he was not someone I was eager to arouse, especially if he'd had a couple. But Sherlock was leading me there and he didn't want to let up.

When I went around to Clyde's door I heard the TV on and thought I'd take a chance. I knocked hard enough for him to hear me over the TV. I waited, then knocked again and waited some more. After about half a minute I heard someone moving about with heavy steps. The porch light went on and Clyde pulled aside the tattered curtain covering the windows on the door just enough to get a look at me. The door opened.

"What the hell, Frances. What are you doing out there on this fecking wild night?" He had a few days' worth of grey stubble on his chin and smelled a little of beer but was half smiling as he growled out the question. I was kind of surprised that he actually knew my name since we only nodded in passing and had never spoken before. "Come on in." He had a slight accent, British maybe. He stepped aside and shuttled me into the tiny windowed alcove off the kitchen with its old enamel-topped table and two wooden chairs and a dusty lamp hanging over it. "Sit here. Let me get you a little tipple." From the pantry he got glasses and a bottle of scotch and put them on the table. "Sherlock, what can I get you?" An open box of Vanilla Thins lay on the counter and he rattled around in it for a couple of cookies that he offered to Sherlock. I could hear the voice of Peter Coyote orating a Ken Burns documentary on the TV. I wondered, who is this man that I've never gotten to know?

"So, Frances, it's been quite a day, hasn't it?" He sat down opposite me and poured a finger into each glass, pushed one toward me and downed the other. To be polite I took a sip.

"Listen, Clyde, I'm not exactly here to visit. It's been a wild day and I'd love to talk to you about it, but one of the kids involved with Ellen, not the one who was just in that crash, is missing and we're trying to find him. Just now Sherlock and I were walking and he took an inordinate interest in the door below, which I guess goes to a crawl space. Can you get me into it?" I pointed to the side of the building where I thought the door was. Clyde's eyes narrowed. "I'm sorry, Clyde, I'm worried about this kid and don't have time for niceties, but I'd love to come back and visit some time." I had no idea how he not only knew my name but also Sherlock's. And this seeming recluse was watching PBS.

"Okay, then, let's go down. We could use the regular stairs but the ceiling lowers below into a crawl space." He paused thoughtfully, rubbing his whiskers with his thumb and forefinger. "Or maybe we should start from the outer door...." He got up and went to a board on the wall with at least a dozen nails in it and almost twice as many keys. As he leaned in to see them better he pulled his glasses from his forehead to his nose. "Here, here's the key to the padlock. Let's go." Sherlock and I followed him out the door.

Chapter 77 – Gerry

I had my headlamp on and tried to train it on the lock as Clyde fumbled with it. The first key wouldn't fit, but the second went in and he turned it. He jerked the lock open, slipped it from the staple and pried open the hasp. The door gave easily and I looked at the ground outside. It was worn enough to be in current use.

A light was attached to the wall. Crouching and aiming the headlamp I noticed steps to a rough dirt path dropping down below the foundation so that once you crawled in you could almost stand. Cinderblock and stone flanked the sides. Sherlock was almost humming with excitement. As we turned the corner in what seemed like a mortuarial labyrinth, I saw in the circle of light a plywood door, also with a lock. Clyde stopped dead.

"What the heck is this?" He inspected it and ran his rough fingers along the seam in the door. Sherlock sniffed it, whined and scratched at the base of the door. Then we heard a muffled noise within, a weak voice.

"Les? Les? Is that you?"

"No, it's Frances. Is that you, Gerry?"

"Give me a minute; we're coming in," Clyde said as we exchanged shocked looks. "I've got some bolt cutters; we'll get this open." He left and I held Sherlock to keep him from scratching too much.

"Gerry, Gerry? I'm Frances, one of Ellen's neighbors. Ellen, your grandmother?" I was almost shouting because I wasn't sure if he could hear me. No response. Clyde was muttering to himself as he crawled through the door to get back down and inside. He came around the corner wielding huge bolt cutters that clipped through the padlock like it was butter. When he opened the door the smell overwhelmed us. Even in the darkness, between Clyde's flashlight and my headlamp we saw it all in seconds. Gerry was on his side on an air mattress. Old towels and rags were piled up in one corner and a five-gallon bucket was in another. Gerry covered his eyes and Clyde averted his flashlight so as not to blind him. Clyde went in and I followed.

"Are you okay?" I reached down to touch him and he recoiled. "Come on, Gerry, we're here to help you. Can you get up?" He used his arms to push himself into a sitting position. He seemed not only stiff but also weak and lethargic. I swung my light around the tiny room, revealing what looked like hypodermic needles among the trash. I pointed Clyde toward the debris and saw him nod.

"Come on, fella, we're getting you out of here." Clyde bent down to take his hand. Gerry seemed reluctant. "Unless you want to stay here...." Gerry took his hand and Clyde pulled him up. Gerry was unsteady so Clyde had Gerry lean on him. "Do you think you can walk?"

"I don't know. I think so." His voice was thick. They stumbled out and crab-walked toward the crawlspace door. I took a last look around. It was appallingly gross. I followed them out. Sherlock looked satisfied.

Clyde sat Gerry in the chair I'd been in.

"How about a cup of tea?" Gerry nodded. "Water?" Gerry nodded. "Food?" Another nod. "I've got some biscuits here." Clyde turned on the electric kettle and put a handful of Vanilla Thins on a plate, then filled a glass with water. Gerry gulped the water, shoved a couple of cookies into his mouth and finally spoke.

"Do you have a bathroom?" Clyde pointed him toward the living room. "Through there to the right. Do you think you can make it?" Gerry stood up, a little shaky, but nodded.

I texted Haggarty.

"Found Him!"

I got an almost immediate text back.

"Gerry? You're kidding!" I texted back.

"Not kidding. In a crawl space under the back of the inn."

"I'll be right there."

"We're at Clyde's, the caretaker; park at the P.O."

"Okay!"

We heard the water running in the bathroom. "He must be happy to be able to wash up a little." All I could think of was how disgusting that little room was.

"Yeah, and to be able to use a proper loo."

We watched Gerry shuffle back into the kitchen and drop into the chair. He barely looked at us, just concentrated on the water and cookies in front of him. Clyde poured water from the boiling electric kettle into a small teapot.

"We've been looking for you." Gerry grunted and avoided eye contact with me. Clyde busied himself collecting teacups, milk and honey.

"Milk and honey okay?"

"Yup." He took another cookie, then paused. "Thank you."

"You're welcome." Clyde brought the tray to the table. "My mother always said that tea fixed everything, and after a hard day it usually did seem to." He filled our cups and added the milk and honey. I thought he probably assumed it wasn't the time to gauge how much or little each of us wanted; we would all drink up and be soothed. We sipped.

I saw Haggarty drive into the post office parking lot and was glad Gerry wasn't facing the window. I got up and went to Clyde's porch. "Back in a minute." Gerry hardly seemed to notice.

"He's inside, having tea." Haggarty gave me an odd look. "He was in the crawl space in the basement, locked up. I think he's been drugged. We saw some needles down there."

"Thank you, Frances. Obviously I have to question him. I'll send a team out in the morning to look over the basement. In the meantime, can you call his father?"

"Of course."

We went in. I introduced Haggarty to Clyde. Gerry looked almost ready to bolt but stayed in the chair, eyeing them.

Haggarty sat down opposite Gerry.

"So what happened, son." Haggarty's tone was kind. Even though out of uniform, he had an imposing and official air. Gerry looked at him and put his palms up to his eyes, his shoulders shaking in a silent sob. I put my arm across his shoulders.

"It's okay. You're safe now."

"Right." His voice was muffled.

"You don't have to worry about Leslie." Haggarty, like me, knew this must have been his concern. Gerry looked up from his hands, eyes red, nose running. I offered him one of the paper napkins Clyde had put next to the cups. Clyde watched from across the room, leaning up against the stove.

"He'll be back. He always comes back." All of a sudden Gerry got up with a panicked look and rushed toward the bathroom. We could hear him vomiting. I went out on the porch to call Gerald senior.

Chapter 78 – He's Alive

"Hello, Gerald?"

"Yes?"

"This is Frances, Frances O'Connor. Remember me from Windham Center?"

"Oh. Yes."

"We found Gerry. He's alive. The officer, Sargeant Haggarty, is here with him now."

"Oh my God! Thank you!"

"I'm sure you want to see him, but we have a lot of questions for him. I don't think you can pick him up tonight, but we'll see about tomorrow. I'll have Sargeant Haggarty call you with more information. Can he call you later or would it be better tomorrow?"

"Really? He's safe? He's okay?"

"Yes, he's okay. We'll probably have to have him checked out by a physician, but he seems okay."

"Thank you. Thank you. I think you can call anytime. So you don't think I can come up and see him right now?"

"I'd advise against that. I'll have Sargent Haggarty call and discuss it with you. We just wanted you to know he is safe."

"Okay. Thank you again, Frances." I hung up and went back in. Gerry was back at the table, still looking pale and disoriented. I motioned to Haggarty that I wanted to talk to him away from Gerry.

"I just called Gerald. He's relieved but wants to come up and probably needs details to put his mind at ease. Can you call him?"

"Yeah, but I really want to talk more to Gerry. I'm afraid he might decide he doesn't want to talk about it and right now he's pretty open. And I think we need to have him checked out, to make sure whatever was given to him isn't leaving any residual effects. I know it's late but I want a team out here to go through the room he was held in, and I think we have a GP on staff who can come and do a few basic tests. I'm worried and really don't want to let him out of our sight."

"Okay. Do you want to stay here or go over to my place?" I could see he was thinking this through.

"Yeah, your place might be best." We went in and found Clyde and Gerry laughing over Sherlock begging for Vanilla Thins. I sat with Gerry while Haggarty took Clyde aside to explain what we were doing and tell him to expect an investigative unit to be coming by, probably that evening. It was already late and I knew their bright lights and crime scene tape would be yet another disruption in our little village. Clyde seemed to take it in stride. We watched Haggarty and Gerry get into his cruiser.

"Clyde, thank you so much for your help in this. I hope you can come by and visit once the dust settles." I shook his hand.

"Frances, I'd be happy to, and maybe I could stroll around the village with you and Sherlock once in a while." He gave Sherlock another cookie and we waved to each other as my dimming headlamp lit our walk home.

The lights were on in my kitchen and dining room. I was glad I'd gotten the books and papers off my table as I imagined that would be a good spot to lay out reports and computers. I showed Gerry where the bathroom was and pointed out the couch and bedroom in case he needed to rest. Haggarty had already brought in his briefcase with papers and investigative tools and computer. I wondered what was safe to give Gerry. Would coffee or tea be better? I asked them both what they wanted. Haggarty chose coffee, Gerry soda if I had any.

I knew this would be a long night and brewed up a big pot of coffee and got a Coke for Gerry, who was slouching in a dining room chair. Haggarty began filling out paperwork and set up a recorder.

"I've got some cold cuts and lettuce; anyone want a grinder? Or what about eggs and sausage?" I wanted to fill the needs of what I knew would be a growing crowd since Haggarty had already called in the team.

"Frances, that's above and beyond. I would love some eggs and sausage. How about you, Gerry?" Gerry, who was visibly flagging, seemed to go pale for a few seconds and then nodded.

"An egg or two, Miss O'Connor?" was his tentative reply. Sherlock had settled himself next to Gerry and leaned in to get his head scratched. I was slightly taken aback that Gerry not only knew my name but addressed me formally. I was sure Leslie had used very unflattering monikers when discussing me with Gerry.

It wasn't long before several police cars pulled into my driveway. I knew there would be a van and more at the inn's parking lot by the post office. My house started to buzz with activity as officers and detectives went back and forth from the inn to the house. In between pots of coffee and shuffling plates of eggs and pizzas that someone brought, I looked out and saw a few neighbors who'd been roused from their slumber. From the gravel sidewalk or the green they watched the inn. It had been a rough twenty-four hours for them. Soon a television van with bright lights and antenna was broadcasting from the sidewalk in front of the church. I knew that Haggarty or his superior would need to approach them and make a statement, but it would be short because it was an ongoing investigation.

Chapter 79 – Long Lost

My old home was humming. Haggarty knew Gerry would be more comfortable in this setting and more likely to talk without censoring himself. He was solicitous, asking if Gerry needed anything, if he was too tired to talk, if it would be all right if a physician checked him out. So far Gerry was good with it and willing to cooperate.

Now and again Haggarty broke away to take a couple texts, one from the physician, who was lost, one from a detective at the scene at the inn saying they'd found the syringes and several packets of drugs of different kinds, probably heroine and fentanyl.

Within minutes the physician arrived and Gerry, who had until that point been subdued, seemed to get nervous when the doctor took out a small syringe and asked Gerry if he could take a blood sample, explaining it was to rule out any danger of disease that might be caused by sharing needles, or drug poisoning, which might be caused by cutting drugs with dangerous chemicals. Eventually, after basic tests including blood pressure and temperature, Gerry allowed the blood sample to be taken.

The physician told us Gerry seemed dehydrated, but other than that not in bad shape, but he had noticed a few needle marks on his arm.

Gerry kept asking about Leslie, but Haggarty was reluctant to tell him what had happened and so repeated that he wouldn't have to worry about Leslie coming back to harm him.

It was well past midnight but Gerry didn't seem ready to rest; oddly he was becoming more animated.

Haggarty filled his coffee cup.

"So, Gerry, how did you meet Leslie?"

"That was so weird. He hit me up on Snapchat. Said he knew I was a UConn fan and did I want to go to a game with him. We started chatting and seemed to have a lot in common. I liked that he was cool and liked the same things I did. He picked me up from school one day and we went to a game at UConn. He has a nice car and I felt special." Gerry took another drink of Coke and looked at Haggarty, who uncharacteristically smiled at him. Beforehand Haggarty had pointed out the recorder on the table and explained that he needed to document the conversation.

"Then what happened?" Haggarty wanted to stay on track.

"Well, we became good friends." Gerry looked down into the Coke can. "We did a lot of things, drove around, went to games, once in a while he'd get a six-pack and we'd get a pizza and have a good time." He took another sip. "Things started to get weird. He had pot, which didn't bother me. Then he brought out coke. I'd never done that and was kinda scared. He called me a sissy until finally I gave in and had some. Then we did something else, we smoked it, but I don't know what it was. It made me feel like I never felt before. We had parked at Hammonasset Beach. He started to talk about how we were brothers. I thought he was just caught up in the drug, but he said it was real. We were both pretty stoned so I didn't know what he meant but he said something like we were brothers from another mother and he laughed hysterically. He said my father was his father. I didn't get it." He finished his soda and as I went to get another, Haggarty with his characteristically straight face gave me a quick glance. Things were coming into focus.

"Gradually he told me a story that I could hardly believe, but I couldn't tell him because he could suddenly get angry and mean. He said my father had knocked up his mother and left her to have the kid and take care of it on her own. He used those words, knocked up." Gerry had a funny look on his face, sad, confused. "He's the one who said my family owed him, and we should get my grandmother to leave him some of her millions. That's exactly what he said, get the old bag to finally give it up, he deserved it and so did his mother who was now apparently living on the dole in a trash apartment in Norwich." Gerry was slowing down.

"So then what?" Haggarty was hopeful.

"We started visiting my grandmother. I hardly knew her; my father almost never visited her. Leslie was trying to get in chummy with her. He was pretending to go to college and that he needed money. He told her the story about my father and she didn't seem that surprised. He got friendly with some of the kids in town, got them beer now and then and they would let him stay at their house. I got to know him well enough to tell when he was lying and when he was going to lose his cool, but he was fun and exciting so I just let it go on." He looked nervous now and pinged the opener on the soda can, picking at it.

"Gerry, we know he's done some bad stuff and something happened with your grandmother, so we just want to get the story from you. Don't worry, we're not blaming you." Haggarty was hoping to get more before Gerry either got too tired to talk or might want to clam up.

"He started to do harder drugs more and selling them. It really scared me. He became nasty. Finally one day when we were visiting my gram, who by the way I was beginning to like, there was a tussle and she fell down the stairs. We both panicked. We watched the ambulance and the cops. It was surreal. I couldn't believe it. After that he became meaner and more controlling, and somehow I just couldn't leave him because I felt guilty, like somehow I owed him something, that I had something he was entitled to. So where is he? In jail? I wouldn't be surprised if he finally went a step too far."

Haggarty avoided answering by asking a question of his own. "What happened with your grandmother? Did he somehow get her to rewrite her will?" Gerry turned his head and focused sharply on Haggarty.

"Yeah. How did you know?"

"We saw the will."

"I don't know how he weaseled his way into it. He'd spent some time with her when I wasn't there. He must have told her a great story–he could do that, spin a great lie and people would believe him. One day he said he'd done it, finally gotten her to rewrite her will." I thought what a mess this would be in probate, an illegitimate child now dead–where would that disposition go, to his mother?

Chapter 80– It's Over Now

"What happened with you two? After your grandmother passed?"

Gerry looked into his soda can.

"He laughed and said he couldn't wait to get his hands on the money." Gerry sniffed and rubbed his eyes with his palm. "She wasn't a bad person, really she was kind of nice." He sniffed again. "Except when she was hurting, then she was grumpy, but Leslie tried to help her. Why did she have to die?" He put his head into his hands.

"Gerry, I think she knew you liked her. She looked forward to seeing you, too. You were in her calendar."

"You think so? Really?" Haggarty nodded.

"We had a fight. Leslie was scared after the cops came and spent time at the apartment. He was afraid they'd find out about him. After they left he broke into the apartment and we stayed there for a while. He told me I had to stay close to him, that we were a team now and we'd get the cash and take off and live the high life somewhere. I think he was mostly afraid I'd squeal, but I felt guiltier than he did and didn't know how to break away even if I could. I figured my father didn't want to see me and I was pissed at him for ditching Leslie's mother. I had to stick with him. We'd found a little cash around my grandmother's and Leslie was still dealing so we were able to live at the apartment for a little while. I knew he was harassing you, Miss O'Connor. He'd talk about you no end, how he was going to get you. He'd catch mice at the apartment and put them in bags to leave at your house." I laughed.

"I may still have a couple in my freezer. It was kind of creepy."

"Sorry. He was very suspicious and cautious. He was watching the street and the parking lot all the time and finally got the jitters so bad that we left and slept in the car for a few days. One day he sort of lost it, said he thought I was going to bring the cops down on us, and that's when he locked me up in the basement. He told me I was as responsible as he was and I would go to jail with him and he'd have his jailbird friends hurt me." Gerry looked around nervously. "Are you sure I'm safe?"

"Yes. You don't have to worry about him anymore." A tone in Haggarty's voice made Gerry turn sharply toward him.

"Is he okay? Did something happen to him?" Haggarty glanced at me. Gerry looked back and forth between us. "What happened?"

"He had an accident. It was very serious." Gerry again looked first at Haggarty and then at me. He knew.

"He's dead, isn't he?" Haggarty nodded and replied.

"Yeah." He paused, then added, "He may have been high; we don't know yet, not until the toxicologist report comes back."

"Geez. I'm not totally surprised. Even he himself said he'd never come to a good end." Gerry looked off into space. We waited. "What does this mean? What's going to happen to me?"

"Well, we still have some investigating to do, but I don't think there will be any charges, or if there are they won't amount to much. We have your statement. If anything, you might be accused of obstructing justice, but under the circumstances you likely won't be charged. You're still a minor. Courts can be lenient, although they sometimes want to set an example, but we'll put in a good word for you." Gerry put his head in his hands and sobbed. Haggarty put his hand on Gerry's shoulder and waited. "It's over now."

"I really did like having an older brother for a while." He sniffed. "Until it got weird."

"Well, your dad is relieved." Gerry stiffened.

"What does he know?"

"He knows you were missing and he was very distraught. I think he was ready to pay a ransom if it came to that. He's very happy you've been found safe. He wants to come and pick you up. It's very late now. We may have him come by in the morning; is that okay?"

Gerry looked down at his hands. "Do you think he's mad?"

"I think he's more relieved than anything."

"What about Leslie?"

"I think you have a lot to talk about." Gerry slumped down in the chair. All the events of the last few weeks that had piled up on him were now in the past. He looked as though the stuffing had been sucked out of him.

"I'm tired." He crossed his arms on the table and put his head on them.

"Come on in here. I've got some blankets and a pillow on the couch." I lifted his elbow and he followed me and sank into my old couch. Sherlock jumped up near his feet and climbed to the back of the couch and soon they were both asleep. The shades were pulled down so the flashing red lights at the corner were hardly noticeable and the sounds on the street were muted.

Haggarty and I sat over what was now decaf.

"What a lot for such a young person to experience. Do you think it will affect him?"

"I don't know," I replied, "but I'll bet he'll be a lot more cautious in the future."

Chapter 81 – The Night of the Bonfire

The events of that day were the talk of the night at the next bonfire on the upper green. It was chilly and the fires, usually three of them in portable pits, were much more welcome than in the warmer months. People gathered around the pits, mostly with bare hands extended to gather in the warmth. It usually started with easy greetings and chatter, and today was no exception. People moved back and forth from the fire to the table where they nibbled the edible offerings, stopping to visit with this group or that, then gathering again around the pits. The smoke blew now this way, now that, and everyone shifted to avoid it but still were magnetically pulled back to the warmth.

I told Haggarty about the bonfire and suggested he join us. I had a feeling rumors would start unless someone was there to clarify, and better Haggarty than me. I saw him drive by and park on the green below and waited for him to walk up. I knew that a week previous a group had been talking about the car crash and finding Gerry. The dust had barely settled, most of the facts were uncovered, and now those who had come tonight would get to hear about it from him. I saw his tall form approaching bundled in a warm wool jacket, and so did several others, who moved aside deferentially.

"Hey, Sarge, how's it going?" I greeted him, wanting everyone to realize he was here. He walked over to the first firepit where six of us had gathered.

"Hey, Fran, I'm going fine. How about you?" Most people knew I was friends with the investigating officer, and now everyone did. I'm sure it was one of the topics of conversation when I wasn't there.

"I'm just dandy," I said, smiling at him. "Want a little snack? I made some sausage and peppers...." I tried to make it sound inviting although now that it had chilled on the table for an hour the congealing fat made it a little less so.

"I brought a six of Black and Tan. I'll have one of those. Anyone want one?" He was speaking loudly enough that I heard someone reply from the third pit.

"I'll have one." To me this was the opening for him or someone else to introduce the topic that everyone wanted more information on, and sure enough Henry Bishop was the one who started it off.

"Thanks." He sounded sincere. "I love these."

"You're welcome." Haggarty popped the top and handed it to him. "So how are you doing? That racket last week in front of your house–did you hear it?"

"I sure did. What a tragedy. Young man's life snuffed out just like that. So what happened?" I saw people move closer to hear what Haggarty had to say.

"It was a tragedy. I can tell you what the investigation has revealed so far, and one of the things is that the kid who was driving, Leslie Goranson, had a mix of drugs in his system." All the side groups had moved in closer and quieted down. "Some of the tragedy was due to a sad early family life. His father abandoned his mother when he found out she was pregnant and left her to have the baby and raise it by herself. She didn't have a job, her mother threw her out, and she went on state assistance. Eventually she turned to drugs and found easy ways to pay for them. So Leslie had a rough childhood." The smoke blew toward him and he coughed, cleared his throat and took another swig of Black and Tan. "This information will come out so I'm going to tell you right now. Leslie, the kid in the car, was Ellen's illegitimate grandson. He was trying to coerce her into giving him money, and she did eventually write him into her will. She died due to a fall that was caused when they tussled over a little cash she was withholding." The group had now formed into one. I heard some sigh, some grunt. "I'm sure some of you know she had been in pain for a while. What you may not know is that Leslie was supplying her with fentanyl lollipops for her pain. I think they helped. Her other grandson, Gerry, had been chumming around with Leslie, and in a fit of paranoia Leslie drugged him and locked him in the basement of the inn." Now there was mumbling. In the back of the group Clyde, who rarely came village events, caught my eye and nodded. When Haggarty paused for another sip people began to ask him questions. I knew this was the balm the village needed, some closure. I moved through the crowd toward Clyde.

"Good to see you here, Clyde."

"Good to see you, Frances." He sipped the Black and Tan he must have helped himself to. "You know, Ellen was really a remarkable woman." .

"How did you know her?"

"We'd get together and watch Shakespeare plays on YouTube. Shakespeare! Who does that? She was very generous, too. Always helping people with money when they came up short or with groceries that might just appear at their doors. She did so much that most people didn't know about and she didn't want them to know. She was the secret Santa, the one who helped people make ends meet, and no one knew. She'd often enlist me to do the giving, slipping around with an envelope here, a box of treats there. I miss her." He sniffed and took another big gulp. It was dark and I couldn't see his face well, but he wiped his eyes with the sleeve of his old jacket.

I heard later that Clyde had been given a decent chunk from Ellen's estate, and probably would pass it on as he had been doing for years. He and I get together for PBS specials on my slightly bigger screen.

Gerry had gotten some keepsakes from Ellen's apartment once it was cleared out to be cleaned and re-rented.

Gerald, with the support of his now ex-wife, had tried to get some help for Leslie's mother.

Haggarty and I went out regularly to discuss some of the cases he was working on. He had one of the mice stuffed and presented it to me in a little glass dome, the mouse sitting up on its back legs holding a magnifying glass and sporting a Sherlock Holmes hat. I laughed until I peed my pants and it's the only thing in my house that gets regular dusting.

Sherlock is getting on, but we still go for our evening strolls and sometimes Clyde joins us.

The village was like a lake that had a rock thrown into it, causing a splash and then ripples, but soon becoming calm once more.

Diana K. Perkins - Chapter 81 – The Night of the Bonfire

Recipes

Chapter 10:

WALNUT SPICE KISSES   2 dozen
Light, delicious cookies, so good you'll want to double or triple this recipe.

Ingredients:
1 egg white
¼ cup sugar
1 teaspoon ground cinnamon
1/8 teaspoon ground cloves
1 cup finely chopped walnuts
25 walnut halves

Beat egg white with salt until stiff. Gradually beat in sugar mixed with spices. Fold in chopped walnuts. Drop from a teaspoon onto a well-greased cookie sheet. Top with walnut halves.

Bake at 250 degrees for 35-40 minutes.

Chapter 11:

BROCCOLI / MUSHROOM QUICHE

Ingredients:
2 tablespoons butter
1 onion, minced
1 teaspoon minced garlic
1-2 cups chopped fresh broccoli
1-2 cups sliced mushrooms
1 9" unbaked pie crust
1½ cups shredded mozzarella cheese
4 eggs, well beaten
1 -1½ cups milk
½ teaspoon salt
½ teaspoon black pepper
1 tablespoon butter, melted

Over medium-low heat melt the 2 tablespoons of butter in a large saucepan. Add onions, garlic, broccoli and mushrooms. Cook slowly, stirring occasionally until vegetables are soft and liquid steamed off.

Spoon vegetables into crust and sprinkle with cheese.

Combine eggs and milk, season with salt and pepper and stir in melted butter. Pour this egg mixture over the vegetables. Add cheese.

Bake 30 minutes uncovered in preheated oven or until center is set well, then cover and cook another 30 minutes.

Chapter 12:

CURRIED CHICKEN

In large skillet sauté:
2 tablespoons olive oil
½ - 1 sliced red pepper
2 chopped onions
4 oz. can of red curry paste from oriental grocer
2-3 pounds chicken, boned, skinned and cut into
      chunks, sautéed until cooked through

Add:
Par cooked carrots
String beans (optional)
Squash
Mushrooms
Broccoli
Kale or chard

Cook until soft enough to eat, then add:
½ - 1 cup white raisins
½ cup coconut milk
¼ cup sesame seeds
1-2 cups cold water mixed with
      2-3 tablespoons cornstarch

Heat until thick. Serve over rice.

Chapter 16:

PEPPERONI AND BEAN SOUP

1 large onion coarsely chopped
2 tablespoons olive oil
1 large stick of pepperoni, quartered the long
    way, peeled and cut into ¼" lengths.
2-3 carrots, chopped small
3-4 cloves garlic chopped or crushed
1-2 stalks celery, cut into ¼" slices
2 cans black beans, rinsed and drained
1 can white or kidney or other beans,
    rinsed and drained
1- 28oz. can whole tomatoes, drain into
    soup and cut up into small pieces

Cook all together until onion, carrots and celery
    are tender.
On the side cook ½ cup rice with 1 cup water
    and add to soup when done.

Chapter 20:

MA'S COLE SLAW

1 large package very fresh coleslaw mix (green
            and purple cabbage and carrots)
½ small purple onion, cut into small wedges
1 cup mayonnaise
½ teaspoon vinegar
2 tablespoons sugar
Dash of salt and pepper

Put into food processor a few small wedges
of onion and maybe ¼ of the coleslaw mix – just to
the top of the blade handle. Using pulse make the
mix "dance," pulsing until all is a finer grind.
Empty into a large bowl and repeat until all the
onion and slaw mix is chopped up.

Add mayonnaise and mix thoroughly; taste
and adjust vinegar/sugar if necessary.

Chapter 22:

WALNUT / RAISIN SCONES

In food processor layer in this order:
½ cup walnuts
½ cup raisins
4 tablespoons cold butter cut into smaller chunks
1 cup + 6 tablespoons flour
½ tablespoon baking powder
¼ teaspoon salt
2 tablespoons + 1 teaspoon sugar
1 egg
1 teaspoon vanilla
1/3 cup half and half

Pulse until all gloms together like dough. Shape into ¾" thick round loaf and cut into 6 or 8 wedges. Bake on top oven rack at 425 degrees for 12 minutes, flip and bake another 6-10 minutes.

Chapter 24:

DATE NUT BALLS   makes 30-40

1½ cup flour
¼ teaspoon salt
1/3 cup sifted confectioners' sugar
½ cup butter
1 tablespoon milk
1 teaspoon vanilla
2/3 cup chopped nuts (walnuts or pecans)
2/3 cup chopped dates

Combine flour and salt, cream butter and sugar, add milk & vanilla, stir in flour, blend in dates and nuts. Roll into 1" balls, place about 1" apart on ungreased cookie sheet. Bake at 300 degrees for 2 minutes. Gently roll in confectioners sugar while still warm.

Chapter 26:

CAJUN CHICKEN

Make rub:

(we quadruple and refrigerate the left over
for next time):

1 tablespoon light brown sugar

1 tablespoon granulated garlic

1 tablespoon granulated onion

1 tablespoon paprika

2 teaspoons dried thyme

2 teaspoons dried oregano

2 teaspoons coarsely ground black pepper

2 teaspoons kosher salt

Combine dry ingredients.

Thoroughly coat 16 – boneless, skinless chicken thighs with rub. Brush or spray with olive oil. Grill over medium heat until meat firm & juicy and juices run clear – 8-12 minutes on one side turn once halfway thorough – or bake in oven at 425 degrees for 20-30 minutes depending upon thickness of thighs.

Books by Diana K. Perkins

Singing Her Alive, award winning novel set in Willimantic and Merrow, Connecticut, recounts a granddaughter's discovery of her grandmother's journal from the 1890s that reveals secrets of a shocking romance between her grandmother and another mill worker, a girl.

Jenny's Way, an award winning fictional tale set in Baltic Connecticut, follows the entwined lives of three families who create a tapestry of local color: a good, hardworking farm family, a family with difficulties and an extended family of women who are supported by the kindnesses of the mill boys they service.

Diana's Pool explores the legend about a favorite swimming hole in the Natchaug River in the small town of Chaplin, Connecticut. Did a girl named Diana jump into the pool and never come out alive? Was it an accident? Was it deliberate? Was it murder?

Summer Ice, set in Coventry, Connecticut is the story of Millicent White's struggle to find happiness in a small village inn. Abandoned by one family, spurned by another and always at the mercy of the inn owners, will she ever escape the drudgery?

The Nonprofit Murders – A retired librarian's frugal lifestyle allows her to amass a fortune, but when her generous trust for local nonprofits is announced she is murdered. An ageing detective, a washed-up reporter, a shrewd librarian and a busybody historian endeavor to solve the mystery the detectives seem to be bungling.

Last on a Match – In 1901 homosexuals could be consigned to insane asylums, and in this award winning sequel to Summer Ice, Felicity White finds herself institutionalized. Although disillusioned, angry and struggling mightily with her demons, she eventually learns to make her way in a world far away from her humble roots.

The Ledge Light – What sends a farm girl to sea to find her way, masquerading as a man to one of the lonely rocks in the Long Island Sound? A broken heart, a thirst for adventure? Follow Martha Green from a Franklin Farm to the Ledge Light in New London.

These books are available on the website:
www.DianaKPerkins.com

Made in the USA
Monee, IL
08 September 2024